THINGS WE DON'T SAY

BOOKS BY ELLA CAREY

Beyond the Horizon
Paris Time Capsule
The House by the Lake
From a Paris Balcony
Secret Shores
The Things We Don't Say

ELLA CAREY

The
THINGS
WE DON'T
SAY

Bookouture

Published by Bookouture in 2021

An imprint of Storyfire Ltd.
Carmelite House
50 Victoria Embankment
London EC4Y 0DZ

www.bookouture.com

Previously published in 2018 by Lake Union

ISBN: 978-1-80019-151-8
eBook ISBN: 978-1-80019-150-1

For my sister, Jane

Chapter One

London, 1980

Lydia placed *The Times* under the kitchen tap and soaked it. Water scurried down the paper until wet black ink rendered the newsprint into a stream, and the foul words were only a soggy, unreadable mess. Soon, the paper flopped uselessly in Lydia's hands. Satisfied, Emma Temple's most loyal friend and housekeeper marched past the remnants of her breakfast, which she always ate well before Emma awoke, toward the rubbish bin in the corner of the kitchen in Gordon Square, tutting as the paper dripped black-stained water onto the kitchen floor. Lydia placed the wet wreckage on top of everything else in the rubbish bin. Should Emma want to see evidence of the accident that had ruined *The Times*, Lydia would simply lift the smooth steel lid of the bin and show her employer its sodden remains.

The best thing now was to carry on. She would not upset Emma's normal routine. Lydia prepared her employer's breakfast in the same way she had done every morning for decades. She would behave as if nothing were amiss, even though everything was about to explode.

Lydia's touch remained sure as she placed Emma's boiled egg on the plate with her morning toast, cutting precise soldiers and placing a glass of bright orange juice on the decorated tray that either Patrick Adams or Emma had painted. Instinctively, after years of service, Lydia smiled at the thought of her employer's delighted reaction to the vivid golden egg yolk and the bright orange of the juice. Lydia loved the fact that Emma still adored color, her face lighting up at the sheer joy of it, even now when she was more than ninety years old.

But unless the article on page five of *The Times* was proven to be wrong, Lydia knew, as she made her way along the narrow hallway to Emma's bedroom that overlooked what she regarded as London's most intriguing square, the life Emma had struggled to build since Patrick's death was about to go belly-up.

Lydia's footsteps sounded like thuds on the hard wooden floorboards.

The paper could have been more considerate! Why publish something damning when one of the players was dead and the other was practically a grieving widow?

Lydia paused outside Emma's closed bedroom door, her rough housekeeper's hand pressing into the handle, her fingers feeling as if they imprinted it as it turned. She would not let her surroundings distract her or upset her. The walls around her abounded with Emma's work and her collection of black-and-white photographs of summers in the country at the old farmhouse that Emma had rented for decades in Sussex and where the Circle felt most at home—Summerfield. The remaining space was peppered with snaps from those summers spent in the South of France...

There couldn't be any truth to the article. It was preposterous. Abhorrent. A disgrace.

Lydia took in a deep breath and opened Emma's bedroom door.

The thing about growing older was that all of one's possessions became imbued with a sense of the past. Emma ran her gnarled fingers over her old jewelry boxes; touching the pieces was as satisfying as wearing the jewelry sometimes. Nothing was particularly precious—not in monetary terms—but to her the string of avant-garde wooden beads that Patrick had painted for her in

France after buying them as blank canvases at a village market stall or the striking, modern silver ring that her late husband, Oscar, had bought for her in Italy in the twenties held as much value to Emma as all the diamonds in the world.

Emma glanced down at her outfit and frowned. Would it work for a talk to a group of schoolgirls today? She never used to worry about such things, but now, a sense of unfamiliar panic rose in her system. Emma regarded her reflection in the mirror and forced herself to smile, but that familiar rebellious expression only looked a little ghoulish on her tired old face now. She'd chosen a vintage shirt for the talk, one she'd painted in while working in the studio that Ambrose had designed for her and Patrick out at Summerfield. Her shoes were brown lace-ups, the sort worn by schoolgirls who trotted around the streets of Paris.

She'd been famous for her complete disinterestedness in fashion all her life—for throwing together odd ensembles that never matched and appearing at soirees in London looking like the bohemian she always wanted to be.

Now, her outfit reminded her how she used to place burnt orange and deep green together on the canvas during the winter, bright fleshy citrus against a vivid green tablecloth, with a sparkling crystal vase of white flowers to cheer things up. The memory satisfied her. Emma liked to be pleased first thing in the morning.

But today, she could not go straight to her studio. It was one of those frustrating days where life was going to intervene and when she would have to wait until the afternoon to work.

Her face, lined and framed with wispy strands of gray hair, peered back at her in the mirror. Her eyelids were veiled with puffs of soft olive skin, but they still held a glint of that something she hoped would never go away. Spirit—perhaps that was what it was.

Emma smiled at the sight of Lydia appearing behind her in the mirror's simple wooden frame. Lydia hovered in the doorway, holding Emma's breakfast tray. Around her was the comforting palette that Emma would never be able to part with as long as she breathed: the walls she had painted with murals of sea mermaids and angels and trompe l'oeil when she first rented this flat with such anticipation and enthusiasm—it seemed hard to imagine that she had been so very young. Now it was almost an effort to simply turn around on her velvet-topped stool.

Lydia blushed, a rush of pink blotches spreading over her once-smooth skin.

Emma looked intently at her most loyal and enduring house-keeper. Lydia did not do blushing. Emma placed a hand on her faded dressing table stool.

"It's the newspaper," Lydia said, her voice holding the hint of a shake, while she placed the breakfast tray on the table in the window. "Wet. Soaked through."

Emma eased herself off the stool and made her way across the room. She leaned heavily on her stick with every step. There had been no rain during the night.

"Don't know what did it," Lydia went on, moving brusquely now, sounding more like herself. "The neighbors watering their potted plants, perhaps?"

"Can you warm the paper in the oven?" Emma fought agitation. She had viewed the goings-on in the world as a crutch since all her friends had gone... the thought of not being able to read and distract herself was annoying, an irritation.

"The newsprint has all run. It's unreadable. I'm sorry."

Emma eased herself into the solitary chair by the small round table at the window where she took breakfast these days. And frowned. This was all wrong. Lydia had placed three red poppies in one of Emma's narrow vases. They sat there, their faces shining out as if nothing were amiss, but the sight of them hit Emma with a jolt. She hadn't thought about poppies for decades... and three poppies? She reminded herself that it was inadvertent on Lydia's part.

They'd said her poppy painting was her finest work, but every time Emma looked at that piece, it caused her pain because she'd been working on it that summer in France. She would not go down that path, not now; there was no point in it. Instead, she tapped her boiled egg with her teaspoon and took a few bites, her breakfast seeming to sit harder in her stomach with every bite.

She placed her napkin back on the table.

"I suppose you could pop out and buy a replacement copy for me, Lydia," she said. How dependent on her routine she had become since Patrick's death.

Lydia bustled about, tidying the room, her gray eyes switching back and forth as if she were a fox. "I don't think we'll have time for that, I mean, for me to buy the paper and for you to read it," she said, her voice high-pitched with nerves. "Are you sure you wouldn't like to go out to the square for a little stroll instead? The blossom is out and has spread a lovely carpet on the lawns." Lydia's words tumbled about too fast. "We could sit on one of the benches for a while."

Emma tapped her walking stick on the floor. "You've been like a cat on a hot roof since you came in."

Lydia remained tight-lipped.

Emma made a wry face and dipped her spoon back into her boiled egg.

After breakfast, Emma made her way downstairs with Lydia right behind her. Emma settled into her favorite old armchair in the living room. White swirls were stenciled across a pale pink fabric and tulips were shaded in light tones of camel and pale blue. One of Patrick's designs.

"I'd best get back to the kitchen." Lydia bustled out of the room and made her way down to the basement.

Emma reached for a book. She had an hour to kill before this talk at the school. She tried to focus on the novel.

Lydia leaned against the kitchen door, her chest rising and pulsing as if it had taken on its own life. She should have known better than to try to trick Emma with washed-out newspapers. Of course Emma would go quiet. It was what she always did when faced with confrontation. But Emma's silence was far more resonant than anyone else's words.

Lydia almost gasped with relief when she saw a bicycle through the basement windows. A pair of familiar feet hauled the paint-chipped old thing up the front steps of the house.

Laura. Lydia bustled back up the stairs to the entrance hall, shooting a sidelong glance at Emma's sitting room door. Emma's granddaughter almost fell in the front door, tumbling over her bike, her copper hair in disarray around her heart-shaped face.

"Does she know?" Laura gasped, her gray eyes wide.

Lydia closed the door as silently as she could.

"*The Times*? I flooded it." Lydia whispered the words. "Drowned it with the kitchen tap."

"Did she fall for it?"

"Not a bit." Lydia indicated with a turn of her head that they should retreat back downstairs to the kitchen.

Laura tugged off her old green coat as they moved down the stairway. The coat had belonged to Emma once.

"Tea?" Lydia moved toward the kettle.

Laura reached up to clasp at the tie that sat on the low neck of her floaty blouse.

She slumped down at the old wooden table. "It makes no sense."

"Oh, dear goodness…" Lydia hated the shake in her voice.

"The portrait has been hanging at Summerfield since… what? The 1920s?"

"Of course it has. Any other notion is nonsense. I have no idea what the article is talking about." Lydia measured out tea leaves and spooned them into the ceramic teapot that Emma had made herself.

"Of course Patrick painted Emma's portrait. He adored her from the moment he met her until he drew his last breath. It's brutal to suggest that it's the work of one of his students or of a copyist. The painting means the world to Gran. She's going to be devastated at any suggestion that Patrick didn't paint her but let someone else paint *The Things We Don't Say*."

"I know."

"It gets worse," Laura said.

Lydia picked up a tea towel and tucked it into the belt of her apron. She poured tea, finding no comfort in the morning ritual she'd carried out every day since she'd worked for Emma… and Patrick.

"The Royal College of Music," Laura whispered. "My course."

Lydia looked up.

"I had to take on a student loan to be able to afford the tuition fees when I started there two years ago."

Lydia was silent.

"That loan is guaranteed by Patrick's portrait of Gran. Gran helped me, not just with tuition but with my rent as well. I try to pay the interest back on the loan with the hours that I work at the supermarket. Gran, more than anyone, understood my need to play the violin. You know that."

Laura recognized the tact behind Lydia's silence.

Laura went on. "Because *The Things We Don't Say* is the collateral for my loan, if the painting isn't a Patrick Adams, then I'm finished. I'm going to lose my music, my career, everything I've worked so hard toward. But what's that, when Gran's going to lose, to be frank, her life?" Laura turned away. And yet she knew she was going to have to get things out rather than hold them in. Not like Emma would do.

Lydia placed Laura's mug of tea in front of her, but the thump of it settling on Emma's familiar kitchen table brought no sense of relief.

Laura stared at the milky brown tea. "Who would *make* such a claim?" She fought to still the break in her voice.

Lydia drew a hand over her gray bun. She'd not changed her style in years. The gaze in her gray eyes was direct. "He owns one of London's most respected galleries in Piccadilly. Didn't it say he was sent to appraise the portrait on behalf of the Tate before it goes into their exhibition of gay twentieth-century artists? So the Tate has now pulled the painting out of the exhibition. As soon as I read it, my thoughts fell to pieces, Laura. All I knew was that I had to protect Emma. Nothing else."

"Lydia, that's what you do. It is why we feel untold gratitude toward you."

Laura glared out at the small courtyard outside the basement, panicked nausea sending her insides into a swirl. "The bank can claim all Gran's assets to recoup the loan if she can't pay the full amount back and if there is any question the value of the painting has decreased. But Gran doesn't have the assets to cover my loan. She's rented all her life, and her own paintings aren't worth a tenth of *The Things We Don't Say*."

Lydia blanched.

Laura's voice sounded hollow in the old basement kitchen. "Lydia, I know this could have repercussions for you. But you're part of our family. Emma would find a place for you, even if we end up in a walk-up in Brixton."

"Oh, Laura..." Lydia's voice trailed off.

"I thought that painting was as solid as Gran and Patrick were all their lives; otherwise I never would have agreed to accept Gran's offer to use it as collateral for my loan. I should never have done so. It was just that the costs of studying music are so vast, and Gran was certain it was the thing to do."

"Patrick *couldn't* have lied to her about his portrait of her. I don't believe for a moment he would have passed off a student's work as his own. Not to Emma. That's the end of it. I'm just certain." Lydia sounded more like herself.

"If only the bank dealt in matters of the heart, Lydia." Slowly, Laura moved across the room. "The press," she said, her voice almost sad now. She pulled the phone free from its socket, where it hung on the kitchen wall. "You mustn't let her answer the phone."

Lydia nodded.

Laura moved toward the staircase. "I'll go and see if Gran is ready for her talk today. I need to think, Lydia."

Lydia nodded. "Oh, you poor dear," she said.

But Laura shook her head. "Don't," she whispered. Sympathy, she sensed, might just break her right now. She placed a hand on Emma's banister and a foot on the first stair.

After the school talk, Laura took Emma to sit in the gardens in Gordon Square. They shared Emma's favorite bench in the corner of the park, where Emma could feast her eyes on the lawns and the trees, which hung like gracious old umbrellas, shading the paths, their new green buds ready for the promise of summer in London. The entire surroundings of this area had been a shelter for Emma all her life; the tall brown houses that surrounded the square were benign reminders that Bloomsbury was a suburb rich with tolerance. It held a special sort of wealth. The University of London, the British Library, and the British Museum were all within a stone's throw of Emma's house. Piccadilly and the commercial art scene where this so-called expert worked seemed a world apart.

Laura had managed to warn the teacher in charge of Emma's presentation at the school to ask the sixth formers not to raise the subject of *The Times* article before Emma spoke. Emma, of course, talked with fierce loyalty to the tenets of modernism, explaining that the most important function of art was to move the viewer, while Laura's eyes had darted to the classroom windows, half in expectation that a news team would start snapping photographs right there.

All Laura could do was reiterate the facts in her own mind before she started the inevitable confrontations she was going to have. *The Things We Don't Say* was out at Summerfield, hanging above Emma's bed in the room that overlooked the walled garden, as it always had done. Emma and Patrick had lived at the country house together on and off from 1916 until his death five years ago, and Emma still spent time down there in Sussex when she could. Even though they didn't own it, Summerfield had been at the heart of the Circle of artists and writers that had revolved around Emma and Patrick since they started leasing during the First World War. It had been a benevolent witness to countless love affairs and writerly and philosophical discussions, not to mention the creation of some of the twentieth century's most forward-thinking art; Laura wished she could have sat at the dining room table and witnessed the conversations that must have flowed among the creatives and brilliant minds who treated the old house as home. Emma had always been its custodian.

The reason Emma continued to pay rent to the aristocrat who owned the farmhouse and its surrounding gardens and fields was because then there was no possibility that she would have to give Summerfield up before her death. It was part of her, and she it. The owner had installed a caretaker to maintain the house while Emma was not there, preserving it for Emma when she decided to go down there to stay.

Patrick's portrait of her was not only a testament to his lifelong love for her but a realization of everything Emma was to the Circle, to Summerfield, and to the new way of living they had pioneered. But still, more than any of that, there was this: He'd never painted a portrait of anyone else whom he knew—none of his friends, none of his lovers. Only Emma throughout his entire career.

While those who admired the Circle viewed Laura's grandmother as a tough, silent monolith, this interpretation was about as far from Emma's real character as a tiger from a dove. No one understood what went on underneath her stoic mask, but Laura knew that what her grandmother didn't say was far more important than what came out when she spoke.

Laura placed her hand on Emma's.

"There is something I need to say, Gran."

Emma's focus remained straight ahead.

"There was a silly article about *The Things We Don't Say* in *The Times* this morning." Why did vital things always sound trite?

"A new critic having a go? You know I decided to ignore them years ago." Emma did not turn away from enjoying the park.

Humor was one of Gran's masks. She was also in her own world. It was obvious that Emma's eyes were taking in colors, dreaming up a painting…

"Something like that." Laura kept her tone light. "Patrick painted you in France in the 1920s, didn't he? That's what you always said."

Emma stirred on her bench. "Patrick started working on the actual canvas in 1923 in Provence. But he finished my portrait in Paris and London while he was traveling in the autumn… and he was traveling with his lover, Jerome, by then."

Laura wanted to reach out and hug Emma. Emma had accepted the presence of Patrick's lovers all his life, because she'd had no choice.

"Did you see Patrick paint the work while you were in France?"

"I sat for him while he did early studies for the portrait. He had this idea that he wanted to make sketches for it when I was young, and then he would paint the canvas when I was in my prime." Emma's eyes crinkled in delight at the memory. "He made such a deal of it, Laura. Such a deal. And when we were in France, he secluded himself away in his studio and worked on his own. Jerome, presumably, saw him paint, but no one else did, and especially not me."

Children ran on the grass, the girls' dresses flapping behind them, their young faces pink with excitement. Laura turned to her grandmother. Emma's face still held a beautiful allure. There was a pride in her, a distinction that was unfathomable, an honest gentility that was timeless. It was dignity. It was the last thing Laura would see her grandmother lose. She would fight for Emma and for Patrick with everything she could, because she knew they were real, knew what Emma felt about Patrick was worth everything, knew that he in turn could never have lied to her about the fact he'd painted her and given her his most valuable piece. The expert was simply wrong. But how to prove something logically that you knew instinctively with all your heart?

That was the thing Laura had to do.

She felt a wave of protection for Emma. Her favorite photo of her grandmother was from the time she was a young woman in Paris, a black-and-white shot against a Parisian street that showed off Emma's deep-set brown eyes and the way her hair fell around her face in loose tendrils. Her skin had been smooth and olive brown. Patrick had been equally breathtaking—dark, handsome, with a glint in his eyes. The old joke was that all of the Circle had been in love with him… well, Emma certainly had been. And his loyalty to her was not going to be proven false at the end of her long, hardworking life.

"Let's go home. I'd like to get some painting done this afternoon." Emma placed her hands on the bench and began easing herself out of the seat.

Laura nodded, suddenly sure about what she had to do. "Gran, I'm going to have to—"

"I'm in the middle of working on a study of the square. Patrick would do a far better job. However, I must keep going. I couldn't bear not being able to paint." Emma stood up, leaning on her cane. She held out a hand, and Laura took it.

Conversation done. Laura knew better than to push on.

Still, she paused one more time before she opened the tall wrought iron gates that led back to the street.

"It's getting chilly," Emma said, her voice firm. "I'm going to have some time to myself."

The gate closed behind them with a click.

Chapter Two

Provence, France, 1913

Imagine: Three handsome young men, fresh out of Cambridge, lounging around a breakfast table in the South of France. Sunshine splashed onto their faces, their low-collared white shirts dazzling in the sun. Conversation flew from politics to art to economics, questioning the very fabric of society and the ethics of what made a worthwhile life, but the men were not immune to the odd innuendo and ribald joke; their chatter was peppered every now and then with a laugh. Discussions were underpinned by a silent agreement that tolerance was the thing. They were to become famous, or infamous, but they did not know that. Not yet.

Bright blooms cascaded over terraces outside the ancient Provençal *mas* they'd rented for the summer, where the circle of friends focused on being young and brilliant and erudite. Secret shaded paths in the local village were the perfect settings for lovers' trysts—and there had been plenty of those here in France, for love came into the Circle in a series of patterns that none of them really understood. Everything was intermingled: their beauty, Provence, their ideas.

When Emma wandered into the room, her bohemian green dress floating around her, she stopped to observe the men, her artist's gaze taking in every detail, lingering on her husband, Oscar, and the different tones his red hair displayed in the light. She would use bright, contrasting colors, not gradations of the same tones, to paint Oscar right now were she to pick up a brush. She was entranced with the post-impressionists and their glorious use of any color under the sun. The avant-garde seemed more relevant, more possible and plausible than ever in the bright light out here in Provence, far more so than in London, where muteness was still expected in art, in decoration, and, even more so, in life.

Emma took in the other men at the table. She studied the contrast between Ambrose's neat black hair and his clear, milk-like skin. From Ambrose she moved her focus to Lawrence—his sensitive beauty, the way he looked at her as if holding a long, languishing sadness that still hung between them.

Emma unlaced her fingers, already stained from an early morning session at her easel. She moved over to the windows to see the colors outside in the garden. Emma was overwhelmed by France. It was as if she were running a race with herself to capture it all on canvas before it was time to return to London.

"Em." Lawrence's voice cut into her reverie.

She sensed Lawrence's gaze still on her and closed her own eyes for a moment rather than turn around.

"You need to eat. You're getting more and more birdlike every day."

Emma moved away from the window and helped herself to coffee. She reveled in the velvety drink here in France.

Oscar remained deep in conversation with Ambrose, who had come down to find the time and space to focus on his research fellowship in economics at Cambridge.

Just as Emma turned around with her coffee, Patrick Adams wandered into the room. Emma reached up a hand to stroke away a tendril of dark hair that had fallen across her cheek. She'd heard about Patrick Adams's legendary poet's beauty, of his olive skin, of the sensuousness of his mouth and his deep-set eyes that seemed to take one in as if he knew more about you than you did yourself. She was aware of the height of his presence and how half of London swooned over him, but no words could prepare her for the reality of a face-to-face encounter.

She watched, transfixed, trying to discern what it was—the warm tone of his voice, how his arrival seemed to imbue the room with something new, a different energy. It was instant and charged and changed, and Emma knew she'd never experienced anything like it in her life.

Her relationship with Oscar had been glorious for a time—of course it had—sensuous, wonderful during their honeymoon in Italy and in London during the early days of their marriage, until he'd resumed his affair with Mrs. Townsend after Emma had given birth to Calum two years ago. Emma remained determined not to react as her Victorian parents would have to her husband's affair and she and Oscar had remained friends.

But was it possible she'd fallen in love with Patrick Adams the moment he'd walked into this room? She stood staring at him, stunned. Was she so full of vagaries that she could be so struck by someone all at once?

The men stood up. Arms patted broad backs, and shirts crinkled over shoulders, the fabric of their white shirts dissolving into yet another dazzling palette.

Emma moved toward the table, taking it all in. She reached for the basket of baguettes, noticing—how could she not?—the way Patrick kept glancing at her. She was drawn to him and felt instinctively that she wanted him close. She helped herself to the local bread, breaking it into pieces and bringing it up to her lips, its crust crisp, its ends pointed and sharp. The tips of the crust pierced the tips of her thumbs.

"You know Em, don't you?" Oscar said. He reveled, as he always did, in the opportunity to be the perfect host. He was such a curious blend of country gentleman and Cambridge elite. The mix had intrigued Emma three years ago when she'd married him.

But now, his bonhomie seemed forced. It was as if he were playing a role, and it was one that didn't ring true anymore.

Patrick Adams held out a hand.

"The famous Emma Temple," he said, his voice holding a lilt.

She sensed everything—the other men's reactions, Ambrose's chuckle, Lawrence's sharp intake of breath, as if a fatal sword had struck him. Her friends were all too whip-smart not to be tuned to what was going on here.

Emma put her baguette down on the bare table as if she were placing a priceless diamond ring down with delicate care. She extended her own hand until it flickered and hovered just within a hairbreadth of Patrick's.

Patrick Adams's eyes danced, while his lips played in a smile.

"How's it going, living down here with your aunt, Patrick?" Lawrence's voice cut into the air between them. Breaking the spell, whatever it was.

"I've been so bored that I've been going to lectures on Marxism." Patrick held Emma's hand for a moment before letting it go, his eyes lingering on hers… in hers.

She hinted at a smile back.

"Have you brought down your canvases?" Lawrence's voice seemed to come from some other place. "I want to take your work back with me to London tomorrow. The Art Society needs them by the beginning of next week."

"I came in my aunt's car," Patrick said. "I stole it from her. The canvases are in the back seat." He widened that smile into a grin.

Emma mirrored him, sharing the joke.

"Let's get them out of the sun then. For heaven's sake, Patrick." Lawrence clattered his chair backward on the hard parquet floor.

Emma picked up the baguette again. She took a bite. The softness inside melted in her mouth, but the crust cut deeper at her lip than it had with her thumb, and the sweetness of her own blood melted on her tongue.

"I still swoon whenever I see him," Ambrose whispered toward Patrick's departing back.

Patrick raised his hand to touch the top of the doorframe as he followed Lawrence out the door.

Emma felt the baguette stick in her throat.

Oscar tapped his freckled hand on the table. "It's becoming widely accepted that Patrick Adams goes beyond talent into genius. While he was studying in Paris for the last two years, he spent his afternoons at the Louvre, alone. Copying the old masters. Extraordinary. He hasn't adopted post-impressionism at all. He's going to break all the rules."

Emma shot Oscar a look.

"Doesn't like Cézanne," Oscar went on. "He has a distinct style of his own already. Lawrence told us they're going to show Patrick's work in a separate part of the exhibition, Em. Putting him with Picasso."

Emma sipped her coffee, wincing slightly as the hot liquid touched her cut lip.

"Are they?" she asked.

Oscar regarded her and raised a brow.

She stood up. "I'm going back to work."

"You don't mind that he's getting that special treatment? His paintings will be separate and distinct. I wish they could highlight your work like that," Oscar persisted.

"Not at all." She spoke the words with the flicker of a feather. But as she left the room, she grasped the folds of her dress, bunching the fabric into a tight little circle until it was fashioned into a knot.

Emma ran her hand up the banister of the wide staircase in the old farmhouse, reveling in the feel of the cold, shining wood underneath her fingers. Light laced patterns into the stairwell, sending yellow shimmers onto the prints that lined the walls, playing around the otherwise invisible dust motes in the air as she made her way back up to her own bedroom and studio after breakfast… and meeting Patrick for the first time. Why did incomparable things happen when you least expected them to?

She wandered into the bathroom to freshen up, splashing her face with cool water. Once Emma was done cleaning up, she couldn't help pulling the curtains aside to glance down at the driveway, where Patrick and Lawrence were unpacking the paintings.

Patrick Adams raised his head, looking straight back up at her the moment she peered out the window. His grin—the excitement of him—was intoxicating. What was it about him that had such an allure? He held a large canvas, wrapped in brown paper. Several other paintings sat in his aunt's little car.

Lawrence burrowed in the back seat, his glasses resting on the top of his head.

With only a whisper of movement, Patrick raised a hand to his lips, and he looked up at her.

Emma swept away from the window and turned around swiftly, leaning against the wall and grinning like a fool. Her friends had told her he'd had several affairs with young men. Even Ambrose had been drawn into Patrick's stellar orbit for a while; they'd lived together for a time before Patrick went to Paris, apparently. Ambrose still pined… and yet she had to trust that Ambrose and Lawrence, being modern, wouldn't blame their broken hearts on others. The sense that she, too, was far out of her depth did nothing to distract her from the irresistible urge to dive in as deep as she could.

Emma moved across to her easel. She'd begun working on a view of the terrace, a composition of two empty chairs with the sun beaming down on them, flickering patterns in different colors on the wicker and shining onto the fabric of the pale cushions while the blue Mediterranean glittered with possibilities below.

"You didn't hear me coming up here."

Emma jumped at the sound of Patrick's voice and the feel of his presence at her studio's open door.

"I assumed you'd left. I don't like being disturbed while I work," she said. She stopped and gazed out at the sea. A couple of boats bobbed in the harbor.

"I told Oscar that I wanted to ask you something about art."

She paused for a moment, her hand hovering over her work.

"Do you like sailing?" he asked, switching tack like one of the yachts out on the blue sea. Still standing at the entrance to her room.

"Not particularly. Unless the company is amusing," she said.

"I've heard that about you."

She put down her paintbrush. "If I have prejudices, then they are only against restraint."

He laughed. "But I understand that."

"I try to make things better in any small way I can."

"Your art does that."

She gazed at her painting. "I always hate what I paint! But, yes, I strive to improve each piece, to make it better than the last; otherwise there seems little point in pushing on. I suppose what I try to do is to express something indefinable, a feeling sometimes."

She swiveled to face him, and he wandered into the room.

"Do you find it easier to live by your philosophies here in France?" he asked. "Or doesn't it matter where you are as long as you can paint?"

"A little of both. Although perhaps I have not found my spiritual home yet…" She stood up, her shoulder brushing against his as she moved past him toward the window.

"I see France as freedom," he murmured.

She looked down at the intense greens outside the window. "I'm afraid our lives can sometimes be reduced to gossip at home. And worse," she said, turning to him.

"It's constant. It never goes away at home for me," he said.

"I can't begin to imagine." What sort of a topic was this, when her feelings were moving in countless nonsensical directions that wanted to ignore who he was, how he lived?

"See that little boat out there?" He came to stand next to her.

Emma looked where he pointed, turning her focus fast, as if clutching at something normal outside the turmoil of herself. He pulled a tiny pair of binoculars out of his pocket and held them gently against her face so that she could peer out at the deep, deep blue.

She leaned closer to him and took in a long breath.

"See the little one, with the yellow sail, with the red poppies painted on it?" he murmured, leaning close to her in turn and guiding the binoculars to the right spot.

"Oh," she said, narrowing her eyes. Two red poppies flapped and floated on the canvas as if they were moving of their own accord. "Yes?"

Patrick took back the binoculars. He rested on the windowsill while she stood opposite him. He crossed his legs and smiled. "I designed the sail for the owners of the boat. Two women. They live together out here in France. They, too, find that things are more liberal here for them."

Emma felt her face redden. She moved back to her easel and dipped her brush into her palette, taking some deep green and focusing with great determination on the soft, lush feel of the brush circling about in the wet paint.

He stayed quiet, and the silence hung between them, but he did not break it for a while.

"Come out with me tomorrow," he said finally.

Emma held her paintbrush in midair.

"I want to show you something. I'd love your opinion, if you'd be happy to do that. That's what I really came up here to ask. And, Emma?"

She waited.

"There's something else." He moved away from the window and strode toward the middle of the vast room until he stopped, standing still on the parquet floor. He ran a hand over his chin and regarded her. "Would you mind very much if I painted you?" he asked, his eyes searching her face.

She looked down at her hands.

"You see, I don't paint anyone I know, as a rule," he went on, his voice low. "I always think that if I were to do that, I would be crossing some line. It's too intimate. My most intimate form of expression. But I'd love, if you would let me, to paint you."

London, 1980

Laura helped Emma up the stairs to her studio before making her way down to the kitchen, where Lydia was chopping vegetables with force.

"That telephone," Lydia said.

Laura could see how these women survived the war together.

"Fourteen calls while you and Mrs. Emma were out. People who are not friends of Mrs. Emma's. Several journalists. Humans are first and foremost gossips, you know, Laura. Sometimes I wonder if, in the end, that is all we are."

Laura ran her hand over the older woman's soft arm. Lydia's ability to run Emma's day-to-day affairs was legendary. Without Lydia's steady support, it was doubtful that Emma would have been able to paint every day.

"Honestly. The questions I was asked! 'Did Mrs. Temple suspect that the Adams portrait of her was a fraud all along, or is the news a complete shock?'" Lydia went on, her eyebrows raising to the roof. "'Would she come on the radio for an interview about the exact nature of her lifelong friendship with the *homosexual* artist Patrick Adams?' 'How does she feel about the fact that the painting could be worthless now that it has been proven'—yes, *proven*, this reporter said—'not to be the work of the artist to whom it has been attributed for decades?' And finally, a woman from New York."

"New York?"

"The *New York Times*."

Laura leaned on the back of a chair.

Lydia paused with her chopping knife in midair.

"That's it." Laura glared at the phone. "Time to set the record straight."

There was a silence.

"It's taken off like a barrel down a hill." Lydia sounded resigned now. "What are we going to do?"

Laura stood up a little taller. "I'm going to confront this 'expert' first. Then I will go to the bank and remind them that everyone knows and accepts that the painting is an original Patrick Adams." Laura pushed aside the dark doubts that had threatened to brew into full-blown worries since her conversation with Emma in the square. If Emma didn't witness Patrick painting the canvas, who did?

"Lydia, surely *you* were in France that summer when Patrick painted her. What did you see? Can you verify that Patrick painted the portrait?"

Lydia placed her knife down and pressed her fingers into the bench. "I was just a girl. It was my first summer with Mrs. Emma, and I oversaw the management of the house in France. I looked after young Calum, but there was a local cleaner to see to all the bedrooms and so forth. I didn't venture into Mr. Patrick's or Mr. Jerome's rooms that summer. As for what struck me, it was that Mrs. Emma and Mr. Patrick had this secret, joking sort of way of communicating between themselves. They tolerated each other's whims and nonsense. It was as if they were their own little circle that no one else could break. There was this quiet excitement between them about the portrait, but to my knowledge, Mrs. Emma let him work on it while she quietly got on with her own art. I do think, with all due respect…" Lydia paused a moment.

"Yes."

"Well, it's just that I do think that the idea of Mr. Patrick painting Mrs. Emma helped temper her worries about Mr. Patrick's relationship with that Jerome. To me, the nature of his portrait of her was just as their relationship was—an unspoken agreement, something of beauty that was between them since they first met. That's how I would describe it. They both knew how they felt about each other all their lives, and they both knew that his painting her, given he never painted anyone else he knew well, was a testament to the depth of their shared love."

"I can't stand this so-called expert already," Laura whispered. "Hate him. I'm going to war." Her words seemed to hover in the quiet kitchen.

"Ewan Buchanan?" Lydia said. "I will join you. I can't stand the man."

Chapter Three

London, 1909

Steady southern light bathed the life drawing room at the Royal Academy of Arts in Piccadilly in a canopy of autumn gold. Emma glanced at the clock, savoring the last five minutes that she could spend here before she was compelled to go home. At half past three, Cinderella-like, she had to disappear. Risking her father's wrath was not worth it. She had to be home to pour tea.

Emma contemplated her work, leaning forward a little in her seat so that the soft blue smock she wore billowed around her slender frame. Her teacher, John Singer Sargent, had started today by demonstrating his method; his head thrown back, he had executed something marvelous from a few strokes of charcoal.

While he was a brilliant technician, Sargent also seemed to Emma a glorious representation of everything she admired about the new ways in art. Light dazzled and flickered in Sargent's work, glinting on skeins of silk, shining on pearls. He eschewed the elaborate skill and unnecessary detail that the other artists who taught at the academy advocated. Sargent believed in getting to the heart of things and argued that was all that was important in art.

This fresh approach to painting, which Emma had studied first in the small book on the French Impressionists given to her by her mercurial father, was beginning to emerge as a new force in her artistic conscience. There was no doubt that she was irresistibly attracted to this idea of bold use of color. She'd always been drawn to the allure of it, and bright tones seemed entirely relevant in the

emerging modern world, far more so than the old, muted colors
that British artists still favored.

Emma gathered her things, painfully aware of the contrast
between the possibility of freedom that seemed so real here and
being forced to serve cinnamon buns to her father's daily visitors
by four o'clock. She would sit through the conversations with the
few matrons and gentlemen who still came to see her father, the
now elderly biographer and literary critic who lived and worked
in an otherwise solitary and temperamental state at the top of the
family's Kensington House.

Emma drew on her cape and pushed her bike out into Piccadilly,
hoisting herself up on the leather seat, pedaling in a firm, consistent
pattern in spite of the swelling drops of rain that pelted her back.
The wind whipped up her hair, causing it to fly around her face
and obscuring her view beyond a few feet ahead. She cycled on,
past the park, where the trees had become shimmering, glistening
versions of themselves, and along to Kensington Road, until finally,
soaked to the skin, her chest hot and heaving, she turned into the
dead-end street where she lived.

Ten minutes later, having unceremoniously thrown off her
sodden dress and changed everything from her soaked-through
undergarments to her water-stained cape, she made her calm way
downstairs, past her family's collection of oddities and the vast array
of Victorian knickknacks that cluttered every surface.

Her eyes darted to the grandfather clock outside the sitting
room as she smoothed down her wet hair, her fingers alighting on
her still-damp cheeks, flushed from the violent effort she'd made
to be here on time.

She was fifteen minutes late.

The sound of her father's loud voice boomed out into the
hallway.

"Don't know where Emma's got to," he proclaimed. "Darned
art school. Teaching women to paint. I've always maintained that

it's important to educate them, though. Complete waste of their lives if we don't. But that doesn't mean we allow standards to slip!"

A general chuckle sounded from the room.

Emma held her head up as she walked into the overheated parlor. She'd learned to stay silent during her father's irrational bouts. Were she to question him, he'd take her out of the academy altogether. So she kept her mouth shut.

The deep green walls seemed to close in on her as she nodded, smiling silently at her father's assembled guests, barely visible in the dark, hazy atmosphere. Two elderly, old-school Oxford dons acknowledged her with the briefest of nods; the wife of one of them and two neighbors looked at her as if she had landed from some distasteful moon. But they were all part of the coterie of friends that Emma's departed mother had kept like a security blanket around her while she devoted the majority of her time to good, charitable works.

"Ah, here's the girl in question," he announced. "You're late!"

Emma raised a brow at the deceptive benevolence in her father's tone. Later this evening, she knew, she would be subject to the full force of his wrath. The evening accounting rituals upset him. He was always telling her they were falling into debt, while expecting her to manage all the family's expenditures since her mother had died. Emma knew that his agitation over the accounts was a mask for the real grief he felt over the loss of her mother. She tried to focus her thoughts on this rather than reacting to him and risking his temper any further.

Emma poured tea while one don droned on and on, only to be interrupted by short, insistent barbs from her father. Emma retreated mentally, her thoughts drifting to Sargent's suggestion that his students travel to see the light in France and Italy. She kept half an ear on the conversation so that she could comment when spoken to.

Sargent's encouragement for her to be bold, to embrace the new emerging world and modernity, seemed almost hopeless in the face of her life at home. In spite of that, she was starting to glimpse freedom of expression in both life and art as an ideal.

If only her painting and her life could merge. How exciting things could become. Emma glanced at her father as he wiped a smear of cinnamon-speckled icing off his chin. His hand shook as he placed his teacup back down on the small table in front of him, beside a silver-framed photo of her mother and a porcelain vase decorated with elaborate gold leaf.

"You're off to do the rounds with Arthur this evening, I trust, Emma?" he boomed. His voice still intonated throughout the room, even though his body, racked with the illness they'd discovered only a few months earlier, was rendering him almost a cripple these days.

Emma laid her own teacup back down in its saucer, but her hand shook in turn as she did so.

"I did promise Arthur I would accompany him tonight." To a ghastly party in Mayfair, then to another in Belgravia. Emma's older brother required her support in society as he determinedly sought a wife, while he saw it as his duty to the family to find a suitable husband for Emma. In short, they wanted to marry her off. She couldn't count the number of times Arthur had told her some sporting chap was keen on her, prodding her to get on with things and be thankful for his attentions.

Two hours later, having endured her father's inevitable tantrum about the household finances, Emma stepped into the family carriage with Arthur.

"I've bought you a horse," her older brother announced, bringing his snuffbox up to his nose and sniffing it as if he were a connoisseur of fine wines. "You can ride out on Rotten Row in the mornings every day. A woman on a horse is always an attractive sight. And something tells me that you would be more alluring astride a mare than most women."

In silence, Emma gazed out the window at the dripping blackness. Carriages swept by on Kensington Road, and Hyde Park looked like a deep mystery in the dark, rather than the wonderland that she had escaped to as a child.

The fan that she held and the long white gloves she had to wear, even the glint of her mother's jewels at her neck and the Malmaison carnation that Arthur had pinned to her dress, seemed like gloomy entrapments ahead of another dull evening.

She'd learned to put men off by seeming distant. She preferred, by far, to be thought cold and aloof than to get caught in any way, having to spend the rest of her life stuck as the wife in a repressive Victorian-style household. At least tonight it was just two parties, and not a house party that lasted an entire excruciating weekend. Having to spend three full days with no space to herself was the worst of all and only caused her to retreat even further into her own interior world.

And yet, when she was at a house party, it was ironic that she yearned for home and the tall house filled with her father's books. At least there was scope for intellectual life there. When her dearest brother Frederick was down from Cambridge, he involved her in wonderful conversations about philosophy, art, economics, and science, all possibilities that seemed almost magical to Emma in their scope. During their childhood, her mother's absence and busyness in charities had given Emma and her younger sister, Freya, the time to read to their hearts' content and, for Emma's part, to draw, and for Freya's, to write.

After they were welcomed into Lady Frances Ottway's charmingly appointed house in Mayfair, Emma occupied herself by sitting in a corner and playing a game of contrast between the sight in front of her and the other thrilling possibility that was emerging in her life right now besides Sargent's lessons—the exciting discussions that happened when Frederick and his burgeoning group of freethinking friends came down to London from Cambridge.

Fiercely intellectual young men, Frederick's crowd was drawn passionately to the philosophies of G. E. Moore, radical writings from 1903 that espoused living a life that valued personal affection and aesthetic enjoyment above all else, a life that contained nothing evil or indifferent, free from materialist philosophy. Such ideas excited Emma to the depths of her soul. It was almost as if someone had put on paper the feelings that bloomed quietly in her mind.

What was more, Frederick's friends represented the pinnacle of Cambridge talent. Their erudite conversations lit upon pacifism as the only ethical and respectful way of life; they would talk of tolerance toward all people, regardless of gender, sexuality, or race. They rejected the structures that dictated social life in Victorian England and saw, instead, personal freedom as the only way forward in the new century.

Emma had come to relish the opportunity to get out of the house with Frederick and the other young men, sneaking away with them to coffee shops in Knightsbridge, where the brilliant young Oscar Temple, Lawrence Irvin, Ambrose Carlisle, and her adored younger brother, Frederick, would open her and Freya's minds and help their thoughts to soar.

Emma almost dragged Arthur out the door of their second obligation in Belgravia as soon as she thought it polite to get away. Pellets of sleet spattered the darkened windows of their carriage, and the horses tapped on the glistening gray cobblestones. Emma's older brother reminded her of her departed mother.

Arthur simply got on with things without questioning the status quo, just as her mother had done, while Frederick questioned everything. It was as if Arthur and her mother before him lived life according to the established pattern that was set out, seeing no reason to challenge society's rules or restrictions. Their attitude wasn't due to a lack of intelligence but rather a contentment in security. There didn't seem to be a need to soar like Frederick, Emma, and Freya so yearned to do.

And as for her father, Emma saw him as frustrated. While he clung to the old social tenets when it suited him to do so and while he clearly missed the way Emma's mother had run the household, Emma wondered if he had held fast to the old ways to please her mother, while feeling the need to stretch his wings in the way Frederick, Freya, and Emma were trying to do. It was almost as if in watching them do so, he became increasingly angry at his own paralyzed state.

Emma had given up expecting any honest affection from her mother as a little girl, and she accepted that she was not going to receive any real warmth from her father.

Color was what inspired her, drawing her away from the coldness of her homelife. Her childhood walks with her siblings and their nanny in Kensington Gardens every afternoon had started it, and she'd embraced getting out of the dark and stuffy house close to the park. Her delicate senses became assaulted and captivated, drawn in by the blowsy, rain-soaked greens and the whites of meadow flowers, the deep reds and brilliant oranges of spring tulips, the fresh air, the blossoms and blue sky and birds. She'd wanted to capture it, bottle it as soon as she returned home, so it didn't get lost. Nature seemed the opposite of rules, so that was what she drew and painted early on. The park.

Her excursions with her father to the National Gallery awakened her in a different way. She felt every bit of the passion in the paintings she saw with such intensity that she could not wait to go home and pick up her pencils to draw. It was in the gallery that she was first struck with the idea that there were no restrictions or rules in the world of the imagination. If nature inspired her to revere color, it was her early viewings at the art gallery that drove her need to capture on paper the otherness that was missing at home and to allow her feelings to roam free with intensity while she worked.

She jumped when Arthur's voice boomed into the swaying carriage, loud over the clack of hooves and the thunder of rain on the windows.

"Did you talk to someone interesting, Emma?" he asked, his bulky body jolting around the carriage.

"Goodness, no," she murmured, half hoping he wouldn't hear, half hoping he would.

"You should make more of an effort. We'll get you out on the horse tomorrow. Get you married by the end of the year." He laughed at his own witticism.

Emma pressed her forehead against the cold window and glared at the wet torrent outside.

As they pulled up outside the house, the horses puffing and stomping with exertion, the footman rushed out to meet them with a large black umbrella, along with Freya, her dark hair loose and wild, her eyes darting to Emma, pushing forward in the rain toward her, ignoring the footman's entreaties to keep dry.

Emma stepped out into the rain, while Arthur took the umbrella, moving inside and disappearing into the house. Emma went straight to Freya, whose face in the lamplight was white as freshly fallen snow. Emma's younger sister took Emma's hands and held them, standing there in the rain, her own hands unduly hot, as if she were affected by a fever. Emma felt something sinister dart through her system.

"It's Father," Freya shouted above the streaming water.

Emma wiped her sodden hair from her face, pulling Freya in through the wrought iron gate. She turned down the footman's offer of another umbrella. Any such protection was going to be useless now. They stopped in the black-and-white entrance hall.

"Half an hour ago," Freya moaned, her voice rising, undeniable hysteria entwining it, vinelike, gripping her features until her face, for the most part a beautiful mirror image of Emma's own, had twisted into a terrified grimace. Emma drew her brows together. The dark dread spread into her stomach, down through her legs. She brought a hand up to the restrictive collar of her evening dress and tugged at it uselessly.

"He's gone!" Freya howled.

Emma heard Arthur shouting at the servants. She took her younger sister in her arms, holding Freya's chattering, shaking body, her hands protecting the delicate hearing that she knew was part of her sensitive younger sister, staring at the empty, still hallway. The grandfather clock struck one o'clock in the morning. Pain pounded searing, flint-sharpened arrows at the very core of Emma's heart, but somewhere—perhaps it was in the distance, perhaps it was in the future—she swore she heard a nightingale sing.

Chapter Four

London, 1980

Laura's bow scratched against the strings, rendering the simmering first movement of Schubert's *Death and the Maiden* quartet unbearable. Her Guadagnini's glistening tones were replaced by screeches that assaulted her ears as she struggled on, trying to play the achingly beautiful violin that the Royal College of Music had lent to her from its collection of rare and special instruments. While the darkness of D minor suited her mood, she was unable to produce anything beyond hopeless, irritated, angry jabs that wrecked the brewing soul of the music, reducing what she'd always thought of as Schubert's brooding testimony to the inevitability of his own death to something insufferably trite.

She shot glances at the other members of the quartet. Marguerite was wrapped in her own world, leading the furtive dark passages as if nothing were amiss with her second violin player at all. Ed's eyes were closed while he played his cello. Laura fought the urge to scream at him to stop. Only Jasper's gaze was fixed on her, until he finally brought her disastrous, distressed rendition of the jagged music to a stop by stopping playing himself.

For the first time in her life, Laura felt as if she were drowning while playing the violin.

"Laura?" Jasper's voice broke the sudden, forced silence while the atmosphere of the fevered music still hovered in Marguerite's charming Covent Garden apartment.

Marguerite's breathing was hard, and her dark eyes glistened with irritation toward Jasper and Laura for interrupting the rehearsal.

Laura focused downward, on Marguerite's smooth cream carpet. She heaved out a sigh and tapped her bow on her knee.

She still battled the agitation that enveloped her as she'd cycled herself into a frenzy on the way to rehearsal today. Her hair and coat flying behind her, she'd ridden through Bloomsbury to Covent Garden, her violin case strapped close to her back. All she could do was picture the wasteland that her life would be without music and the desolation that Emma would feel were she to learn that the man whom she'd adored all her life had fobbed her off by engaging some student to paint Emma's portrait, not bothering to lay a finger on his paintbrushes himself.

Laura sat, useless. Helpless. Her plan to fight this, compiled with such confidence at Emma's house, seemed futile when aligned with the possibility that she might lose her music for good. Because if she couldn't play at the level that she was beginning to attain at the Royal College, then there was no point playing at all. It was hard to explain the soaring nature, the closeness that she'd been able to achieve with her music since she'd started studying there. Being among students who understood what she felt when she played and who felt the way she did about not only music but life, had opened endless possibilities. Up until this morning, it had seemed as if there were no limits when it came to either music or opportunities for her career.

The idea that she could achieve her dream of being a soloist, traveling and working in Europe, motivated her to strive to attain that elusive level of interpretation that was as close to the composer's intentions as she could get. The point was to achieve complete oneness with the music—no distance between her and what she was interpreting. This meant more to Laura than anything else in the world. If her music was taken away from her, she would only live a limited, dull, gray life. How was she supposed to continue on without music, and who was she if she was not a violinist?

"Let's go from bar thirty. Laura's entry. Again." Marguerite frowned at the page, focused as always.

Laura peered mute and hopeless out at the tops of the trees in the street.

A siren sounded in the distance.

How could the world continue as normal when someone's life was falling apart?

Laura felt the shuddering possibility that she seriously might lose it all.

"Do you want to take a break and have a chat?" Jasper asked, resting one of his sensitive musician's hands on her forearm.

"I don't know what to say," she managed.

"Ten-minute break, guys." His voice was merely a murmur.

"Keep it to that." Marguerite's French accent seemed to lend further irritation to her voice.

"Sorry." Laura placed her violin on her chair.

"Come on, Laura." Jasper stood up.

Laura followed him out onto Marguerite's small terrace. What if the bank closed in on her and Emma straightaway?

Once outside, she hovered, aware of the sunlight trickling only scant warmth onto her face.

"Talk to me," Jasper said.

Laura looked across the small terrace, her eyes only half seeing the London rooftops. Covent Garden. Emma said she'd loved living so close to the theaters when she moved to Bloomsbury after her father died. She'd reveled in being able to walk home in the evenings to Gordon Square. Where would either of them go if they couldn't afford to live in Bloomsbury anymore?

Jasper stood close enough that she could almost reach up and brush her lips against his. The attraction, hopeless as it was, that had always lingered in the air when they were together still hung between them, as if it were a phrase from some old song.

And that was the rub. It was part of the reason that Laura felt such a strong sense of kinship for her grandmother. Emma had always been in love with Patrick in the exact same way that Laura knew she loved Jasper.

Her grandmother's love for Patrick was something that was never going to change. The Circle's critics called it a tragedy that Emma had loved a gay man all her adult life—and now Laura was grappling with the very same thing. How Emma's critics derided her for sacrificing her own happiness for a man who could never love her the way she needed to be loved. Others, more sensitive biographers and art historians, described Emma and Patrick's long-standing mutual devotion as one of the most romantic love affairs in artistic history—comparing it to that between Elizabeth Barrett Browning and Robert Browning. Laura, for one, knew only too well that what Emma and Patrick shared was real. It was a beautiful relationship, despite what the gossips said.

And while Lydia and Laura would do what they could to protect Emma, Laura knew that the sum of Emma's parts was far more complex and finely wrought than she ever showed to the world or even to those around her.

If some art critic proved that the man Emma had adored all her life—the man who was her rock—had lied to her about the most treasured symbol of their entire relationship, then Laura had no confidence that Emma would want to go on living in this world.

Patrick's death had shaken Emma to her core. They'd planned to be buried next to each other in the old churchyard near Summerfield. Patrick was already there... but with Emma's heart broken by Patrick's death and then again by this perceived betrayal, Emma might follow sooner than Laura was ready to say goodbye.

Quietly, Laura talked to Jasper. He ran a hand through his shock of dark hair that never did what he wanted it to do.

"She's putting on a brave face, I take it," he murmured, his eyes widening as they always did when he was being serious. His almost translucent cheeks were flecked with pink. "As for you, I can't even begin to imagine." He pulled her into a tight embrace.

Laura continued to stare hard at nothing over his shoulder. "I've only hinted at the problem to her. If I have my way, I'll sort the entire thing out before she knows the extent of it."

"The guy who put the idea out there's an art dealer, you said?"

"A well-respected one, according to *The Times*."

Jasper held her at arm's length, his eyes scanning her face.

"Once I've spoken to him, I'll go to the bank," she said.

"Good God, Laura."

"We'd better go back in. There's nothing else I can do now."

She made her way back toward Marguerite's elegant French doors and reached for the handle. Normally when she discussed things with Jasper, she came away with a spring in her step, but now, all she felt was heaviness. She could not bear to lose the string quartet as yet another casualty should she not be able to continue with her studies. They'd formed in their first year at the Royal College of Music and had started off playing at weddings. Now they were trying to get commissions to perform around the country—in churches, at local concerts and such places. Who knew? It might go somewhere. It could go anywhere were they to secure the interest of an agent and, even perhaps, a record label. But they all knew that in order to have any hope of getting an agent's attention, they simply all had to keep their standards high, they all had to keep striving to improve, and that meant Laura too. If Laura were forced to give up her studies at the Royal College, she'd have to step away from the string quartet. The implications went on and on.

"Even though Patrick was gay," she said to Jasper, "or perhaps because of it, I know he loved Gran more than anything in this world. It didn't matter, you see." She leaned her head on the door, sensing Jasper standing right behind her. "It was real. I know it was." Sometimes the heart didn't have boundaries; emotions and individual feelings were complex, not binary. Love wasn't one thing or another, gay or straight, black or white—love was the full palette.

She swiveled to face Jasper, her eyes luminous.

He reached out and stroked her cheek.

"If we don't get back inside to the Schubert, Marguerite's going to lay an egg," Laura muttered.

Nausea roiled in her stomach when she sat down to play again. It was becoming a nasty accompaniment that she wanted to rid herself of as soon as she could.

Ed rested a hand on the back of her chair. "Are you in love, darling?" he asked Laura. "Is that what that was about?"

"Only with me," Jasper said. He was deadpan, and Laura adored him for it.

"*Alors!*" Marguerite said. "I suggest we get on with it. Now."

"That's why you play first violin, Marguerite." Ed grinned. "We all love it when you crack the whip."

They all raised their instruments in perfect unison, holding their bows aloft, ready for the music to start.

Chapter Five

London, 1909

Three things happened in succession after Emma's father's death, and those three things changed her life for good. She moved herself, Frederick, and Freya out of the tall house in Kensington; Frederick died; and Emma married Oscar Temple three days after she lost the brother she adored.

It was surprisingly quick to pack up the house in Kensington, sorting through her father's curios and moving all his Victorian furniture into storage or selling it. Emma worked with the focus of a demon. She knew in her heart that it was no longer tenable to remain in the rambling dark house. Freya slipped into a distressing state after their father's death, angry with Emma for her practical approach, while mourning, dreadfully, her lost childhood and, in some ways, Emma thought, the parents she'd never had.

Emma could not sit by and let Freya descend into complete melancholy; she also could not shake the sense that all the house did was remind them of their father's death. When somebody dies in a house, their death can permeate it. The stench of it and the sadness never quite go away.

Emma knew her conflicting emotions about her father did not help. She battled with guilt at the irrepressible sense of freedom that took flight in her soul after he was gone. No longer did she have to be home by four o'clock every afternoon. She was becoming drawn even more to Frederick's circle of Cambridge friends now that Arthur was, at last, courting a suitable woman. All at once, Emma had liberty to make her own choices.

Arthur's marriage was the final catalyst for the move that she knew she had to make. Freya took their brother's departure as another loss. Emma continued cleaning out the house.

She'd been living two lives until now. One was centered around the world at the Royal Academy of Arts. The other, at home, was focused around her father's demands, but that life was gone. What if she now had a chance to merge the sense of freedom she felt when she painted with a whole new way of living?

She was starting to become interested in something even more radical, the new idea of abandoning all form in art. The concept of abstract art was fascinating to her, this idea of seeing art entirely as a means of individual expression, whose purpose was to strike an emotional reaction in the viewer, no matter what form or structure it took on—if any.

Absence of structure, of form, of tradition swelled into a glorious new hope. All this seemed enticingly linked with Frederick, Oscar, Lawrence, and Ambrose and their fervent discussions about the value of personal freedom above anything else in life. Frederick's friends were becoming closer to her than her own family—modern, secular, inclusive, and radical, they refused to be subjugated by conservative and religious dogmas. Their discourse flew around new ways of imagining what a home, a family, and a career could be.

Emma's father, an atheist, had raised her to forsake traditional religion, but her brother and his friends' ideas seemed to bring her father's ideas to life. They rejected capitalism, misogyny, traditional views of marriage and family, as well as imperialism and any notion that Britain was somehow superior to other lands. *Principia Ethica* was the Cambridge group's replacement bible. It espoused joy and color in aesthetics instead of restraint, freedom to love instead of repressive morals and marriage. It embraced the notion that family did not have to be limited to those who shared a bloodline. The ideas opened up a complete turnaround of what moral values should be. The views resonated with Emma, and she became obsessed with the idea of creating a new life.

She knew she was searching for a way to heal everyone after her father's death. What if she could finally live by these sensible principles—kindness, tolerance, the application of reason to a problem? If the world could see beyond countries and kings and languages and war and even monogamy, what could be achieved as a society and as individuals? And yet, it would not work for just her to live by such new radical ideas; she needed to gather around her those who felt exactly the same way.

Once Arthur finally married, Emma was no longer required to accompany him to endless events. She sold the horse he'd bought for her, and her life became more entwined with Frederick's, while her younger sister, Freya, also started to take a keen interest in the ideas the young men espoused. Freya's mind took to it all like a streaking cat—she was erudite, sharp, and well able to keep up with the educated men. She began submitting articles to *The Times* Literary Supplement and reviewing novels. One of her reviews was regarded as definitive.

Freya wrote and Emma painted—and with serious intent. Emma kept searching for somewhere to live. Someone at art school mentioned Bloomsbury—the home of the British Museum, the British Library, and the University of London, not to mention the Pre-Raphaelites, Dickens, and Charles Darwin. The theater district in Covent Garden was only a short walk away. More important, Bloomsbury was a world apart from Kensington society and the life that Emma was starting to view as utterly false.

When she found the house in Gordon Square, Emma knew she had found her new home. The large brown town house had picture windows that flooded the rooms with light. It overlooked the fenced-off square opposite.

There was plenty of space for Emma, Freya, and Frederick to have their own rooms both to work and live in. Emma negotiated the rent and had the entire house painted a fresh, light white. She pulled down the old curtains, left the floorboards bare, found modern furniture, and kept only a few of her father's Turkish rugs along with the family's collection of wonderful books. She decorated the new furniture with modern throws for warmth as a rebellion against the Victorians' tendency to shiver in front of the fire. She hung some of Frederick's friend Lawrence's early paintings on the wall in the living room.

Emma layered in all sorts of delicious rebellions—including the absence of napkin rings and the taking of coffee instead of tea after dinner.

Once they were settled, Frederick began hosting Thursday-night discussions at home. Emma spent her days at art school and her evenings at the theater or with whoever of Frederick's friends were in London. Finally it seemed she was living life on her own terms.

When Frederick's friend Oscar Temple started showing an interest in her, Emma wasn't sure about him. She was aware that all the men in Frederick's circle of friends found both her and Freya fascinating. They'd inherited their mother's dark eyes and long chestnut hair. She'd certainly felt flushes of attraction to the rounds of interesting men whom Frederick brought home. But often she wondered if she was more lit up by their ideas and their minds than by any thoughts that they might be contenders for her heart.

She had no desire to give up her independence, even though Oscar proposed twice.

Until Frederick died. After three days of feeling out of sorts, he was struck by typhoid and gone at the stroke of a hand.

Emma collapsed with grief and took to her bed. Oscar Temple was the one who remained by her bedside for those first vital days. When he asked her to marry him once again, finally, Emma accepted him. And the reason she did so was simple. He made her feel that there was some possibility of keeping things together after the devastation of Frederick's death. Nothing could replace Frederick, but with Oscar by her side, she could continue to live by his tolerant views. Emma wanted to gather her beloved brother's friends around her and hold them tight, as if in some way, they would again give her the connection to Frederick that had been severed with such a cruel hand.

Their honeymoon in Italy was a revelation. Oscar was an experienced lover and a charming companion. Emma for a time was content.

When she became pregnant, everything changed. Oscar resumed his affair with the married woman he'd been seeing before they were engaged. Then Emma collapsed with grief for the second time since Frederick's death, and it was their friend Lawrence who looked after her.

Her affair with Lawrence started after her son's birth. Lawrence's wife had been in an asylum for more than two years; there was no hope of her recovering, and he was lost. Although Emma found him charming, she was not in love with him. She was still bruised after Oscar's sudden turning away from her. But, in spite of the feelings that tore at her, she was determined not to judge Oscar. Lawrence made her feel appreciated and seen rather than invisible, just when she most needed that to be the case.

But ultimately, while she valued Lawrence's kindness and friendship, there was not enough of an emotional connection with him to pursue their fledgling love affair. Because she did truly want to be in love with someone, Emma knew she had to pull away from Lawrence, but she did so tactfully, citing the reason that she wanted to be a mother, wholly, to Calum and to paint for a while. Lawrence was his usual accepting self, but he threw everything into his career.

When Patrick arrived in Provence, Emma was ready to fall in love. If she had believed in fate, timing, or serendipity, then she would have said that his arrival in her life, like Oscar's and

Lawrence's, was part of a pattern. She would have said that it was meant to be.

London, 1980

Laura walked from Marguerite's house to Covent Garden Station, her thoughts in turmoil. Once she'd arrived at Bond Street Station, she took a shortcut down a narrow lane, glad of the tall, shadowy buildings with their windows protected by bars. For some reason, the run-down old street was reassuring when she was about to walk into the heart of illustrious Mayfair.

Ewan Buchanan's art gallery might be in the smartest part of London, but it was also the part of London that Emma and the Circle had rejected outright. There was no doubt Emma had been successful in forging a life far apart from the commercial side of things, but it seemed ironic that this very world had the power to topple Emma from her life's achievement with one fatal blow. Well, sod that. Laura would stop that happening if it killed her first.

As she made her way into sophisticated New Bond Street, Laura wanted to close her eyes as a chauffeured Bentley swept along the road, a glamorous insignia gleaming on its polished black door. The shops that lined the street vied for attention, their banners showcasing famous logos outside windows filled with discreet and luxurious displays that most people could only dream about owning. Laura stopped outside the elegant gallery where Ewan Buchanan worked.

Her palm, sticky with sweat, slipped on the brass handle as she pushed the glass door open. She took in the cool, vast space for a moment, until she stopped to stare at one of Patrick's paintings, stark and beautiful, on prominent display.

Laura took a step closer. It wasn't any old painting of Patrick's either, if there were such a thing. This was a rare abstract, one of the few remaining examples of Patrick's short fling away from realism before the First World War, when he had worked in collages in an effort to elicit emotion from the viewer using only mosaic-like patterns and color. Patrick had been strongly influenced by Picasso and Matisse at the time. He met Picasso in Paris while studying there, and the two men had kept in contact over the years. Not many of these experimental pieces had survived after Emma and Patrick's shared studio in London was bombed during the Second World War, but here was one rare example right on this wall. So this gallery knew what they were about.

After several moments, Laura made her way across the elegant space to the empty receptionist's desk; it was an expensive antique in walnut wood. Carved with curlicues, it seemed to float on the pale marble floor. Laura waited a moment before the inevitable clip of footsteps echoed into the room.

Even though Laura had grown up surrounded by sophisticated artists in Emma's circle, she couldn't help but gape at the woman who appeared from a room in the back. The receptionist who swayed toward her wore a swirling caftan, her sharp cheekbones highlighted by the way her hair was pulled back sharply from her face.

"Good afternoon," the woman said, her eyes narrowing as they ran up and down Laura's old trousers, her scuffed shoes, and her ill-fitting brown coat.

"Hello." Laura fought the tremor in her voice. "I was wondering if Ewan Buchanan was free by any chance?"

A frown passed across the woman's face, but then it was replaced by a knowing look. "I'll see, Miss…?"

"Taylor. Laura Taylor. Emma Temple's granddaughter."

No hint of friendliness marred the disdainful expression on the woman's face. She sighed and reached for the phone, the only suggestion, apart from Patrick's collage, of the modern world in a room that seemed entirely devoted to glorifying the aristocratic past, a time when only certain people were admitted to places such as this and were allowed to purchase certain things—although, had all this changed so very much? Laura felt a wave of sympathy toward Emma and the Circle's strong beliefs as the distinct sound of a male voice answering on the other end of the phone echoed in the room.

"Ewan. I have a *Laura Taylor* here to see you." The woman pronounced Laura's name as if she were something distasteful that deserved to go in the trash bin rather than be admitted to the gallery. No mention of Emma Temple.

Did the woman know who Emma was? If she was as commercial as this gallery, Patrick's would be the only name that caused her to perk up her ears where the Circle was concerned.

Laura wiped the hand that wasn't clutching her violin down the side of her coat.

"Mr. Buchanan will be out in a few moments, *Laura*," the woman said, patronization oozing from every syllable. "You can take a seat over there."

Laura moved toward the pair of Chesterfield sofas that sat in a back window overlooking a courtyard decorated with sculptures and a fountain, along with a selection of immaculate blooms. She perched uncomfortably on the edge of her seat and put her violin down, rubbing her shoulders where they ached from the long hours of practice that she had to put in for her exams.

After what seemed an interminable wait, she glanced up sharply at the sound of footsteps clipping across the floor. The woman in the caftan disappeared as if she were exiting stage left.

Laura leaped up and stood face-to-face with a man who was a little taller than she and who looked to be a few years older—in his early thirties, perhaps. Laura held his gaze, and Ewan Buchanan held out a hand, smiling, a dimple appearing as if on cue in his left cheek.

His handshake was firm.

"What can I do for you, Laura?" Charm and confidence oozed from him like steam curling from a china pot.

She fought down the ridiculous flash of intrigue that flickered through her at the sound of his Scottish accent.

"I am Emma Temple's granddaughter," she said.

"I see." He startled a little on the spot.

Laura glanced around the gallery. She should get them out of here. Talk to him on neutral ground. A park would do the trick. Perhaps a pigeon would come and perch on the shoulder of his Savile Row suit, dropping something particularly repugnant right on his tailored arm.

Laura shook away the murderous direction in which her thoughts were going. "I'd like to talk to you about *The Things We Don't Say*, Mr. Buchanan," she said, keeping her tone light.

"Ewan." He met her gaze and ran a hand through his dark-blond hair. "I can understand that you would. Laura, how about we go to a little place down the street? It might be better to talk there."

"How charming." Laura fought to keep the sarcasm from her tone. He held the door open.

"After you," she said.

"You go first."

Laura made her way out, holding in the words that wanted to escape in a torrent until he stopped at an elegant café on the nearest corner and held the door open for her again. Laura couldn't halt her continuing cynical thoughts as she followed him through the café's elaborate glass entry. The floor was swathed in red carpet, and the walls were lined with gilt mirrors that would not have looked out of place in Versailles.

"You call this a little place?" Laura asked, genuinely perplexed. She turned around and nearly walked into his chest.

"Would you like tea?" he asked politely.

"Coffee. Black. Strong. Thanks." She took a deep breath and perched on the edge of a red plush velvet seat. If there was a dress code in this opulent café, she'd be kicked out before she'd ordered a thing.

Ewan caught a waitress's eye and waited while Laura ordered a double espresso. He ordered Twinings Tea with a twist of lemon.

When her coffee arrived, she swigged down the strong black liquid as if it were whiskey and gathered her strength.

"What could have possessed you to assert that the Patrick Adams portrait of my grandmother was done by some student? And what gave you the right to go to the *Times* rather than approaching Emma Temple first? After all, didn't you think she might have something to say? An opinion to contribute on the matter of her own portrait's authenticity? After all, my grandmother is an artist in her own right."

He lifted his teapot and poured before taking a slice of lemon with the pair of tiny silver tweezers that had been provided for such a delicate operation and placing a slice in the porcelain cup.

Emma would hate the porcelain, Laura couldn't resist thinking.

He stopped with his teacup held aloft.

"I'm sorry," he said, his voice dropping an octave or three. "I honestly, truly am."

Laura lowered her voice. "You know, I've grown up around artists, and I know a thing or two about the shady side of commercial art. You're a dealer. You know how to make a buck." She winced at her brazen choice of words. Emma and Patrick never, ever discussed money. It was just not something they did. "Getting yourself a name in lights while simultaneously ruining the reputation of the recently—and, I have to say, conveniently—*dead* artist Patrick Adams seems beyond the pale."

He remained silent.

Laura focused her thoughts on her darling gran. "Wouldn't it be preferable to sell some painting for an inflated price in order to make a cheap buck?" Buck. There it was again. Laura sat up in her seat. Avoiding conflict may have underpinned the Circle's philosophy, but sadly it was one thing that was not going to work now.

Ewan placed his teacup down in its saucer and showed that dimple again. "Laura—let's take a step back here. You've jumped to the wrong conclusions."

"Do you have any idea what the ramifications of your claim would be for Emma and for Patrick's memory?" Laura held his gaze.

"I have a distinct feeling you're going to tell me."

"I'd hate you to think you could exploit Patrick's memory in this way."

"I would never go to the media," he said.

Laura ran her finger around the rim of her white saucer. This time when she spoke, her words came out as if she'd measured them with one of the exquisite silver teaspoons that were doled out in this gilt-edged café. "How did your opinion of Patrick's work get out then? Because it seems extremely convenient from where I'm sitting—you get the fame and people see you as the expert on the Circle, while the elderly Emma, who to you is an easy target to exploit, is made to look like a fool. But you forgot about me." She shook her head at him. "Research is always a good idea."

"The work was about to be exhibited at the Tate. I couldn't stay silent, Laura." He crossed his elegant legs.

"Perhaps we'd best go straight to stage two," Laura said.

His smile was tight.

"You are a salesperson."

"No."

To Laura's surprise, a hint of amusement passed across his face.

"Yes, you are."

He raised a brow at her and waited.

"You are trying to sell a rare Patrick Adams in your gallery right now. You kill a few birds with one shot—you set yourself up as 'the expert,' reassure everyone that the piece you have up for sale is authentic, make a name for yourself as the bloke who quite rightly exposed that the portrait of Emma was not in fact by Adams, and sell the collage for a drastically inflated price. I'm telling you, it won't work."

He eyed her. "You've inherited your grandmother's wild imagination, but you clearly don't have her tact."

Laura felt a stab below her ribs. *Don't rise to him.*

"*The Things We Don't Say* has been at Summerfield since Patrick Adams completed it in 1923. Emma Temple, my grandmother, was there when it was painted. Were you? Patrick told her he was painting her and only her. All his other portraits are of people he hardly knew. That makes your claim even more sensational, does it not? You become the famous one."

"I had to tell the truth. It's not an Adams. I don't know how many times I have to repeat myself." The Scottish accent was a dream. He curled his *r*'s and rolled his tongue around every word.

Laura forced away that reaction and, instead, made herself go on. "On to part three. You make the claim, increase the value of the 'real' Adams collage in your gallery, and—game, set, and match—go straight to the *Times*."

"Why are you certain that it was I who went to the *Times*?"

Laura gasped. "Please do not say anything more to the media unless it's a retraction of your statement, which has no basis. My grandmother is considering suing you for damages." Laura closed her eyes. Let's hope he knew nothing about the Circle's philosophies… pacifism, acceptance of others, respect, tolerance. And the fact that neither Emma nor she could afford to sue anybody, let alone a dealer in Mayfair.

"Emma is a modernist," he said. "You and I both know that she won't sue. She will try to approach this with reason. Did that trait escape you?"

Laura pressed her lips into a hard line. He knew more than she thought. "Exploiting an old woman and damaging the reputation of a dead artist is no decent thing to do."

"Believe me, it's the last thing I'd do, Laura." He loosened his tie. She looked at him.

He pushed his teacup away. "You said you know a thing or two about the commercial side of art, but you have no idea how far exploitation and falsehood can go. It's not an Adams. I can't sit here and tell you it is."

"But you went straight to the *Times*—how is that not disrespectful and exploitative toward Emma?"

Ewan ran a hand over his chin, his slight stubble catching in the old-fashioned lights that hung over the golden-framed mirrors. "I've told you, it's not what I've done."

"How can that be?"

"My appraisal of the work was released to the *Times* because the Tate can't exhibit the piece. The portrait had already been included in the catalog, but it's been removed. People were expecting to see it, so the news was reported to the media, but not by me. *The Things We Don't Say* was a drawcard for the Tate's exhibition on homosexuality in art, partly because it's been stored at Summerfield privately forever and obviously because Patrick was gay. His relationship with Emma intrigues people; it's Patrick's and Emma's devotion to one another throughout their adult lives that draws people even more to the Circle. Without their extraordinary love story that crossed every boundary we know as a society, the painting wouldn't have held such allure. I'm sorry you've taken this entirely the wrong way. I want to make sure that Patrick's memory isn't exploited, not the other way around. I don't know what happened or how it happened, but the painting that's hanging at Summerfield was not done by Patrick Adams."

"How can you be so sure?"

Ewan tented his hands on the table between them. "It's a dead certainty that the painting is not his work. I know it for sure. I'm sorry. That's all I can say."

"No. It is absolutely his work, Ewan."

Ewan looked over to the side, seeming to catch, for a brief moment, a glimpse of himself in the mirror before turning sharply away.

The sting of it for Laura was this: The only person who could authenticate the painting, who had the real authority to put this entire matter to rest, was dead. Professor Rivers, a Cambridge don whose parents had been outside members of the Circle, had produced a biography of Patrick that was recognized as definitive. He'd devoted his entire academic career to early twentieth-century British art, with a focus on the Circle. His word was so respected that Laura knew even Ewan would have to back down. But without the professor's backup, if the Tate had withdrawn the painting and would not exhibit it, and with no real argument except Emma's word, the only person Laura had to rely on was herself. Engaging a lawyer was out of the question, and time was her enemy. With crucial second-year performance exams looming, which would determine the place she'd get in the college's orchestras and ensembles in her final year of study, Laura knew she was stuck.

Ewan looked uncomfortable.

Laura frowned at her empty coffee cup.

"It's not something that I wanted to happen. I'm not trying to exploit anyone, and I'm certainly not out to make a quick 'buck.'"

Laura eyed his Savile Row suit, the way his polished cuff links sat just so on the white cuffs of his pressed shirt. "Why are you so adamant?"

"I'm sorry. I'm just sure. The painting is a spectacular imitation of his style, I grant you that. I was as stunned as you are when I realized it was not his work. It was the last thing I was expecting, believe me, but there is something that tells me without doubt that the painting is not a Patrick Adams."

"You can't just say that." Laura almost whispered the words. "You and I both know it. Brushstrokes? The age of the canvas? A lack of Patrick's trademark ingenuity? What exactly did you see? Because it strikes me as extremely odd that Emma slept with the painting above her bed for decades and noticed none of this. She's got a pretty good eye for a piece of art, and Patrick lived at Summerfield for decades with that painting right in the house…"

Ewan took in a shaky breath. "The first thing we look for is the name of the artist on the canvas. The work is not signed."

Laura waited.

He leaned against the table a moment. "Following the artist's name, there's quality. It's not something I can reduce to words; it's instinctive."

Laura sensed herself frowning.

"It's as if, when I'm called out to authenticate a piece of art, I'm looking for that overall something that makes the work an Adams. Then, there's no definitive documentation to prove that the portrait is by Adams: no certificate, no exhibition or gallery sticker attached to it. The portrait has never been bought or sold. We can't rely on supposition. As a professional, I cannot in good faith verify the authenticity of the painting."

"You need to tell me what makes you so sure," she said, her words sounding as if they came from another person. "It's all too vague."

"It's exactly the same as it is with a piece of music," Ewan said suddenly.

Laura's gaze sharpened.

"Authenticity is paramount in all art."

Laura was silent a moment. When she looked up, he'd already pushed back his chair.

"I have to go," he said. "I'm sorry. I have a meeting now. I can't do anything to help. All I can tell you is that the painting is not the work of Patrick Adams. There's nothing else to say."

"Ewan—"

But he'd gone. Swept out of the coffee shop in a flurry of chic designer suits and slicked-back blond hair.

"That's not quite the end of it, if you don't mind," Laura murmured as she placed another pound down on the table. Ewan was clearly rattled. He'd forgotten to pay for his tea.

Round one to whom? All she knew was that she had to bring on round two and fast.

Chapter Six

Provence, 1913

Emma reveled in the soft feel of brush against canvas, the way the morning light warmed her shoulders. The tactile nature of her work was comforting. As she detailed the slight cracks in the wicker on a chair in her painting, she kept her eyes focused on the ruptures and splits in the wood. And was aware, completely, utterly, of Patrick standing in the middle of the room waiting for her response.

"Why me?" she asked him. "Why would you want to paint my portrait when you don't paint anyone else?"

She kept going, allowing herself to be drawn in by the almost pearlescent colors in the wood.

"Because you understand it, Emma. You understand what it means to *have* to paint. Painting, for me, is the need to capture something that captivates me, to hold the very essence of something for one moment from the fleeting nature of time. You and I both know that with art, we at least have some way of expressing our feelings, to glimpse beauty. I see something in you as a person that I not only recognize in myself but that I want to express. That I have to express. It's all I can say."

Emma laid her brush back down. She rested her hand next to her on her stool. Her painting had become a blur in front of her eyes.

"What I see in you is the same thing that yearns to be expressed in myself," he said. "Painting you would be my way of capturing that essence that I saw in you straightaway and, in a small way, turning you into something eternal. I don't know. All I do know is that I have to paint you, if you will allow me to do so. I don't ask it lightly. The reason that I don't, as a rule, paint those people I know well is for that very reason—I know them. But with you, I feel that I know you, but while we are both artists, I also sense there is something about your character that remains elusive, that I respect and seek and will never fully understand. But I still want to try to capture it on canvas, to express it, because I find it beautiful."

Emma shifted her gaze out the window. She remained silent. The boat with the two red poppies on it still floated in front of her eyes.

"Very well," she said.

She closed her eyes when she heard his intake of breath. "Thank you. I promise I will not let you down. If you don't like it—"

She laughed; the tension broke.

The little boat started moving faster across the surface of the sea.

"The two women who own the little boat have commissioned me to paint the entrance hall in their chateau. Would you take a look at it with me tomorrow? I'd value your thoughts."

Emma stayed quiet.

"I've seen your portrait of Lady Somerville. Your use of color is breathtaking," Patrick said.

She looked critically at her work in progress.

"Frederick told me what you'd done at home in Gordon Square," he went on, sounding genuinely enthusiastic. "I heard about your decorative abilities, which is one of the reasons, I confess, I snuck up here to look at your work. And I'm sorry, I know you have things in your past that are... Well, Frederick did share with me some of the difficulties you had with your father. I hope you'll forgive my candor, but I did know Frederick well in London."

The sudden thought crossed Emma's mind that Frederick could have been in love with Patrick as well. Oh, dear God, she had to halt her feelings and thoughts sometime. She looked at him.

His focus was down at the floor, his exquisite profile thrown into perfect relief. His beauty was extraordinary. The more she watched, the more she felt the desire to paint him, in turn. Patrick's eyes were warm when he brought them up again to look at her. His character was clearly so complex. He had moved through three stages in the last few minutes—intensely emotive, to earnest, to warm and genuinely brotherlike. His clear warmth toward Frederick made her feel even closer to him again.

"I could pick you up in the early afternoon at, say, two. That way you could get in a morning session of work, then another one after we return. I won't keep you too long."

She nodded almost imperceptibly.

"I could meet you out front if that suited you?"

"Yes."

"It will be good to have your ideas. Lady Thea and her companion, Beatrice, are an interesting pair. But I think you'll like them very much. No, I'm sure of it."

He lingered a moment in the room before turning and walking out the door.

London, 1980

Jasper and Laura were the first to arrive at chamber group rehearsal in the Royal College of Music late that afternoon. Spring sunshine bathed the Amaryllis Fleming Concert Hall with light. Laura had already spent an hour wrangling with one of the pieces they were rehearsing—Mozart's *Divertimento in B Flat Major*. Stuck in a rehearsal room, she'd had to force herself to focus on achieving delicacy in the fast runs that the violin solo required, its brilliance lying in the need for complete accuracy and a lightness of bowing that her hands just did not want to execute today. Her mind was too busy trying to grasp on to a plan for approaching the bank next... unless they called her first to rescind their loan for her college fees, which was highly likely at this point.

"Have you read the *Evening Standard*?" Jasper sat down with a thump in the empty seat next to Laura in the first violin section.

"Please don't tell me you read that." Laura leaned her head on his shoulder.

"Oh, darling, you have to stop the whole thing. I have every faith that you can." He moved closer, scanning the stage as other members of the orchestra started appearing. Jasper lowered his voice. "Tell you what, the Scotsman's gorgeous—the evening paper had a photo, no holds barred and all that—heavenly dimple, cheeky smile, amazing skin tones. Can't you seduce him or marry what has to be his fabulous bank balance and force him to retract his claim?"

In spite of everything, Laura felt a smile play around her lips.

The room went quiet. The conductor stepped up on the dais.

Jasper rested a hand on her shoulder before standing to move back to the viola section. "Call on me. Whatever you need, I'll help."

Laura lifted her bow, her heart hammering in her chest. Rachmaninoff would suit her feelings far better than Mozart right now unless someone gave her the option to wring Ewan Buchanan's neck.

Her private lesson, directly after the rehearsal, was a disaster: she'd not gotten past the first bar of the Bartók *Solo Violin Sonata* that she was performing at the end of term. After three-quarters of an hour wrangling with the fiendishly difficult counterpoint and the left hand's pizzicato while the right hand required sublime legato in order to make anything work, her teacher called it quits early, sending her home. Laura's steps were heavy as she moved down the stairs outside the grand redbrick building that housed the music school. Instead of a head full of inspiration, Laura had a gut full of worry. And three violin students lined up to teach after supper this evening.

She made her way along Prince Consort Road before turning up Exhibition Road toward the Tube station. She'd rung Lydia at lunchtime, asking her to promise to protect Emma at all costs. One thing was for certain—Laura could trust Lydia to keep the media at bay. But for now, she needed to catch the bank manager before closing time. Laura had to know the extent of what they'd do to recoup their loan, if anything at this stage, and then she'd put the pressure on Ewan far more specifically to get him to retract his ridiculous statement and fast.

Once she was on the train home, sandwiched among five people and wedged under someone's armpit, Laura stared out at the black tunnels until they reached Russell Square. She strode up the road to her flat on Bernard Street, right around the corner from Gordon Square, where Emma still lived. The sense of the Circle living on in Bloomsbury seemed to hang about in the streets and the old garden squares, and now, being back here lent Laura at least some sense of security, having come away from the pretensions of Piccadilly's and Kensington's innate grandeur.

She made her way into her basement room at the bottom of the dingy house that, nevertheless, held a few failed attempts at politeness. The woman on the second floor had installed heavy chintz curtains in an effort to make the place look a little smarter than it really was. An old fan light decorated the main entrance on street level, but Laura had to go down a flight of steep, rutted, old cement steps to reach her basement studio, and no matter how much she swept the ground outside her front door, loose bits of rubbish and detritus always fluttered down from the street. She lived only a few steps from the Tube station, which rendered her street worlds away from Bloomsbury's elegant squares and Emma's and Patrick's artistic past.

Still, all these factors meant the rent was a million times cheaper than anything else in the area, and she could be near Gran. Laura dropped her key on the small table by her front door, turning on lamps as she made her way into the single room that she called home, a sense of overwhelming protectiveness engulfing her at the sight of her bed with its quilt designed by her grandmother and the cheap, old wooden table they'd found together at a flea market years ago, brought to life by Emma and Patrick, decorated with Emma's particular painted circles and Patrick's fluid human figures. These charming touches lent a whimsical air to the otherwise dull and cramped space. How dare anyone threaten it! Laura slumped down on her sofa.

Up until now, the biggest obstacle in her career had been her mother's antipathy toward Laura's chosen life path. Emma's daughter, Clover, had broken away from her own mother, rejecting Emma's bohemian lifestyle and setting up a small, quiet life in a village. Laura's mother worked in the local library, while spending the rest of her time keeping an immaculate house. And yet Laura knew that, as a child, Clover had been talented. Emma had encouraged her daughter as much as she later encouraged her granddaughter. Clover had once played the violin, decorated ceramics, and made up volumes of sketchbooks that Emma had shown Laura when she was small.

But in the end, Clover had rejected everything about the Circle and fled her artistic heritage. Marriage and stability meant everything to Clover—a practical means to an end.

When her phone rang, Laura half wondered if it would be her mother checking in on her during one of her rare, random phone calls. Clover must have read the *Times* article, unless the newspaper had not reached the depths of the countryside.

"Miss Taylor."

Laura took in a sharp breath. Not many people knew the sound of their bank manager's voice by heart. She did.

"Ivan," she said. Heaven help her if he read the *Evening Standard* as well.

"I know this is short notice, but do you happen to be free to come in this evening to talk?"

So. He'd gotten to her first.

"As a matter of fact," she said, running a hand over her brow, "I was going to come and see you." She said goodbye and stood up again, grabbed her light coat, and threw it over her shoulder.

Half an hour later, she sat opposite Ivan Mansell in the bank in Highgate's Euston Road. Laura gazed out through the slim gaps in the venetian blinds to the wide street, where men and women dressed in smart business attire moved with purpose up and down the sidewalks.

"I'm afraid," Ivan said, "that if the painting's provenance has been called into question and the Tate will not include it in their exhibition, then under the terms of our agreement, we will require a portion of the loan to be repaid immediately."

Laura felt her throat close over, tight.

"I'm sorry, but we did explain this at the time." Ivan sighed, wiping his hand across his bald head. "I know the work was authenticated by your grandmother, a long-term client, and Professor Rivers also provided enough evidence in his biography of Adams to satisfy the bank of its provenance for the purpose of a loan. However, now we have everything that the professor assumed potentially thrown on its head."

"Ivan—"

He held up a hand. "I'm sorry, but the painting's provenance has been put into question by the leading twentieth-century British art gallery in the country. If the painting cannot be included in an exhibition at the Tate, then we should not be using it as collateral to fund a bank loan any longer. The questions raised immediately reduce the value of the work and therefore the value of the collateral of your loan."

"But the claims are not proven beyond all doubt."

"Yes, but now the painting's validity *is* in doubt, and unfortunately, should you be unable to pay back the amount due, we have the right to acquire your grandmother's assets." Ivan pulled out a handkerchief and wiped his brow. "Relying on art as collateral is risky, but I never anticipated that something like this would happen. It hasn't happened in all the years I've…" He stopped. "May I ask if you are quite all right?"

Laura shook her head.

"I can give you and your grandmother a little time to gather the funds. But the bank will want surety, I'm afraid. Prepare yourself. It won't be long. I wanted to warn you right away. In fact, I didn't want to let this day go without informing you of our position on the matter. It is definite. I'm sorry."

Laura felt as if she were floating somewhere else.

"How long will we have?" she managed to say, but her words were a shadow of her normal voice.

"Not long. I can't see them letting it slide. Once again, I am sorry."

"Can you remind me of the portion of the loan that needs to be paid back?" She knew, but maybe, surely, she was wrong.

"It's right here in the small print." Ivan moved the agreement over for Laura to examine.

Laura leaned forward and read, "Fifty percent. Fifty thousand pounds." She raised a shaking hand to her head. Even her parents did not have anything like those sorts of assets in the bank.

Laura fought the urge to be sick.

"Have you any questions?" Ivan asked. "I'm happy to give you further clarification. I am saddened for you, Laura. I know how much your music means to you."

"Ewan Buchanan has no justification for his statement. I've already spoken to him, and he can't even tell me his reasons for stating that Patrick's painting is a fake. I need some time. I'm asking you for some time."

Ivan blew out an audible breath. "I'll try and stave off my superiors. But I have little hope that I'll be able to do so for long. A month would be generous. Two weeks might be a more likely scenario."

"Two weeks?"

Ivan stood up and reached out a hand. "Have you got somewhere you can go, Laura, someone you can be with?"

She managed to shake his hand. "No, I have students coming this evening. I have to teach." But her own hand trembled. Laura stumbled out of the bank, threading her way through the crowded street. Her legs seemed to barely work. She moved like some strange shadow of herself down to the station and made her way to the Northern Line and home.

Chapter Seven

Provence, 1913

Patrick appeared at the front door of the chateau in Provence in a pony trap the day after he'd first met Emma. She'd hardly slept the night before and had risen early to play with Calum before his breakfast. Ambrose had offered to play with him this morning, and the nanny Emma had employed would see that her little son's routine was all in place. Patrick stopped his horse and raised a brow at Emma, who stood ready on the front steps. Excitement blended inside her with anticipation and nerves in one heady, delicious blend.

"Borrowed the cart from my aunt's groomsman," he said, cheerfully patting the horse, clearly not bothered by the idea of driving about the fashionable Côte d'Azur in an ancient pony trap.

Emma eyed him from under the wide brim of her hat. She'd rolled the sleeves of her white lawn shirt up to her elbows as if she were a washerwoman about to plunge her hands into a basin of dirty clothes. She felt something flicker through her at the sight of the paint stains on his fingers, and she reached her equally decorated hand up to take his.

"I have to warn you," he said, walking the horse on down the driveway out to the wide country road beyond, "Lady Thea Rose and her partner, Beatrice Connelly, are quite the pair of outright saphs. I hope they won't shock you."

"For goodness' sake. It makes no difference to me. Surely you know that."

She shot a look toward him and saw the way his eyes crinkled at the sides.

"Chocolates?" he asked, producing a box of elegant chocolate creams.

"You do make me laugh," she said.

He held out the box with one hand while driving with the other. "Chocolate and insouciance are the perfect ways to deal with infidelity in a husband."

Emma startled a little at his candor. Had he been studying her so carefully yesterday that he'd sensed what was going on with Lawrence, Oscar, and her? Or what had he heard?

"All you need to do is to remind yourself that you really don't need him around," Patrick went on.

"Your audacity on such a fine summer afternoon is unique," she murmured, eyeing the tempting box of dark chocolates in a myriad of exotic shapes. A detailed description of each of them was imprinted on the lid of the wooden box. She chose a peppermint crème. "I am beguiled by your complexities." That was not quite right. She was starting to fall for them…

Gently he reached out, taking the chocolate from her hand, his fingers brushing hers for the briefest, most delicious of moments. Emma opened her lips, and gently, he placed the chocolate on her tongue.

Emma almost swallowed the chocolate whole.

"What I don't like," she said, once she'd swirled the crème center into a small sliver in her mouth, "what annoys me in a man more than infidelity in a husband is a man who makes promises, then doesn't keep them. It always leaves me wondering whether he ever meant what he said in the first place—whether I can believe anything he will say in the future."

She allowed the sides of her lips to turn up when Patrick grinned.

"I try to deal with vagaries in men in the most reasonable way I can," she explained. "Otherwise, we may as well get out dueling pistols. As I'm a pacifist, I resort to reason when dealing with them at all times." Emma frowned at her sudden outburst. What had possessed her to say all that?

She reached up and held on to her hat.

Patrick stopped the horse, turning to her, his face more serious. He reached out for a moment, laying his hand on her arm, before turning into the silent country road that led on through the lavender fields.

He stayed quiet.

Emma felt heat stain her cheeks.

Finally, Patrick halted the pony when they came to another crossroads. "Talking of convention versus taking a more tolerant approach to things, Thea and Beatrice are a bit of a conundrum to me. Their way of life is entirely independent of the conventions back home, and yet, I find their house and garden fastidiously neat. It's hardly bohemian in the way most of us live. I'm not sure why they live that way, but I can't help worrying that by presenting an immaculate front to the world, they are trying to prove that they are not... what people say they are... in some way, obscene for loving each other the way they do." His voice cracked.

Emma took a quick glance across at him, stopping herself from staring or showing her startled reaction to his close proximity on the little cart. Their shoulders almost touched, and she wanted to drink in the exquisite line of muscles in his arms. She felt a much stronger pull toward him than the frisson of excitement she'd felt yesterday.

"It must be unfathomably difficult," she said, wanting to acknowledge his struggles, without saying anything direct.

"At home, women are able to love each other and to live together in relative peace. They are not outlawed, but even still, there's some judgment; it is far freer for them here in France to be who they are, to live and to love with still less condemnation. For men, it is almost impossible..." His voice trailed off.

Emma nodded. She wanted to understand and accept him for who he was, but here was the rub—she was sensing strong signs that he might be showing a real interest in her, and she wanted him to do so, despite all she knew about his romantic history.

"You know, you have the reputation of being somewhat exclusive yourself, Emma," Patrick said, urging the pony on, shooting an amused glance toward her.

She felt her heart lift a little at the lighter tone in his voice, while it dropped at the meaning behind his words. "No!"

"Only socializing with your Cambridge friends? Looking down on any discussion other than the intellectual? Fleeing off to Bloomsbury? And you, in the middle of it, an artist… people see you as very exclusive indeed, Mrs. Temple."

"I don't classify myself as an intellectual, though," she murmured. "Not at all. Not like the others."

"Perhaps another artist in your close circle would be a welcome balance," he offered.

Emma gazed sharply out at the sea on her left.

"I admire your confidence in striking out," he went on, his voice still with that honeyed hush. "I'm intrigued by your determination to live on your own terms, no matter what."

"I confess, though, that back in London," she started tentatively, "I did find myself wanting to retreat from the world, not only in my life but also in art. I started experimenting with abstract forms—I suppose I wanted to break things up. I couldn't see, for a while, explanations for any of it—the world, people, life after Frederick's death. But out here, in France, it is different. The light and nature make the real world so astonishing that it's something I want to be part of fully while I am alive. It's something I want to paint. I'm not sure that abstraction is right for me after all."

"I completely agree," he murmured. "I played with abstraction myself for a while too—I'm still intrigued by collage. I keep coming back to realism but in a new, modern way. Do you know what I mean?"

Emma nodded. She was finding it impossible to view this discussion in the way she viewed the intellectual banter that she had been drawn to since the early days with Frederick. There was something far more intimate and personal about the way Patrick was addressing her. He really seemed to hear what she said and didn't say.

"I want to bring a sense of constancy into Beatrice and Thea's chateau," he went on. "To soften their sense of isolation and to remind them that they are part of the ongoing nature of things. In the classical world, beauty and love were appreciated in different ways. People such as us were not always frowned upon as we are in our time. I'm interested in the truth that lies behind the mask they put on, and I want to inspire them to be confident in themselves. I worry that they live with such military precision."

"The military…" Emma veered on to that conversational path, keeping her focus on the road ahead, even though her thigh was touching his, and she could lean her head on his shoulder if she wanted to. "Ambrose, Lawrence, and Oscar talk of nothing else but politics. Should there be a war, the government will require Ambrose's financial expertise, Lawrence will most likely try to be acquitted from service, and Oscar, no doubt, will take on some helpful role in London."

"I could *never* kill another human being." Patrick's words held such urgency that Emma felt her whole body respond as they approached the chateau. "I try to accept people as they are, entirely. I believe that if we all accepted others as they were, the world would be better for it."

It might be what I have to do with you, she thought, *or I will lose you. Another artist in our circle of friends would be… perfect; it would round things out.*

Right then, he leaned across, and her breathing quickened before, suddenly, he dropped a kiss on her forehead.

The intimacy that she felt with him seemed so heightened that she could hardly breathe. "If I am a little exclusive," she whispered, "it's because I surround myself only with the people I like most. Yet sometimes, I feel alone."

"You've made a little circle for yourself within your circle of friends, and you need someone who understands you entirely, who is there for you. I'm happy to do that."

Emma took in the house beside the cart; her heart beat like quick fire.

"Beauty in nature is eternal," he murmured. "That is why you are drawn to it. Love is also eternal. If you love your circle of friends, there is nothing wrong with that."

"I'm glad we've got that sorted," she whispered.

He smiled as he gently coaxed the pony to move on.

London, 1980

After her foray to the bank, Laura let herself into her little studio. She closed her eyes and wrapped her arms around her body, which seemed, rather than being its usual conglomerate of feelings and thoughts and busyness and productivity, dead. As if nothing were left. On automatic pilot, she went over to the fridge, pulling out the two lamb chops she'd bought for dinner, striking on the gas on her stovetop, placing a pan on the hob. She prepared a salad, but then once her meal was ready, she thought she was going to be ill. She had half an hour until her first student for the evening would arrive.

Hopelessly, she gazed around the room, her eyes alighting on her violin in its case. She stood up, moving toward it, the need to play seeming overwhelming. To get away from the banality of this world—from money and vagaries and people and… everything.

There seemed to be no hope of any answers. What sort of explanation could there be for this? None.

Once she'd taken out the beautiful Guadagnini, forcing herself not to think how she may not be able to pick it up in a month or two weeks or after however long the bank decided to take back her loan, she placed the mute on her violin. She raised the beautiful instrument to her shoulder and tuned up, thankful as always for the fact that she'd been given the gift of perfect pitch. She knew the moment she stroked the strings with her bow that she'd be able to play, even if she had only a short time tonight. As her instincts danced over the first movement of her adored Bach Double Violin Concerto, the opening notes seeming to hold such depth and power all at once, she realized that it was strength and beauty Bach displayed in his wonderful music, and those things were exactly what drove Emma in her life.

The more her violin swept over the notes, the more Laura came to know what she had to do. She may not have the answers yet, she may never find out whether Patrick painted that portrait or whether she would be able to go on doing the one thing she loved more than anything in the world, but she did know a solid truth: Emma was still alive, and Emma should not be pushed aside from anything. While Laura's first instincts had been to protect her grandmother, to stop Emma's heart from becoming even more bruised than it had been for years loving Patrick when he was not able to love her back in the way she needed to be loved, the fact was Emma the one person who knew more than anyone else about this whole situation. What was more, Laura believed, like her grandmother, that people should not be excluded or judged or deemed to be unworthy because of their age or because of anything else.

She began the slow, lilting second movement, the notes drawing out in exquisite beauty, and in her head, the sound of the second violin's voice sang along next to her.

She would take Emma out to Summerfield, and together, they would both look at the painting.

The simple truth of Bach's theme carried her away to another place. She leaned into the music. Her violin sang. The second movement always sounded to her like a lone lark telling a story of loss, of love, of people who sought something more beautiful than was found in this world, while at the same time, sadness in the music seemed to encompass something that was gone, never to come back. The way the notes hung in the air also called of uncertainty. Perhaps some things were never meant to be told. And maybe there was a beauty in that.

The last note lingered as if it held all the mystery on this earth. All that remained when she stopped playing was silence, tarrying like haunting questions.

She forced herself to sit down and eat the food she'd prepared. She would be logical, as Emma always was—or as Laura always perceived her to be. For sometimes, what we think we know about others may only be correct in our imaginations, but perhaps our imagination gives the truest interpretation of the world. Laura had to help her grandmother see that what they had all believed for so long was its own fact. And the only way to do that was to take Emma out to Summerfield, to go and look at *The Things We Don't Say* and allow Patrick's work to speak for itself. And then, Laura would get the woman who she honestly believed knew and loved Patrick better than anyone else in this world to confirm that the work was definitely his own.

The following morning, Laura gazed out of the taxi that they'd caught from the train station in Lewes as they approached the serene South Downs; the line of high hills sat behind Summerfield, protecting the old farm from the wild weather that blew in from the nearby south coast. She'd telephoned the caretaker to tell him they would be visiting today. He was going to be working on the farm and would not be able to let them in, so Laura had Emma's own key safely in her handbag. Emma sat in silence beside her. She seemed to have retreated into her own world ever since Laura told her about her meeting with Ewan Buchanan. Laura knew better than to probe.

Laura clasped her hands in her lap. The local taxi driver seemed to have picked up on their contemplative mood as they made their way up the rough, isolated track that led to Summerfield. She hardly heard Emma as she thanked the driver and paid the fare; Laura's eyes raked over the old farmhouse as if in hope that it would give her answers instead of all these questions that life was throwing at them right now.

But all she could do when she looked at Summerfield's dear facade was sigh in despair. Paint crumbled on it; the climbing roses that spread up the front of the building ran rampant, their gnarled branches intertwining in elaborate knots. The garden beds that edged the lake were overgrown, and the lawn was blousy with the last of the spring bulbs, waving like silent ghosts in the light breeze. Laura gazed upward at the cracked paintwork on the eaves, at the water stains that ran down the outside of the house, taking in the guttering that was pocked with holes. Emma's beloved lake was only resplendent with algae these days.

Laura turned the key in the peeling front door.

Resisting the temptation to bend over and shake out the doormat that was strewn with dead leaves and rose petals, she went inside. At once, the dim interior engulfed her with the past.

She went ahead of her grandmother, aware of her stillness, of the way her footsteps were slow in the hallway, where once they would have tripped along the bare floorboards. Laura glanced left into the dim dining room, where Emma and Patrick's painted motifs covered every surface, from the door panels to the table and chairs. The old house seemed to draw Laura in even further the deeper she went.

Being here only cemented her view that Ewan was wrong.

Emma's steps were measured and steady in her old brown lace-up shoes. She arrived in her bedroom—the room where so much had played out.

Laura had to bring her hand up to her mouth when she caught sight of Emma's bathtub—the bath that Patrick had installed for Emma so that she could soak and think in her favorite room. The patterns and flowers that decorated its sides looked as if they could have been painted this morning. Emma's small wooden writing desk sat in the corner of the room, a photo of Emma's mother on the top right-hand side. A sheaf of notepaper was laid out as if abandoned.

They both moved toward Emma's single bed. It sat, lonesome against the wall, facing outward to the walled garden, where she used to take her breakfast on summer mornings. The blinds were halfway up, and sunlight beamed in from the flower garden outside.

It was as if by some unspoken agreement that they both looked to the portrait at the same time. Laura watched Emma, as she tried to find answers from Patrick's interpretation of her when she was young. She hung on the wall as she'd always done, seated, her gaze slightly to the side. She rested her chin in one of her hands, her long fingers reaching up to her cheek. The rings on her fingers glinted as if they, too, held untold secrets, and behind her sat one of her own paintings, a cluster of oranges and lemons that she'd put in a vase when Patrick sent them to her after a visit to Spain. Emma's green dress highlighted the tones in her olive skin.

"Gran," Laura said, "shall I take it off the wall?"

Emma nodded. Laura moved the bed.

Silently she eased the painting off the wall, trying not to stare, not to feel everything at once at the sight of the darker patch of paint on the wall that looked like an unwelcome stain once the portrait was gone. With Emma padding along behind her, Laura carried the portrait down the hallway to the farmhouse kitchen, where rows of beautiful, thick cream earthenware mugs that Patrick and Emma had designed together still hung on hooks above the sink. Emma's parents' blue-and-white platters sat in a row above the old range where Lydia had always held court. Laura glanced toward the staircase that led up to the attic from the kitchen, stairs that Lydia used to descend from her bedroom down here, each morning, for all those years.

It was as if the house was bursting with the past. No one was ever going to live here in the way that Emma, Patrick, and the Circle had done. Laura held *The Things We Don't Say* upright, then laid it out on the old farmhouse kitchen table, where they could examine it with proper care.

"I don't know why he never signed it," Emma murmured, standing close, peering at the space where an artist's signature would go. "But just by looking at it, we can see that the canvas comes from the 1920s." Emma reached out her hand, as if she were about to touch her portrait, only to let her fingers stay while in front of the frame. "Next, let's look at the details," Emma said.

Laura felt respect for her grandmother's quiet professionalism.

"It's got all the hallmarks of Patrick's work," Emma went on. "He always used different colors to tone a painting, and look at the way details are blurred—some things are left a little unfinished. See, if you look closely, the features on my face are a little hazy."

Laura nodded. "It always looked a little unfinished to me. As if he was going to come back to it sometime…"

"No. I, too, used to blur faces. You see, it's to show that we could never know a person entirely. That was why we believed in treating them with respect, because we can never inhabit another person's feelings, thoughts, ideas."

Laura searched her grandmother's face. The irony of this statement was not something on which she wanted to focus just now.

"Look at the way he only hints at the folds in my green dress. It's realism but with a touch of abstract modernism in his execution—that's just what we did. And see, the influence of Cézanne there, and here, with the almost flat representation of the fabric on the chair. I can't see that some student could have attended to all this, nor could they have captured the hallmarks of Patrick's innate style.

"I have no doubt it's his work. I think we could easily get an auction house to back us up, but I am so sure, darling."

Laura reached out and stroked the back of Emma's paint-stained hand.

"I have another suggestion," Emma said. She raised her head from the painting and eyed Laura. "We make a counterstatement to the *Times* ourselves."

Laura felt a flicker of warmth in her system. Dear, clever Gran.

"A little wicked, my dear," Emma went on, "but perhaps just this once we could not be pacifists?"

Laura caught the light in her grandmother's eyes and grinned.

Chapter Eight

London, 1980

Late that afternoon, Emma stood, silent in her hallway once Laura had gone home. She'd put on a brave face with Laura. It was what she always did. And in any case, if Emma had learned one thing in this life, it was that understanding of others came only with the acceptance that we were all flawed and vulnerable, just in our own unique ways.

But Patrick? Was he capable of lying to her? They'd avoided conflict, but did that mean they'd not told each other important things?

She could look at the painting today and say that it was his work—that was certain. But still, she could never push aside the pain she'd felt that summer in France when Jerome had been living with them and loving Patrick. Sometimes, she knew, pain was something she'd constructed herself, by imagining a problem that might not exist. Emma knew she was susceptible to such things, given her wild imagination and her need to give in to it in order to carry out her work. And yet, deep down she had always been in conflict over the extent of Patrick's love for her.

Emma made her way up the stairs to the studio at the top of this house. She sat at her easel. Work had always been her salvation. Goodness knew, it had saved her through two world wars.

But now, what sat in front of her was a gift for Laura, a portrait of her. Emma knew there was a chance it would be the last piece she ever did. She'd rendered her granddaughter in a chair, ironically, much as Patrick had painted Emma. But Laura gazed straight at the viewer, confronting head-on whoever was looking at her. There was no hint of Laura looking away or avoiding anything. If character was what Emma was trying to capture, Laura seemed far more straightforward a subject than herself. Or was she? The fact that Emma had begun the faint sketch of Laura's violin in the painting now seemed awful, brutal. She would not, while she had breath in her body, cut the violin out.

But how to prove without doubt that Patrick had painted her? Intuition was one thing, but Emma's own memories were only confusing her when she tried to look back. It seemed that what she did remember were only the times that were the brightest flowers in a vase full of everyday blooms. What if she simply couldn't recall some momentous detail of what may have transpired that long-ago summer when Patrick put paint to canvas for her portrait? Emma worried that her inability to recall the past would cause Laura to lose the career that Emma knew would save her granddaughter from the worst that life could throw at her.

Thinking about it all was so very much harder without those she loved who'd lived through everything with her—Patrick, Ambrose, Lawrence, Oscar, Freya. Dear Calum. Sometimes, looking back, life seemed to fold out behind her like one endless stream of loss.

And yet, the memory of all the people she'd loved kept them alive in her heart. But her memories were only her own interpretations, a myriad blend of feelings, emotions, and thoughts that, in the end, were nothing to do with how others felt, thought, and behaved. Memory, in the end, existed only in the imagination. It was just a story we made up.

Emma looked down at her folded hands in her lap. So that was all she had to work with—a story of some long-ago artistic life. If working through her own past was a daunting and complex task, then saving Laura's future was looking more impossible than anything she'd ever faced. And she was ninety. It had to be almost time for her to let go of this world.

But both her beautiful granddaughter's future and Patrick's memory were worth fighting for.

Emma nodded, as if making some final deal with herself. She went to the telephone, collected her glasses, picked up her address book, and opened to B. For Bank. She would start to make steps herself. Patrick's biographer might be dead, but there were other people to whom she could reach out.

"Good afternoon," she said when Ivan answered his direct line. "It is Emma Temple."

"Mrs. Temple."

Her bank manager had always seemed like a measured person. So how would she best get through to him? Mathematics? Logic? Surely a bank manager lived by such things. He wouldn't be moved by art or beauty, as all her old friends were.

"Your granddaughter has been to see me," Ivan said. "I've explained where we stand. I'm sorry."

"I know. But it is a shame that the person in question is no longer alive to put this… problem to rest," she said.

There was a pause.

"Mrs. Temple—"

"Emma."

"I can't do anything except give you a couple of weeks. I know you understand the finances only too well. I'm sorry. I really am. I don't know if she told you the time frame."

Emma traced a pattern on the delicate painted wood of the little table on which her telephone sat. Of course Laura had not worried her with that.

She closed her eyes when she spoke. "I am willing to give away everything I own to pay you back, Ivan, but I can't sit by and let Laura lose her reason for living."

There was a silence down the line. "I believe she does not want to cause you distress in turn. But I can't get away from the agreement."

Emma reminded herself that the man was only doing his job.

"I have no doubt that the portrait is Patrick's work. We will prove it is so, and I'm sure everything will be fine. Please be reassured that I will keep in touch with you and ensure you're updated on any developments. Laura and I will do our utmost to keep the loan going, and please be aware that there is not, in any way, any deception on either of our parts where our relationship with the bank is concerned."

"Of course not."

Emma said goodbye and hung up the phone. Slowly she made her way back to her painting and picked up her brushes.

Who could verify the painting if the one expert on the Circle was dead? An auction house? But then the very person, the expert curator who'd been called out to appraise it, had claimed it was a fraud. He'd probably worked at Sotheby's before owning this gallery himself.

Emma knew she could waste time getting other opinions, but her best bet was within her. She had to remember the past. Freya had started the idea that people were like books. We had no chance of knowing them at all beyond the titles that sat on the covers. And she and Patrick had been struck by that idea—and so they'd blurred faces in their art. Had Laura picked up the irony of that in his portrait today? Well, it didn't matter. What mattered was that somehow, Emma was going to have to prove that theory wrong.

Provence, 1913

Patrick passed his cigarette to Emma while they waited on the steps of Beatrice and Thea's chateau. His fingers lingered on Emma's; his eyes narrowed behind the smoke.

Oscar had taught Emma to smoke during their honeymoon in Rome. They'd both laughed at the disapproving stares she'd received from Englishwomen. Now, she tapped the ash off the end of the cigarette and took in Beatrice and Thea's charming garden, which spread before them surrounded by cool, mysterious cypress trees.

"An independent woman is still seen as a difficult one, you know," she said, extending the cigarette back toward Patrick. "I'm probably just as outcast as you even though I am not of your persuasion. We will both have to be strays…"

Patrick held out his hand for the cigarette, blowing smoke rings that were both sexy and resonant with attitude. He was elegant, exotic, the most attractive of men. Her attraction for him was worlds away from what she'd felt for Oscar or Lawrence. Now, it was clear to her that those relationships had been protective, born, first, out of Frederick's death and, next, out of Oscar's betrayal. But with Patrick, it was as if she was finally meeting with someone on her own terms. That seemed fascinating to her. It was almost as if he were a mirror image of her own complex, creative, questioning self. And she had no problems confessing that she liked that.

"You're not difficult," he said. "You're extraordinary. The most extraordinary and interesting woman I've ever met by far. You are nothing like other women."

"Is that supposed to be a compliment to my sex or not?" She couldn't hold back a laugh.

An amused expression passed across his face in turn. "I'm not trying to be offensive. Just honest. I'm saying that I'm intrigued by you, and I'm telling you that you're not difficult. You're delightful. And bloody attractive." He nudged her.

She threw back her head and laughed louder now. "I still think that a woman who wants to be more than decorative is viewed as trouble." She leaned back on the front steps, stretching out her legs and lifting her face toward the sun.

"Just be yourself. It's too hard to be anyone else," he said. "On the other hand, being a sodomite, I am thought of as either a harmless lunatic or a criminal." He sat up, changing tack like the little boat with its poppies out on the sea. "Emma, would you mind very much if I started to make some preliminary sketches of you? Right now? I want to make up hundreds of sketches before I take my brush to the canvas for you. It will be my ultimate gift to you, you know that."

Streaks of white ran across the otherwise eggshell-blue of the sky. Emma inclined her gaze downward to his hands and regarded them under her eyelashes. The heady, roguish, light-headed attraction she felt toward him was overwhelming her. Were her body and mind playing tricks on her? And was there any possibility that Patrick might not be playing tricks himself?

"I don't mind if you work on the preliminaries now," she murmured. And watched him as he pulled a small sketch pad out of his pocket.

He undid the tie that bound the leather notebook together, turning the leaves until he came to a fresh white page.

Emma entwined her hands in her lap. She gazed out at the garden, unable, for some reason, to stare directly at him. A flutter of nerves, excitement, she knew not what, danced through her system. But she shouldn't be nervous. Goodness knew, she'd sketched countless models herself at the Royal Academy, not to mention Freya, Frederick... her father.

"I don't subscribe to the Sitwell Circle. I'm not some dandy or a cliché," Patrick said, his tone conversational.

Emma swiped a glance down at his sketch pad before just as quickly turning away. He had already captured her expression so closely to the way in which she viewed herself as to be almost uncomfortable to see it.

"We are all lumped together in this sort of Wildean aestheticism," he said. "And yet, we are individuals. As different from each other as anyone else. Why do we humans persist with convenient ways of categorizing each other when we can hardly begin to work ourselves out?"

"From what I know of my circle of friends, sexuality can be as complicated and individual as human nature," Emma said. She couldn't help but be honest about how she'd lain awake last night, her mind wandering over delicious thoughts about Patrick. There were far more colors in this world than black and white.

"I hope you didn't mind my raising that Frederick told me about your father and about the restrictions he imposed on you because of your sex," he said.

"They were difficult years."

"Frederick told me other things, Emma. I don't want to probe, but…"

"You had a very open relationship with my brother?" She spun around to face him all of a sudden. "I cannot tell you what it means to me to speak of him, to sit with someone who was truly close to Frederick—who got beyond discussions about politics, economics, and the world. Please, do not in any way hold back!"

He placed his charcoal down a moment before reaching out and taking her hand. He held it. "Emma," he said, "for one thing, you know Frederick adored you."

She sighed, wanting to drink this man in. Frederick had opened up her world in ways that no one else had done or could do. Had the timing been different and had Arthur not married and her father not died when they did, she would have ended up like so many women, the possession of her father and then owned by a husband, with no control over the way she lived. She owed Frederick her freedom and marriage that did not restrict her in any way. She knew, for her, at least, this was a vital thing to have as an artist, as a person, and as a woman.

"He said that your father had terrible rages and that the way you dealt with them was to shut yourself off. He worried that you withdrew into your own little shell and didn't talk about things."

"I suppose, in some ways, it sounds as if I were weak, putting up with his temper for so long. But it was impossible to rationalize with him when he was in a rage. Reason would not work, and I could not appeal to his heart while he was in a state, so I shut myself off. I withdrew. It sounds dreadful, I know, but I could only escape and start a new life once he was dead because I had no means of supporting myself or Freya while he was alive. If I'd had my own income, I would have left, because sadly, sometimes, the only thing you can do is walk away when other people's behavior is never going to change. I am determined, always, to be able to support myself."

The colors in the garden seemed to merge into one misty fog.

Patrick leaned closer and started to speak, but just as he did, the sound of horses' hooves crushed his words. Women's voices rang loud and confident over the rattle of carriage wheels on gravel.

Patrick closed his sketchbook and stood up at the same time as Emma did. He rested his hand on her shoulder for a brief moment. Emma felt her whole body react as if it were on fire. And told herself that he was probably only being brotherly.

She stepped down toward the welcome and yet unwelcome interruption. Emma knew now that she could spend the rest of the day—of her life—talking with Patrick.

The open carriage stopped in line with the front steps to the house. Patrick indicated that Emma go ahead of him to greet the two women who sat in the velvet seats.

"Dearest Patrick! We saw the pony trap and thought you'd either sent your manservant to apologize, which simply would not do, or you'd forgotten altogether and we had some dull visitor instead of you, at which point, we'd have to hide in the hydrangeas. Oh!" The woman who spoke stepped down onto the gravel driveway and peered up at Emma. "Who is this? What an interesting outfit! You do collect such wonderful people, Patrick. *Vous êtes Française?*" the tall woman asked Emma in loud French.

"No, I'm not French. I'm Emma Temple, of London." Emma reached out a hand to the dark, angular woman, who met Emma squarely eye to eye. Her outfit was made of what looked like Japanese silk—wildly fashionable given the ongoing fascination with Japonaiserie that still crazed the wealthy sets. She looked to be in her mid-forties and had that certain confidence women of that age often bore.

"The infamous Emma Temple."

Emma tilted her head to one side.

Before Emma could respond to Beatrice, a shorter woman alighted from the carriage, wearing a loose caramel-colored frock that draped her curvaceous body. Pearls wafted from her neck down to her chest. "I'm Thea," she said. Emma noticed the beads of sweat that lined her forehead.

She shook both women's hands.

"Patrick's talent astounds us. Took the opportunity to grab him while he is here. We want something unusual and striking to decorate our front entrance hall," Thea said.

A manservant appeared and opened the front door. As Emma wandered into the cool interior, she noticed that Patrick was right. Everything was, indeed, immaculate. A bowl of flowers sat on a perfectly placed walnut table, and the books that were next to the vase in turn were stacked one on top of the other with military precision. The foyer was decorated with a swirling staircase, the banisters full of gold embellishments and curlicues. So these two had not abandoned wealth. They clearly held different values from those of the Circle. How varying and complex rebellion could be...

"I've been wondering about the ancient Greeks—their open ideas toward love in the classical world. I admit, at first, I wanted to lighten up the tone in here with some of my favorite male circus acrobats, but I think timeless love would be perhaps a more enduring and appropriate theme in these surroundings than frivolity," Patrick said, marching into the middle of the entrance hall and gazing at the wall that ran down next to the stairs.

Emma eyed him. He seemed to have switched out of the intimate mode he'd adopted with her to take on the demeanor of the professional artist he was without batting an eyelid. That was utterly compelling, too, she had to admit.

"I've been thinking about a masked ball to reveal the murals," Beatrice said, her voice high-pitched, as if holding a sense of excitement.

Patrick regarded the woman a moment. "Good idea, but I'd like to consult Emma and ask her opinion before I discuss my final proposal with you, if I might?"

"Oh, I see," Beatrice said, eyeing Emma with something that looked like respect. "We shall leave you both to consult."

Emma wandered closer to the pale, smooth wall. She reached out her hand, touching the wonderful blankness of it. The idea of working alongside Patrick to shape, condense, and order her own sensations into the permanence of art was entrancing. It was one thing to work by oneself, but to collaborate with someone who felt the same way as she did, well, that was something wonderful.

Chapter Nine

London, 1980

Two days later, Laura sat in the train with Jasper, holding Emma's rebuttal in that day's *Times*. Jasper pulled a cigarette out and placed it between his lips, leaving it hanging there unlit as the train approached Highgate Station.

"Bit desperate, isn't it?" Laura shot a sideswipe at him and, in spite of herself, laughed.

"Nope." He pulled the cigarette out and waved it around. "Forward planning"—he threw an arm around Laura's shoulder—"always reduces future stress."

A chill slipped through Laura's system as they stepped off the train onto the platform. People rushed by in the evening crowd. They were all intent on going on their own trajectories. A woman sighed with annoyance as Laura stopped in the middle of the platform, wishing she knew which direction her life was going to take.

Her nerves swooped like kites as she started moving toward High Street. She half listened to Jasper's chatter, but no matter how hard she tried to plan what to say to Ivan, she ended up going around in circles. If Ivan wouldn't accept Emma's opinion that the painting was Patrick's—seriously, what then?

Her next step could be an auction house, but as Emma pointed out, Ewan had worked in just such a place, so how would the bank decide who was right and who was wrong, even if another appraiser came to a different conclusion than Ewan had done? Surely the woman who was the subject of the portrait and the intimate friend and onetime lover of Patrick Adams would have credibility when it came to verifying his work.

Today's *Times* felt like a sixty-four-thousand-dollar question rather than the answer she'd hoped it would be. While Emma had lashed back at Ewan, making bold statements about the portrait that would leave only the most die-hard cynic with any doubt that it was Patrick's work, the bank was firm about the fact that *any doubt* was a problem.

"Yikes, Laura!" Jasper's voice broke into her thoughts. "Promise me you won't end up like that!" A young woman heaved past them pushing a stroller laden with two babies. "She looks exhausted, darling. Promise me…"

"Oh, it's exactly how I'll end up. Pushing prams around all day with a smoke hanging out of my mouth—a convenient marriage is one way out of this mess."

"Won't let it happen." He stubbed out his cigarette on the ground.

They stopped outside the glass walls of the bank. Laura heaved the front door open and gathered herself inside on the orange carpet a moment. Jasper moved over to a stand of brochures, looking absurdly out of place in the bland environs of the bank. His jeans were torn at the knee, and his pointed shoes would be at home on a vaudeville stage. Today, he wore a fedora.

When Ivan came out of an office, Jasper wandered back toward her and placed his hat on her head.

"I've got to go," she said. She handed the hat back.

Jasper squeezed her hand. "I'll window-shop while you do your stuff. Will keep an eye on the bank for you to come out."

Laura shot him a panicked look. "If the bank won't budge—"

"Just stay focused. On you and Em."

Laura nodded, her whole body shuddering now, and went toward Ivan's office. When he indicated that she should come in, Laura handed her copy of the *Times* to him and sat down.

He scanned it and sighed.

"Laura," he said, "we've seen the article, but I'm afraid I can't give you good news. The fact is our area manager was skeptical about your loan when we signed it up. The only reason he agreed to it was because your grandmother has been a long-standing client. But it has always been clear that any doubt thrown on the value of the painting turns everything on its head for us." Ivan leaned forward on his desk. "There's no easy way to tell you this. The bank is going to have to entirely rescind the loan. You can have two weeks, but I'm sorry, there is absolutely nothing more we can do."

Laura eyeballed the wall behind him. Two ugly paintings were the only thing that decorated it, if one could use that word. A filing cabinet sat, dull and gray.

She leaned back, slowly, in her seat, her hands gripping the armrests.

"I'm sorry, Laura," he said.

She looked up. Such a bandage of a word.

"I suggest, in this case, that you talk to your parents. See if they can help you finish your studies."

"They don't have the funds to do so."

Ivan tapped his pen on the desk. "I'm sorry, Laura. But you have to see that in our position, we can't—"

"I want to ask you to give me four weeks. Four weeks to prove Ewan Buchanan wrong."

"Laura—"

But she leaned forward in her seat. "I've never missed one repayment yet; I'm working a part-time job, teaching violin students; and when I graduate and finally get a position in an orchestra, I'll start paying back the principal. But in the meantime, tell me what exact proof you need."

"We'd need Ewan Buchanan to retract his statement to clear up any controversy. Let me put it this way: if the Tate relied on Mr. Buchanan's opinion before allowing the piece to be exhibited there, then the bank would also be confident that if Mr. Buchanan changed his mind and convinced the Tate to exhibit it after all, we could continue with the terms of your loan. You could seek another opinion, but at this point, we'd need the museum to be confident that the portrait is an Adams. At the moment they are not. They chose their expert, and they are following his advice, just as they should do."

Laura rose up taller in her seat. "But shouldn't the possibility that the work is Patrick's be given a fair chance to be investigated? Two weeks is hardly a reasonable amount of time."

Ivan tented his hands under his chin.

Laura pulled her hands out from underneath herself, realizing she'd been sitting on them.

"I can see your point, Laura," he said finally. "But I have my answer."

"I need time to get to the bottom of this."

He waited. "I will ask, one more time."

Laura shook his outstretched hand. She managed to walk out the door, stepping into the late-afternoon sunshine and shading her eyes from the sudden glare to spot Jasper leaning on a park bench like an Adonis.

He leaped up and moved over to her.

"Well?" he asked intently.

"I'm going straight to confront Ewan now," she muttered, starting to walk. "No time to waste. They won't take Emma's word as testimony. While it's tempting to get another opinion, it's very clear to me that I need to cut this off at the source. And that's Ewan Buchanan. I'm trying to get the bank to give me four weeks, but at the moment, I only have two. And very little, if any, possibility they'll extend that at all."

Jasper kept pace alongside her. "Do not let Ewan fob you off again."

The chuckle Laura let out was dry. "Oh, don't you worry. Never, Jasper, could I be accused of doing that."

*

Half an hour later, Laura stalked her way up New Bond Street alone, determination propelling her along as she approached Ewan Buchanan's gallery. But then, she stopped. Laura felt in her handbag for the business card he'd handed to her last time. She turned the corner to Brook Street in order to find a phone box. When she spotted one, she slipped inside, pulled out a few coins, and cleared her throat, dialing the direct number listed.

"Ewan, it's Laura."

"Hi."

She forced herself not to focus on the pair of women in expensive dresses who waited outside the phone box. It would not do to take out her irritation on them. "I'm not going to beat around the bush," she said. "Are you free? Now. I have to talk to you."

The sound of him flicking through papers seemed to ring down the phone line.

Laura closed her eyes. Rational. That was what Emma would be. Laura clung to her tendency to channel what Emma would do when faced with awkward situations.

The two women outside the phone box gave Laura pointed looks. Laura rested her forehead on the phone.

"Laura, I'm not in a position to say anything other than what I've already told you—"

"You are not in a *position* to say what? I need more information from you, at the very least. You owe us that." Laura measured each word as if drawing out the lengthiest possible notes on her violin.

"You do have to understand that I'm not able to talk about this, Laura. I never wanted to do you or Emma any harm. But I had to tell the truth. I'm sorry."

Laura stayed quiet.

"Where are you at the moment?" He sounded strangely close now. It was almost as if they were having some quiet conversation on an old sofa in an intimate café, rather than between a phone box on a crowded London street and an office in an art gallery.

"Around the corner from your gallery."

"Look." She heard his sigh as if it, too, were right next to her. "Do you want to come in here? There's not much I can do. I'm honestly sorry."

"Not in there." She fought panic. His gallery was the last place she wanted to be.

He sounded urgent, almost fervent now. "Go back up Brook Street toward New Bond Street. Turn left and then take a right up Dering Street. There's a little pub on the corner called the Duke of York. You won't miss it. I'll be there in five minutes."

Laura hung up the phone. Her hands clenched into two tight fists.

She pushed open the door, registering in some dim way that the two women who were waiting for the phone box stepped to the side, eyeing her as if she were an oddity from a faraway place. Laura made her way back up the street, her brow furrowed and her head down against the gathering breeze. Gray clouds hung low over the buildings, laced with strange streaks of yellow and black. Laura forced her swirling thoughts to focus on the one thing that mattered, but it was getting harder and harder to put it all into one concrete plan. It seemed impossible to separate the need to protect Emma from the invidious implications for her own career and from the grim prospect of moving Emma out of her beloved home. And then there was Summerfield to lose.

Multipaned windows ran along the facade of the Duke of York. Window boxes filled with colorful petunias swayed in the bilious weather, bright against the kaleidoscopic sky. Laura pushed open the double front doors and made her way past a group of elderly men sitting at the bar. The place was otherwise empty. At least Ewan had chosen somewhere they could talk in peace. She ordered a glass of wine, sat down at a table by the window, and focused on the wildness outside.

When Ewan swept in, his shirtsleeves rolled up, his blond hair disheveled from the gathering wind, he seemed too well dressed, an out-of-place, striking presence alongside the drab old men who propped up the bar. Laura sat a little taller and wished all of a sudden that she'd worn kitten heels instead of her scuffed brown boots.

He strode over to her table, holding out a hand. The sense that he was an anomaly here seemed even stronger now. It was as if he was following some old boy's code. Nevertheless, Laura held out her hand to shake his. She was determined to play this professionally. She would not give in to the swell of emotion that was rising deep inside her. But her heart thumped in her chest and bile rose up into her throat, making it impossible to breathe easily while she watched as he went back to the bar to order a beer.

"I'm hoping that you'll take the opinion of the woman who lived with Patrick Adams seriously." She put the newspaper article down on the table once he was back, as if she were placing down chips, a bet in a gambling den.

He looked dismissive. "Nothing is going to make any difference, Laura."

"You have to see the truth," she whispered.

His head shot up for a moment, and he caught her eye for a brief split second before turning away sharply. "I said I'm sorry. No matter how I might want it not to be this way, it just is."

Laura leaned, her fingers pressing into the table. "This is the last thing I want to share with you—"

"What is it?" he asked, his eyes hitting hers.

An involuntary stab shot through Laura's system at the way she was sensing his sudden shifts. She couldn't help but think that his movements were like those of a fox caught on the edge of a rabbit hole.

"It's not just about Patrick's reputation." She punched out every word. "The painting is being used as collateral for my loan to study at the Royal College of Music. I only have one year left of my master's degree, but without that loan, I can't afford the tuition. I worked my heart out to get into the college, and I have performance exams in a couple of weeks. This is more than important, Ewan—every step I'm taking leads me closer to my dream of playing in one of London's best orchestras, traveling even as a soloist in Europe, doing what I love for a living every day. But without that bank loan, I will have no choice but to drop out and finish for good. Playing the violin is the only thing I'm good at. It's my passion. I have no hope that you'll ever understand. But I swear, I'm banking on the hope that there is at least a shred of humanity inside the heart of a person who deals in the commercial side of art."

He raked his hand through his hair.

"Ewan, while I'm training to be a musician thanks to the value of *The Things We Don't Say*, I'm working long shifts in a supermarket so I can eat. I teach private students, and every paycheck goes straight toward the interest repayments of the loan. The school has loaned me a Guadagnini violin to play—it's become part of me; I'm extremely attached to it. As far as I know, I could have it for my entire career. I don't know if you have any idea what it's like to hold a priceless instrument in your hands, to have the opportunity to nurture it, to make it sing and soar…"

He wouldn't meet her gaze.

"Then there's my grandmother. Everyone who knows anything about the Circle knows that Emma loved Patrick Adams. She is strong, a passionate, talented artist who worked hard all her life. But have you any idea what it might be like for her now that you, a random stranger, have come along and announced to the world that the person who fed her soul for more than sixty years lied to her instead?"

His lips wrenched grimly downward.

"You come along when she's more than ninety and say to the world that Patrick never painted her, even though he always told her that he did? Emma made great sacrifices for her relationship with Patrick. He was gay, but Emma loved him in spite of his relationships with men, in spite of the fact that he could never be the man she needed him to be."

"Laura—"

"No, Ewan, Emma gave Patrick Adams a home, she supported him so that he could paint, and he famously gave her a place to rest her weary head whenever she needed him. They are to be buried next to each other in the churchyard at the village nearest Summerfield."

Laura glanced up at him, and she swore his eyes were glittering, but she had to finish what needed to be said.

"Your announcement that the universally recognized symbol of their love for one another could be based on a falsehood will destroy something—it will kill her faith in him, in the person she loved. If Emma dies with your allegations hanging in the balance, I could never live with myself. You need to retract your statement. And I need you to do so now."

Silence hung between them.

Laura waited a few beats. She lowered her voice even more. "I want you to announce that you made a mistake. Put this right." She pushed the newspaper that lay between them closer to his side of the table. Ball in his court. He had to make the next move.

The old men at the counter laughed at some joke or another. They seemed content, happy; no one was messing with their precious lives… because life was precious. Emma's life was important. She, as an individual, deserved respect toward her memories, her story, not some jackass coming along and messing everything up.

"Laura, believe me, I understand where you are coming from, and I hate this, but I cannot retract the statement." Ewan's voice hit like bullets out of a gun. "I just can't…"

"Did you hear anything I just said?"

"How much is the loan?"

"One hundred thousand pounds. There was no way I could afford to go to the college under any other terms. Like I said, I'm working two jobs to pay off just the interest until I get a position with an orchestra. But without my tuition, I have no hope of playing to the level that I need to attain in order to get a job in an orchestra or to have a career in music."

Ewan tented his hands.

"The bank," she went on—there was not a chance in heaven she was going to give up—"is threatening to recall half the principal in two weeks because the authenticity of the painting is in doubt. You've thrown it into doubt. Emma knows the painting is Patrick's work. We need you to rescind your statement."

"There's no other way of guaranteeing the loan? Your parents? Family?"

"I don't have parents with a trust fund in place for me. If that's what you're asking."

"No." He looked at her, his expression dark.

Laura fought a derisive laugh. Look at him. He had his first-class path—expensive education followed by fine-arts courses at a top university, then a job as an appraiser followed by a partnership in the chic art gallery in Mayfair—written all over his face. How could he possibly understand hours and hours of practice, alone, in her unremarkable bedroom in a small, nothing special village in deepest Hampshire?

"I'm sorry. I wish I could help. But I can't. Taking out a loan and using art as a guarantee is spectacularly risky. I'm surprised the bank allowed you to do it."

"Patrick Adams was one of the leading figures in modern art. The bank has had a relationship with Emma for years—they allow paintings to guarantee loans, Ewan. It's not something they don't do."

"But still."

"If I can't pay them back that half principal in two weeks, money that we are supposed to conjure out of the blue, then the bank can and will recall all Emma's assets instead. But her furniture and her own artworks don't amount to nearly what's required. She never achieved the recognition or fame that Patrick did. Her work sells in the hundreds, not the thousands of pounds, and she rents her houses, both in London and in Sussex. She always has. So she'll lose the homes she's lived in for decades and have to move, aged ninety, into much cheaper accommodation. Away from the Circle's two spiritual homes—the places that fed both their art and their souls."

Ewan paled.

Laura focused on his untouched glass of beer.

"I am so sorry, Laura."

"We know that Patrick painted Emma in the South of France during the summer of 1923. Before that, he made preliminary sketches of her in preparation for what was going to be a most unique work. Patrick never painted people he knew, you see. But still, he painted Emma. Doesn't that tell you something about *The Things We Don't Say*?"

"I understand the Circle's theories and I know about Emma Temple and Patrick Adam's relationship."

"How on this earth could a student or a copyist have any hope of capturing her inner truth, of capturing what moves anyone when they look at the portrait of Emma, in the way Patrick has done?"

His jaw tightened into a tight, hard line.

"Patrick gifted the portrait to Emma. He told her he painted her. What possible reason or motive would he have had to lie to her about it?"

"I wasn't there. You weren't there."

"Emma was."

"I can't lie professionally."

"Can you honestly say that you are an expert in the Circle's art? Because with all due respect, it seems very odd to me that we haven't heard of you until now."

Ewan raised a brow, but when he spoke, he sounded more resigned than cocky. "I worked as an appraiser at Sotheby's for twelve years, specializing in twentieth-century British art. It's also what my gallery handles—and it has done so since the early decades of this century."

How predictable this was turning out to be.

Ewan reached a hand across the table, leaving it halfway between them. "Tell me something. How is this affecting your music? Can you still play?"

Laura swallowed the lump that appeared in her throat. "It's up and down."

"What are you playing right now?"

She glanced at him. If she was not overwhelmed by his perfidious actions, she would say that the expression on his face seemed genuine. "Bach and Bartók." She frowned.

"Bach is my favorite composer," he murmured in turn. "You know, it's funny, I always come back to him."

Salesman, she thought, and realized how Emma-like she sounded.

A car approached up the narrow street, its headlights shooting a distinct beam of light in the darkness that gathered under the murderous black clouds.

At this moment, Laura was unable to find any words to say.

Chapter Ten

Provence, 1913

Emma ran her hands down her paint-smattered smock and hovered while Thea, Beatrice, and Lawrence inspected her and Patrick's hard work at the chateau. She regarded her shoes—flecks of green and ochre decorated the brown leather lace-ups, colors that were resplendent in the murals decorating the walls of Thea and Beatrice's entrance hall.

Emma had no doubt about Patrick's talent, having worked with him these past weeks; were she honest, she regarded Patrick's vision and creativity as far superior to her own. For her, painting was like a slow burn—it was the one thing she relied on. It was always, always there. But for Patrick, it was as if artistic inspiration struck like a series of wild flames, each one needing to be tended until it burned out, and then he moved rapidly on to the next.

She'd become enraptured with the way he flew from thinking about the project at Beatrice and Thea's chateau to his own private projects. Ideas came to him throughout the day while they worked together, lighting him up like streaks of gold embedded in rock. He'd decided, stunningly, to paint a circle of men in the end, inspired by the ancient Greeks.

The muscled men posed in a series of glorious formations, their arms linked, some dressed in the classical robes of the ancient world, others only half-dressed, some of them naked. Their bodies were painted in a bold, figurative style against a background of mottled sky and vibrant grass. Goddesses looked down upon them with approval. Each male form was in a state of movement, causing the eye to move, in turn, around the room, creating an effect where the viewer felt at no distance from the work. Time did not matter. Their beauty—that was eternal. Their strength was their vulnerability.

Patrick and Emma had painted from dawn until evening for three weeks straight. It was vigorous, exciting work.

Lawrence took a shot with his camera, the noise ricocheting through the echoing space. "I have good news, Patrick," he murmured, his eyes still on the breathtaking, larger-than-life images.

Thea and Beatrice remained quiet, their expressions ones of contented admiration.

"I've managed to get six of your paintings accepted for a major post-impressionist exhibition next year," Lawrence said. "You'll be exhibited alongside Picasso, Matisse, and Gauguin again, but this time, the exhibition will be a major public event. I'm hoping that exhibiting Picasso and Matisse in such a major way will finally open the British art world to their striking talent. And I want you to be shown right alongside them as Britain's answer to modernism."

Patrick rested his paint-stained hand on the stubble that flecked his chin. "I am completely honored. But Emma did half of this. It was an equal proposition for us. She should be represented too."

Lawrence glanced across at Emma. "I'm always going to be putting Emma's work forward. We're hoping to get your two latest French pieces into the exhibition, Em."

Emma held out a hand to Lawrence. His hair was disheveled, and his eyes were bleary. She knew he was taking no breaks here in France, and back in London he was building a reputation for racing off to an art meeting in Brussels, then returning to London and attending a party straight after he arrived back. He was like a man in a whirlwind—art critiquing, writing, and lecturing, and now he was on several boards; on top of that, he was setting up a collaborative art and design workshop in London, to which he'd asked both Patrick and Emma to contribute. His plan was for artists to share in the profits of the sales. He'd found premises for a potential gallery and workshop in Bloomsbury's Fitzroy Square.

Thea took off her round spectacles and swiveled around from her close inspection of the murals. "The fact that you've painted men in a house full of women delights me. You never lose your sense of humor, Patrick."

Patrick smiled, a lazy, sexy smile; Emma couldn't help that thought… then she admonished herself. She'd loved working alongside another artist. No, she'd loved working alongside Patrick. But what happened when they returned to London?

She and Calum would live in Gordon Square, while Oscar moved about. Out here in France, she'd been able to work so furiously only because she had left her baby in the care of the wonderful nanny she'd found for him and because Ambrose had taken a thoughtful interest in her little boy. She spent time with him in the early mornings, and in the evenings she would play with him before he went to bed. Back in London, she wanted to spend more time with him—that was a consolation, and not a small one.

But Emma looked down at the way the shapes fitted together on Thea and Beatrice's perfectly polished floor and fought the feelings of inescapable loss that roamed around inside her at the thought that this project was over. Would she ever have the chance to work with Patrick so closely again?

Emma ate lunch on the terrace with everyone, only to remain lost in her own particular thoughts. Baguettes and ripe tomatoes were tempting and full of color, along with local cheeses and wine. Patrick was in fine form, leading the conversation, delighting in showing Thea and Beatrice a little kaleidoscope in which he was placing a moving reel made up of tiny paintings he'd done. The exquisite patterns ran in front of the viewer as they twisted the kaleidoscope reel. He'd been trying to mimic the transient nature of sensations, with the unique idea that as each image came up, one would feel a new sensation as it passed. He had used collage, color, and pattern to achieve this effect. Even though he and Emma had agreed that realism was probably their natural means of expression, they were still playing a little with abstract at times.

"Em, how did you find working alongside Patrick?" Lawrence asked, his voice sounding as if out of the blue.

Emma looked at the way he twirled his wineglass around on the table. She suspected that his gray eyes read her thoughts sometimes behind those thin-rimmed glasses he always wore.

"Won't you find it somewhat dull going back to working alone in London having painted alongside the dashing Patrick in the South of France?"

Do shut up, Lawrence, she wanted to warn. *Don't say the unsayable. Be quiet, for goodness' sake.* To her horror, she felt her cheeks burn. Silence fell over the table. She sensed Patrick watching her with the intensity of a flame.

"Tell me, Thea and Beatrice, in which village do you buy your bread?" she asked, keeping her tone as even as the smoothest of lakes. "It is the best I've tasted."

She knew Patrick's eyes remained on her, and she smiled and smiled at Thea.

But Lawrence, darn him, roared with laughter. "Darling Em. So typical. Where do you buy the bloody bread?"

"In Uzès," Thea answered, her measured tones matching Emma's to a T. She arched her brow. "And bread, Lawrence, is an inordinately serious subject here in France."

Beatrice began a loud conversation about an exhibition in Aix.

"Promise me you won't fall in love with him," Lawrence said in Emma's ear. "Everyone does. Not you too."

She lifted her chin. "Do tell me about the design workshop you are conceiving in Fitzroy Square, Lawrence. I think it's a marvelous idea."

Emma didn't look at him. She knew what the expression on his face would be—eyes downcast with the hurt she was causing him. She hated to hurt him. And yet, she couldn't stop the flush of excitement that spread through her at the thought of the party that Beatrice and Thea were holding to celebrate the completion of the murals here in their beautiful chateau tonight.

Once twilight had slipped into velvet darkness, Patrick arrived at Emma's studio door freshly washed and dressed for Thea and Beatrice's party. She'd spent a couple of hours working on her current painting after they'd returned from inspecting the murals, and now, she felt curiously naked in her smock as he stood in his dinner suit in the dimly lit room.

"They let me into the house," he said, surveying her up and down. "Lawrence and Ambrose were in the middle of some political discussion. I thought I would come up here and keep you company instead."

Emma wiped her hands on a cloth. Turpentine and the deep smell of oil paint had imprinted their strong scents into her skin. She'd fought with a flush of worry over Lawrence this afternoon, and yet here she was, devastatingly attracted to Patrick. *What a roundabout we all play on when it comes to falling in love.*

Emma placed the cloth on her workbench. In any case, she reminded herself, no matter who was in love with whom, Patrick was right. It was a relief not to have to discuss politics and economics all the time.

And yet she did sometimes wonder whether she was deliberately looking to find a part of her circle of friends that was exclusively for Patrick and herself. No matter how much she fought to create a free, new style of family that broke the confines of what she had endured, sometimes it still seemed that the tightest circle was the lonely bubble in which she found herself. But maybe that was the way things were in life. Was it possible to ever truly know and love another person entirely? Thank goodness for Calum, for her baby.

She smiled at the time she'd spent playing with her two-year-old boy earlier this evening in the garden.

Emma glanced up at Patrick and couldn't resist smiling even more at how handsome he looked. Whatever the answers were to her questions, whatever barriers she had to face, it seemed particularly vital right now to live in the moment, because that, Emma realized, in the end was all we had. Particularly with the talk here in France about neighboring, frenetic Berlin being on the march. Germany had become an explosive mixture of modern technology and nationalism, with a kaiser who was restless and wanted a new shining navy to compete with that of his British cousins. Downstairs, Emma knew that Lawrence, Oscar, and Ambrose were talking of the new Balkan War. Whatever the outcome, they all agreed on one thing—total avoidance of conflict; killing and hatred went right against their pacifist beliefs. All Emma's male friends would do everything they could to avoid actual fighting in any war.

She stood up and made her way across to her open bedroom door.

"I suppose I should take a bath," she said, pulling off her smock to reveal her skirt and blouse.

She started to unbutton her shirt, feeling a little reckless as he followed her into her bedroom. But if freedom and tolerance was their philosophy, then there had to be no boundaries at all. All should have the freedom to love whom one chose at any time… and Emma was well aware that no one had a choice with whom they fell in love.

She moved through her bedroom, her glance taking in the pink sunset that glowed outside the window like a beautiful hint of things yet to come. Emma made her way toward the bathroom that she had all to herself here in the house.

She turned on the brass tap on the claw-foot bathtub, running her fingers under the warm water, pouring in her milky-toned bath salts and waiting while the water became chalk-white. She unfastened her skirt—knowing full well that Patrick hadn't gone away—and pulled her blouse over her head until she stood in her undergarment, thin, loose silk that floated around her body, hiding parts of her and exposing her forearms and her bare legs just below her knees. She reached up to tuck a few stray tendrils of hair into her loose dark bun, turned off the tap, and stepped into the bath, her transparent slip floating around her body in the water.

He sat down on the wooden chair in the corner of the room, crossing one leg over the other. And pulled out the sketchbook he'd been using to make preliminary drawings for his portrait of her.

"Do you mind if I make some more sketches of your face... your hair? And I want to capture your hands."

She smiled her assent, slipping back into the warm, scented water and into an awareness that felt both natural and exquisite at the same time. Whatever was between them was a rare bird indeed. Was this love?

The connection she felt with Patrick ran like a streak of light between them every time they were together. She was drawn to him in a way she'd never been drawn to anyone in her life.

Emma picked up the sponge on the side of her bath and soaped one extended leg.

"I feel bad about Lawrence," she said.

"Don't," Patrick responded, resting the sketchbook on one crossed knee. "For all his cleverness, he's an active, doing person. He's not reflective enough for you. You're too different. There's nothing to feel guilty about."

Emma focused on the way water ran down her arm in clear rivulets, sliding off her skin, wet and sensuous. She slid her head back into the bath.

Was she destined to love in triangles? Her, Oscar, and Mrs. Townsend; Lawrence, her, and Patrick? Patrick, all those men, and her...

Emma sat up abruptly. Water cascaded and rippled down her body—her hair clung damp to her neck. She reached out and collected her towel from the chair by the bath. Emma pulled out the plug, and as she stood in the bath, her face hot with steam and her hair wet, she looked at him, feeling wounded. And yet, what had he done?

"Most women would be panicking about that," he said, his hands moving, quick-fire, with his small piece of charcoal.

"What?" Her voice seemed too sharp through the hazy steam from the bath.

"The fact that your hair is now soaking wet. But you just stand there, your hands still spattered with paint, and you don't care. I love that about you."

Emma picked up the towel that was on the wooden rail beside the bath and began drying herself.

"Whether you adorn yourself or not tonight for the party, it won't matter either way. Everyone adores you, Em. You need to know that."

Everyone? Emma stepped out of the bath and made her way across to her bedroom.

"Would you like me to help you choose?" he asked, his voice quiet. He put the sketchbook back in his pocket.

But everyone loved Patrick. They didn't love her. He smashed all the rules.

"I'm not sure what to put on," she said, keeping her tone light.

"Want to play dress-up?"

Silently she slipped off her wet undergarment, leaving it to pool—a wet skein of silk on the wooden floor. She dried her naked body in languid strokes while he fossicked in her wardrobe. She watched the way his hands slipped around her small collection of dresses. Emma pulled fresh underwear out of a drawer, and a new slip, and made her way to stand behind him.

"How about I go and raid the house for you, see if there is anything in another bedroom that belongs to someone else? Surely we can borrow things. It's hardly stealing," he murmured.

"What a good idea," she said. "Perhaps there's something left here by some French ingenue last summer?"

"There's plenty of spare rooms in the house. I'll go and search, see what we can find for you to play with. Sound good?"

She nodded up at him, and he slipped away in his elegant dinner suit.

Emma moved across the room to her dressing table. She dabbed a little powder on her nose and stained her lips with rouge. She'd never enhanced her eyes with anything. They twinkled back at her, large and brown and sparkling.

After a few moments, he returned.

Emma gasped when he held up an apricot silk dress, its bodice beaded and low cut in the shape of a square. The skirt flowed, and the soft fabric was looped into a knot at the knees.

"It's beautiful," Emma breathed. "Where on earth did you find that?"

He held a finger to his lips. "It was in the first room I went into. You have every reason to adorn yourself," Patrick said. "There's no need to hide anything, Em, and no need to be surprised when you attract a lot of attention tonight."

She stood up from her little stool. The problem was that she didn't want other men's attention.

"Turn around," he whispered. "Enjoy yourself. You're allowed to have fun, you know. Allowed to let go."

She raised her hands above her head. Behind her, he slipped the garment over her body until it hugged her curves across the bodice, flowing softly around her legs. Silently, he did up the buttons that ran down her back. And slowly, she moved to face him. He reached around, tugging at the loose bun that had held her dark hair all day while they painted, and let it tumble in a cascade of wet, deep-brown curls down her back. Next, he reached for the crystal vase of orange blossom that sat on the dressing table behind her and placed a sprig in her hair.

"Heavenly," he murmured. "Let's go now…"

By midnight, everyone was dancing on Thea and Beatrice's terrace. Tea candles decorated the tables, flickering honeyed light into the dark, warm night. Champagne glasses cut of the finest crystal and shimmering glass bowls of strawberries lay about like the remnants of some extravagant feast.

Beatrice and Thea knew exactly whom to invite to a party. The guests tonight were other bohemians who shared in Emma's and her artistic friends' liberal views; they would not judge Patrick, Ambrose, Thea, or Beatrice for who they were.

While Patrick flitted around the gathering, Emma felt freer than she had in years. Her only obligation was to her darling son, Calum. She wasn't married to any man except Oscar, who right now did not count; she wasn't tied down now by being in love with Patrick. She loved the way that tonight, he gave her the leeway to be herself, while letting her know that he was right here and that he could, at an extraordinarily deep emotional level, satisfy her, while not making her feel in any way obliged. She only hoped whatever this was between them would last beyond this magical time in France.

As she sat on a rug out on the lawn in the early hours of the morning, her legs stretched in front of her while her shoes had been scattered off who knew where, she watched him and wondered whether an immensely close connection with a man of his leanings couldn't be one of the easiest relationships in the world.

As the dawn rose in the eastern sky, it was Ambrose who was, as usual, cuttingly astute.

"It seems that Mrs. Townsend takes Oscar, Patrick takes Emma, and I will be left responsible for young Calum."

Emma caressed the silk folds of her apricot dress. A secret smile formed on her lips as she sensed Patrick stirring nearby.

Chapter Eleven

London, 1980

Laura leaned against one of the long corridors in the grand redbrick building that housed the Royal College of Music. Nausea, wrought by fear of losing everything, had become her only regular accompaniment now. She forced herself to eat but often found herself staring blankly at the fridge in her tiny studio, unable to conjure up the motivation to prepare food anymore. She'd spent the last couple of shifts at the supermarket in a daze—and she knew that her poor violin students had suffered a lackluster teacher this week.

Jasper appeared alongside her. He'd caught her eye while he chatted with a group of students farther up the hallway. With exams looming, everyone was in a panic heightened by nerves and mounting pressure to excel in their performances. The idea that, once they graduated in a year, they would all be in competition with each other for coveted positions in orchestras ran among them like an uneasy thread. The fact was, no matter what instrument they might play, some of them would get jobs, and some of them would have to miss out.

Laura had just botched another violin lesson. The second in a row. She'd had to walk out, her hands shaking and her face pale with shame. She could not talk openly with her teacher. She had to resolve matters herself. There was a queue for miles to get a place to study here, and Laura was not about to risk any gossip spreading that she could not afford to pay her fees or that she was unable to concentrate on her music anymore.

"Come on," Jasper said, taking Laura's elbow, hauling her violin up from where it sat next to her on the floor and clasping it in his hand. "Let's go somewhere quiet and talk."

Jasper moved to a private spot in the common room and sat down opposite her on one of the low, wide leather seats. And waited, reading her, she knew, in a way that no one else could.

"Sorry. I'm not much company," she said.

"Don't be ridiculous."

Laura scanned the room. Other students sat alone, hunched over scores, their faces twisted in their own particular silent concentration.

Laura glanced at the exam timetable that was pinned to the board. Two weeks until she had to perform the Bartók. Right now, she was playing both it and the Bach Double that she adored with the delicacy of an elephant. When she picked up her violin, it was as if she couldn't see past the next note.

"Emma would have dealt with this as smoothly as if she were running her hands down a silk dress," Laura said. "She got through two world wars; kept her relationships with all the men in her life intact, including an ex-husband, a gay man whom she loved, and another man who loved her all his life; raised two children; and had a career doing what she is passionate about… I can't even make it past college without hashing everything up. And destroying Emma's and Patrick's artistic and personal reputations single-handedly, while losing Emma her home to boot."

Jasper took her hands in his own. "No. You are talented and capable. You work hard. I think, like Emma, you have a genius for your art, but now, don't you see, here's your chance to show your genius for life."

Laura leaned her forehead against his. "You have no idea how valuable you are to me," she murmured. And she reached out, touching his face in a way she had never done before, because touching was something that they just didn't do, no matter how close they were. "I'm so lucky to have you."

He smiled at her. "And I you," he whispered back. "All you need is proof of what you already know. Emma is still alive. And while she's alive, you have hope of putting this right."

Laura bit her lip. "I struggle with the effects of this on her health."

"If only we could protect the ones we love from the problems in the world," Jasper said. "It's what we try and do."

Laura stood up. She hauled her violin onto her back and held Jasper's outstretched hand for a moment. "Go and practice, Jasper," she said. "Please don't put your future at risk, whatever you do."

"I have such faith in you and Emma as a team. You are the strong ones. You're both cut from the same cloth."

Laura hugged him, but as she moved out toward the entrance, guilt about the dreadful effects of this on Emma sat like a slippery stone in her gut. She moved down Prince Consort Road and turned toward the station. Getting Emma involved even deeper and risking her feeling even more emotional pain than she must already be experiencing was the very, very last thing she wanted to do.

Emma let Laura in the front door herself as evening fell over Gordon Square. Laura waited, charmed by the way the door opened slowly and by the fact that Emma's brown lace-up shoes were the first thing she saw, even though her heart ached at the way Emma's feet puffed with age and seemed almost stuffed into her old leather shoes.

"I've rung the bank," Emma announced, looking up at Laura with a determined expression on her face. She pushed her frame toward her living room and faced Laura in the middle of the lovely space with its large picture windows. Every time Laura came in here, she felt the spirit of the parties and the intellectual conversations that had happened in this house lingering about. It was extraordinary to think that Ambrose, who had become a famous economist, and Lawrence, one of the leading lights in the art world during the twentieth century, both had been Emma's closest admirers and loyal friends, not to mention the love she'd shared with the famous modernist artist Patrick Adams. Surely one day Emma, too, would be recognized as the major breakthrough talent that she was.

"I've told Ivan that it means nothing to me to let go of this house," Emma announced. "Instead of paying such high rent, I shall move into cheaper accommodations and hand over everything I own toward paying off your loan so that you can keep studying. There is simply no other way."

Laura pressed her fingers into the back of the nearest upholstered chair.

Emma eased herself down on the sofa, placing one of her exquisite decorated cushions behind her back.

"How could anyone even consider kicking you out of this house, Gran? Everyone knows how connected it is with your friends in the Circle. I can't imagine, quite frankly, anyone else sitting between these walls. And one day, if they do, the place is going to resonate with all the wonderful conversations that you held here."

Laura's glance tore around the room, landing like a fluttering moth on the wooden framed photographs of Patrick, Lawrence, Ambrose, and Freya. Friendship had been the heartbeat of their extraordinary group.

·"You are not losing your home, your reputation, or your life over this. You've fought bigger battles, Em, with quiet determination and strength. I, too, am determined to do just that now. Although I do wish I had inherited a little more of your patience."

Emma looked out the window, a vague smile passing across her face. The trees that lined the edge of the square sat still, silhouetted against the streetlamps that had just turned on.

"It's all in the past now, though, Laura." Emma spoke softly in the waning light. "Whether we like it or not. It's what happens, dear. You can't hold on to what has gone."

"That's true, but you need to protect what you know is truth and look after your own interests, Gran."

"Laura…" Emma's voice trailed off.

Laura came to kneel in front of Emma. "I hate to have to ask you to do anything, but can you try to remember if Patrick left any notes, evidence, diaries, clues? Is there anything remaining at Summerfield? Shall I go there and look? Any photographs of him painting the portrait? What about the others—did they keep diaries? And are you sure there are no preliminary sketches that he did lurking around anywhere?"

After a silence, Emma finally spoke. "There's nothing at Summerfield. I cleaned everything out as they all died, one by one, Lawrence, Oscar, Patrick, and Ambrose. I gave all Lawrence's, Ambrose's, and Oscar's things to their relatives. It seemed right to do that, even though they had their own rooms there, you know, and they were my family. And now they are all gone. As for the preliminary sketches of me that Patrick did, they were burned during the bombing of our studio in the war."

"Gran"—Laura moved over to sit on one of her grandmother's dining room chairs—"can you tell me what you remember about the time the painting was done?"

Emma eased herself back into her cushion. "While Ambrose contributed to the war effort from August 1914 by landing an economics post in the War Office, Patrick did what he knew best. He painted, cataloging his horror at the war. I suppose we retreated from the atrocities of life and set up an alternative. I couldn't see another way…"

Laura regarded Emma. How she needed Emma to get to 1923. But the pinpoint approach she needed her to take was clearly not on the table this time…

"Patrick's mother was raised in Australia. Did you know that?"

"No."

"Patrick's mother traveled to India when she married, accompanying Patrick's father there. She was appalled that Patrick would not enlist at the outset of war that summer in 1914. He registered as a conscientious objector."

Laura stayed quiet.

"Patrick tried to go to France during the First World War. He was offered a position designing stage sets for a production of *Macbeth* in Paris, but he was turned away and then hassled back in England, at Dover, because he was not contributing to the fighting."

Laura sighed. "War, like love, is never black and white."

Emma shot her a glance that held remnants of a far younger woman's sharp gaze.

"The art that Patrick created during the war was his contribution; like all art, it lives on beyond his death, and his recordings of that time were not wasted, nor were they a waste of time, even though he was a pacifist. Although he did more than paint."

Laura waited.

"During the war, modernism became frowned upon. It was viewed as 'foreign' and 'new' when patriotism and a turning to all things traditionally British became de rigueur. Nationalism was the force that drove Britain through those dark years. The feeling in this country became utterly conservative in a world that was trying to become modern, and those who were not patriotic in the face of the war were seen as betraying us all."

Laura looked out the window. War was no place for sensitive artists who could not kill another person, and the fact that Patrick was gay and that was illegal at the time, and Emma was a woman who believed in freedom of love... How their values and beliefs must have been up against the wall. And yet, the most profound art often came from conflict.

"So you leased Summerfield in 1916 and got Patrick a job working as a farmhand once conscription was introduced."

"It seemed a simple, sensible solution. He had started working in East Anglia on a farm, but the local villagers hassled him. Not least because of his sexuality. But during that time, while he was subject to all that attack, ironically, was when we became especially close for the first time. He came to stay with me when I went out to the countryside to escape London with Calum."

Laura waited.

"But then something happened."

"Something happened?"

Emma tapped her arm on the sofa. "So! Anyway—back to this day and age. Ivan won't accept my refutation in the *Times*?"

"Wait—"

"I will do everything I can to get to the bottom of it, to find the truth, and to ensure that you can continue with your music. To me, that is the most important thing. I can live anywhere, dear. I'm not worried about that. All I want is for you to have that one precious thing in your life that will always be yours. It should be the one thing that no one can take away from you. I cannot die thinking that there is any risk you might lose your music."

Laura knew better than to ask her grandmother anything more on the topic she seemed to be avoiding.

"Circles, while interesting thought patterns, are not useful when getting to the bottom of a linear problem," Emma went on. "In some ways, trying to remember is like searching for one specific grain on a sandy beach. I need to examine everything before I find the one piece of information that contains the truth we need."

Laura slumped down in her seat. "Alternatively, I could go and belt Ewan over the head and make him confess to inventing the whole story."

Emma chuckled. "I do adore you, darling. You know I never had any time for bores, and since you were a little girl, I knew you were never going to be one of those… that was part of my problem, I suspect. People had to be either fascinating or fun for them to intrigue me. But that is beside the point. I just wish I could remember something concrete. I am frustrated, you see."

Laura took in the still, quiet room. While Emma's influential friends' ideas and beliefs seemed simple and clear enough, there was no question that their lives and their feelings toward each other had been woven into a complicated, tangled web. How Emma was going to get to the bottom of what really went on behind the scenes in her circle, Laura had no idea.

Chapter Twelve

England, March 1916

Emma removed the scarf that she wore to protect her hair and laid it on the large worktable in Lawrence's new workshop in Fitzroy Square. His venture provided the perfect conduit for Emma to keep in touch with Patrick now that they were back in London. She, Patrick, and Lawrence had become joint directors of the studio, situated in a charming house on the corner of Fitzroy Square in Bloomsbury, a short walk from the house that Emma shared with Calum, his nanny, and occasionally Oscar, along with visits from her circle of friends. Lawrence's studio, set up just before war broke out, housed artists' workspaces upstairs, a large collaborative workroom, and a public showroom on the airy ground floor, where customers could browse the workshop's designs.

Lawrence remained the driving force behind the venture, and what motivated him was a passion to see some of the ideas of modern art—bold use of color and simple forms—translated into other creative outlets: fabric, furniture, and fashion design.

He also viewed the workshop as a way to nurture the careers of his many artist friends, to give them a chance to earn a living decorating furniture and textiles, while working on their real passions as artists at the same time. The studio was collaborative and profit-sharing. It offered select customers decorating schemes for their homes. Patrick and Emma's murals at Thea and Beatrice's chateau had inspired a handful of socialites in London to follow the idea; printed curtains, fabrics, and murals were all featured, and Emma started to design bohemian, free-flowing dresses using Patrick's fabric designs.

Lawrence picked up talent by visiting exhibitions and art schools. The artists worked part-time at the workshop, and as employment at the studio was informal, some artists worked at the workshop for only a short time before moving on. The workshop's existence was supported by a small elite artistic and literary circle—those few aristocrats who were willing to experiment with the avant-garde in their homes.

Press coverage was never flattering, and while the workshop did sell a few expensive commissions, the itinerant nature of the artists, their sometimes volatile relationships with each other, and the fact that Lawrence was funding the majority of the enterprise's costs from his own pocket rendered the financial rewards to be very slim. And yet, there was no doubt that this was where Emma started to view Patrick as a partner in her work.

"Something odd happened this morning," she told him, pulling her hair out of its confining bun.

He looked up at her, his face still wearing that concentration that took over while he worked.

She came to stand beside him while he put down the brush that he was using to apply delicate patterns to a fabric design; the quietness in the studio, the almost misty atmosphere had become to Emma a haven and a refuge from the constant reminders of war. Both she and Patrick acknowledged that they used the space as a way to come together and try to create something beautiful in spite of all the horror, now that almost every day the newspapers were filled with double spreads of graphic photographs of the fighting that was going on across the channel in France.

"There was a visitor, unwelcome, I would think, here before you arrived this morning," Emma said.

Patrick ran a hand through his dark hair, the muscles in his forearms flickering in the lamplight.

"A dealer, Patrick. He wanted to talk to you about representation. But exclusive. It would mean you couldn't work for Lawrence anymore."

"Well, the answer to that is simple for me. I could never abandon Lawrence. He is part of the family."

"Will you tell him no?"

Patrick shrugged. "Of course."

As if in some unspoken agreement, members of the Circle always came first in all dealings, both business and personal. If there was a choice between financial gain and loyalty to their friends, the latter won every time.

Emma searched Patrick's face. She reached out a hand again, only to draw it back. While the decision to reject a dealer who could offer financial reward might cause him to shrug, she knew that he was wrestling far more troubling demons than that. And yet, she wasn't sure how to help him.

Patrick was one of two male artists who worked here now while nearly every other male in the country was at war. He remained steadfast. He refused to fight on the grounds that he could not kill another human, in spite of the manner in which he was harassed whenever he walked in London's streets.

Bloomsbury was only a tenuous haven for him. London was in the grip of wartime hysteria—women handed out white feathers to farm laborers who remained in the countryside and to men in the cities who did not enlist. Innocent people were victimized, and the talk was of nothing but war. His life was becoming shaded by withdrawal, not only because of his pacifism, which was endemic to the entire circle, but also, she knew, because he worried about links being made between his homosexuality and his refusal to fight.

Emma had begun to conceive of an idea as to how she might be able to help with both problems, a way to protect her male homosexual friends by offering them a safe haven in some way, where they could be accepted as they were rather than derided as shirkers. Patrick had received his pardon as a conscientious objector at the war tribunal only a few days earlier, and Emma knew that in order for him to be able to stay away from the conflict, he had to find vital farmwork, and soon.

She rested a hand on his shoulder and looked at what he was working on. "Stunning," she murmured, taking the design, which was a delicate rendering of flowers on pale yellow fabric, in her hand. "Imagine the inspiration you could find in the countryside."

"I hate to think of the suffering of other men." He leaned his head on her hand.

A cloud passed across Emma's features. So far, four of Oscar's friends from Cambridge had been lost. Oscar was seeing out the war and maintaining his pacifist beliefs so far at Mrs. Townsend's country home, while Ambrose was occupied in the War Treasury Office, and Lawrence had received a pardon due to his poor eyesight.

Emma swiveled Patrick to face her. "I've found the place for you," she said. "We can keep Calum safe. And Ambrose can come out on weekends. It's in Sussex, and the house is called Summerfield…"

He leaned heavily on the workbench.

"I'm going to look at it tomorrow." Summerfield and keeping Calum, Patrick, and her circle of friends safe were already intertwined together in her mind as at least some small way of living through this dreadful war.

The following morning, Emma made her way to the old farmhouse. It was down at the end of a rickety lane filled with potholes, deep in the Sussex countryside. The nearest village was fifteen minutes on foot. The fact that Summerfield sat in isolation in glorious unspoiled countryside below the Sussex Downs was one thing, but knowing that the farmer who owned it was seeking help from someone exactly like Patrick rendered it almost meant to be. Emma pushed her bicycle up to the front door and took in the wild, unkempt garden and the pond overhung with willow trees. The surrounding fields sat in silence filled with crops that needed to be tended while all the regular farmworkers fought in the war.

Emma propped her bike against the front wall of the old house, placing it so it did not disturb the climbing roses, whose still-green buds dotted the paintwork. Daffodils had just started to raise their heads in the grass that surrounded the pond in front of the house, and a bank of narcissus had already popped up under the great willow tree, but even in today's sunshine, the air was cold. Emma preferred not to dwell on the inconveniences here; there was no running water or electricity in the house. The first few months were going to be tough, and heaven knew what the next winter would be like without electricity. But that was a minor inconvenience. Safety for the people she loved had to come first.

Emma had worked out her finances with great care, factoring in that Oscar gave her an allowance to supplement Ambrose's generous offer to help pay rent in return for a room in the house for himself. Ambrose had cleverly invested her inheritance from her father, or what was left of it, too, allowing her at least some financial independence. She would never be rich, but she had enough to live on if she were careful.

Emma hoped that as Calum reached his fifth birthday, hardly understanding that he was growing up in a broken family, he would not miss Oscar very much. Calum had come to view Patrick as a sort of lovable and fun older brother, an uncle of sorts. Having Patrick here with Emma's son would be perfect for the little boy. Apparently Calum told his nanny that he thought all the adults around him were mad. Everyone else's parents in London talked of nothing but German submarine campaigns and the fact that the country had just declared war on Portugal. The word *war* was never mentioned at his home. He also wondered why his house in Bloomsbury had a bright red front door when everyone else's was painted staid dark green or black.

Now Emma opened the deep-blue front door of Summerfield. At once, she was hit with the reality of the low ceiling in the hallway, which was narrow, with four rooms leading off to either side. The floors were bare of any rugs, and the boards were dusty and pale. Ugly curtains hung from the windows that overlooked the garden. Emma swept into the first room on the left, pulling back the closed drapes, letting what little cold sunshine there was beam into the house. There was a fireplace and enough room for a large table in here, along with a little door that led to the kitchen behind. She moved back to the hallway, to the room on the opposite side. It afforded a fine view of the pond and had a charming window seat. Emma's imagination painted curlicues and perhaps wood nymphs dancing around the windowsill. This would be the living room; she'd have to find comfortable chairs, and she'd install bookshelves for the part of her father's collection that she would bring down here.

Her shoes clattered in the silence, and it felt more than strange being here alone. She'd not brought Calum, as she was unsure of the state of the house, but she'd told the little boy how she was going to find them a place with a proper garden this morning, and he and his nanny had seemed entranced. Emma had to remind herself that she'd never, ever be on her own if she could help it.

She ducked her head into the kitchen. Her mental list included a dresser and perhaps some blue-and-white china, although gradually, she and Patrick would replace her parents' old crockery with modern pieces thrown on the newly acquired pottery wheel at Lawrence's workshop. Thick cream plates and mugs would be just the thing to hold in her paint-stained hands after a long day's work.

As she marched upstairs, her hand running over the banister, which, surprisingly, was of highly polished wood, she glanced with satisfaction at the long, narrow hallway upstairs that led to three bedrooms off to the left. To her right, she made her way into a private wing that had two bedrooms and a small dressing room between them.

One bedroom would be for her, one for Calum next to hers, and the other three large rooms would be perfect for Patrick, Ambrose, and any other guests—Lawrence would come regularly, of course. Oscar and Mrs. Townsend, she knew, would occupy one room when she could convince them they were perfectly welcome in her house.

Emma sighed. It was all bare and ghostly, yet seeming to wait to burst into life. And perfect for what she needed for Patrick. A blank canvas. Exactly what she liked.

She'd already gained approval from Mr. Hicks—the tenant who managed the attached farm while leasing it in turn from the aristocracy, who owned all the land around here—to paint, wallpaper, and decorate the rooms as she pleased. Emma was thinking about dove gray, which she was going to blend with a chalk white from the local soil to give a soft background to the paintings she would hang to brighten the house. She'd make new curtains to Patrick's designs.

Emma needed color and beauty around her like some people required the trappings of wealth. She'd decorate all the door panels with her particular circles and geometric shapes, while Patrick could contribute his moving figures to the woodwork if he were not exhausted by all the farm labor he'd have to carry out.

Emma stood in the room that would be her bedroom, looking out over the walled garden, which she'd enhance with sculptures, another passion that she and Patrick had taken up together.

Everything was slipping into place. Emma reached into her pocket for the letter that still lay tucked away there.

Fitzroy Square, Sunday

My dear Em,

It seems that while I cannot stop your train of action, especially your move away from London to such remote countryside, I am laid at your feet with admiration for the way you are handling everything in your life. Because you've quite simply got yourself exactly what you wanted. You've got rid of my attentions while keeping me as a devoted friend, kept your relationship with Oscar intact, and are juggling what I know is your grand passion for Patrick with typical great aplomb. You're going to save him and keep him sane, while raising Calum on your own.

All this while producing works of art that, in my humble capacity as an art critic, I think are extraordinary in their modernity and scope. I love that your deviation away from abstract after a short flirtation with the form shows an extraordinary openness to your own independent feelings in spite of fashion, especially given the nature of our world and the forceful nature and influence of strong opinion on all things in the world at present.

You somehow manage to distill conflict and peace into one harmonious whole, recognizing that both exist in our world. You find a remarkable harmony between the two. If only there were more people like you, perhaps our young men would not be dying in France.

You clearly have a genius not only for art but also for life.

Yours dearly,
Lawrence

Emma gazed out at the garden as she made her way back down the wooden staircase to the hall. She moved out of the open front door, locking it and standing a moment on the small step outside. Something troubling had swelled in her. Was she now regarded as some sort of saint?

Knowing she was being irrational, Emma almost fell toward her bicycle. When she reached it, she leaned her hand on the handlebars and took deep breaths. Lawrence was right, and yet also so wrong at the same time. His words were kind and exquisite, and yet they upset her for some reason that she could not quite pinpoint.

What he did not say was that she was handling her life well only because she had no choice. If Patrick could not love her in the way she needed to be loved, all she could do was love him and accept him for who he was.

While she rebelled against traditional marriage and the stultifying idea of being a kept woman, still she could not quite grasp in her hands what she wanted.

And yet, it seemed imperative that she keep up a facade of placid contentment and personal peace in the absence of being fully loved. Otherwise, she risked losing that which she did have, which was not enough. How ironic. Was she only doing the same thing as she would have done had she chosen to be conventional?

She decided to push her old bike up the uneven track, opening the farm gate and then closing it tight shut, throwing her left leg up onto the pedal, flicking up her skirt as if she couldn't care less, when she actually cared about everything more than she could ever admit. As she made her way up the narrow lane, head down as if her life depended on it, she cycled fast toward the one person she wanted to see right now—and the other reason that taking on the lease at Summerfield made perfect sense.

Ascombe, the home of Freya and her new husband, Henry, was a three-mile bike ride away. As Emma weaved along the narrow country roads, the discomfort that played around her insides billowed into something that seemed impossible, unthinkable. All the while, she asked why, when she believed that rationalism was the only way to deal with this life, was she left at the mercy of her own uncontrollable feelings for Patrick? How was she supposed to reconcile that with her theories?

Freya maintained that *why* was a useless question to ask. And yet it was the question that Ambrose, Oscar, and Lawrence seemed to debate in endless circles, looking for answers. But were there answers? What was the reason for the ghastliness of the war? There could be no reason for the fear and dread that every parent faced each day, only to be pathetically grateful if their sons had been spared from death's merciless scythe while others were being cropped like wheat by some force none of them could control.

Why seemed the most futile question in the end. Emma guessed that the only answer came back to G. E. Moore—a firm belief in friendship, no matter what, and the pursuit of aesthetic pleasure. But she was doing that, and still, she had her moments.

Her circle of friends had all sworn to atheism before the war. And yet, where did her love for Patrick come from? Because at times, she swore in turn that it almost felt divine. The love, acceptance, and kindness she felt for him were far beyond anything she understood or could control. How did rationality, which she believed in, explain feelings of unconditional love for another person whom she was not supposed to love? Perhaps it was just a loophole of her imagination, something that was forbidden, which she should ignore because it was well out of the bounds of what society wanted her to do.

She dropped her bike out front of Freya's house. The first thing her eyes landed on was her sister, sitting and writing, framed in one of the French doors of the tall house. Freya said she felt complete here, able to curl up with a book or write after long walks in the countryside. The woods around the house were silent, still fresh and dewy in the morning and yet starting to thaw out as the increasing sunshine spread yellow light down from the clear blue sky.

But Emma frowned as she made her way to Freya's study. Here was the difference: Freya's husband adored her, and he was available fully to her. It was as simple as that. Their lives were hardly conventional—Freya was not going to have children, and she was determined to build a career as an independent writer of both critical essays and novels.

While, like Emma, Freya was largely formally uneducated in comparison with the men who surrounded her, she could well hold her own with her acerbic wit. She was experimenting with her individual, striking form of modernism, writing books that were rollouts of the subconscious, random scatterings of the thoughts that run through our heads every day, while managing to convey character and some sense of narrative at the same time. Her work was thrilling and bold. Freya was the person Emma needed to be with right now.

Emma stopped, one hand poised on Freya's French door. The panic she felt had started in what was going to be her bedroom, which she would never share with Patrick because Patrick was not coming alone to Summerfield. Rupert, his latest lover, a man to whom he seemed closer than any of his former male friends, was going to be at Summerfield too. She'd saved Patrick from condemnation, but unwittingly, she'd collected his new lover. Where on this earth did that leave her?

Freya appeared at the door, her gaze running down Emma's figure. Emma knew she must look a wreck. She felt ashen. There was no doubt she would look ashen too. She raked a hand through her hair.

"Em?" The sun shone incandescent on Freya's face, which with its large brown eyes and rosebud mouth was not quite a mirror image of Emma's face. Freya's gaze was rich with questions, while knowing all at once.

"Oh, dear God, come in," Freya said, opening the door wide, stepping aside for Emma to enter her sanctuary of a space out here.

Emma marched toward the mantelpiece, glaring at the elegant modern clock that Henry had bought for Freya so that she didn't entirely forget the time while she wrote. Emma leaned heavily on the mantel, resting her head in the crook of her arms. Her breathing was labored. Sudden, unexpected physical pain seared through her chest.

Having closer proximity to Patrick had seemed like a heaven of an idea in so many ways, but was she really going to cope with him sharing his bedroom with Rupert, right across the hallway from her own room, every night?

She did not look at Freya, instead focusing on the dew on the lawn. It was even colder here at Ascombe than it was at Summerfield, buried as it was in the middle of the woods. Ghosts were supposed to haunt the house, but Freya loved that about the old place.

"I am beginning to wonder where, in the middle of all this, my interests lie, Freya," Emma blurted out. "What is there of me? For me?"

Freya angled over her desk, placing her fountain pen back in the inkwell. She drew her arms around herself. "It will either resolve itself or it won't."

But Emma was in no mood for her sister's wit. It was not practicality that she needed—it was rare for her to feel this way, but she just needed someone to listen and understand.

"What if he leaves me completely for Rupert?" Emma knew she was panicking. Her thoughts, like those of Freya's characters in her books, were tumbling unconscious out of control in one direction. The wrong direction? She was only terrified that she was right.

Freya reached out and took both Emma's hands in her own. Freya's touch was cool and firm. For once, Emma's sister looked decisive, in control when Emma needed her to be just that. Thank goodness Freya was not in the grip of one of her own bad turns such as had come over her in the years after their father's death. While Emma knew she had to be the strong one, the older sister who looked after her fragile younger sibling, she thanked goodness for the times when Freya, in turn, did exactly that for her.

"Emma," she said, "you are giving Patrick the home he never had growing up while his parents remained in India, the home and stability that he never will have with these serial relationships he has with other men. You are the one constant in his life. I have no doubt of his feelings for you. No doubt, Em, at all."

Emma fell into Freya's shoulder, letting her sister stroke her hair.

"In a time of war, he wants to be with you, Em. He wants you close. You have to focus on the fact that he's wanted that since he met you."

The first weeks at Summerfield were relentless and cold and tough. While Emma fought with her own guilt about being away from the potboiling reminders of war back in London, there were still harsh intrusions from the deadly conflict in France even here in Sussex. The sounds of gunfire ricocheted across the Channel as Emma worked in the garden, audible even with the South Downs as protection.

Even if she avoided newspapers, unable to tolerate the graphic horrors outlining the marauding and killing of adolescent boys and young men that flooded the streets of London, it was impossible not to be swept up when awful news came through of friends' deaths in the Somme. At times she would look at Calum playing in the walled garden under the watchful eye of his nanny or she would play games with him and look at her sensitive, growing boy with his delightful inquiring mind and have no idea how parents with sons at the front lines coped, knowing that they might get a dreadful telegram at any moment.

When Ambrose arrived, as he did most weekends, overstimulated and yet exhausted from his work with the war treasury, his eyes were like two tiny bright dots in his pale, sun-deprived face. He'd bring tragic stories of more men they knew or sons of friends, lost at sea or maimed or falling from the sky. Boys whom they'd entertained in Bloomsbury, part of their wider social group. Boys who would never again live as Emma did freely here at Summerfield.

Her melancholy spread, worsening as the weeks went on. Sadness flowered inside her for the ongoing war, but still, she could not face having anything to do with the ghastly conflict, even though women were working as nurses and in administrative jobs in London.

Patrick and the tall, fair-haired, muscular Rupert, the younger son of an aristocrat whom Patrick had met through Ambrose, buried themselves in labor, pushing their bodies to the breaking point out in the hard, unforgiving soil, delivering spring lambs at all hours of the night, harvesting wheat, tilling the land as so many generations had done before them in an effort to keep the home fires safe. Patrick knew his contribution did not hold a slim candle to the risks other men took and the sacrifices other families made, but the idea of bloodshed and hurting another human still sickened him to the core.

In the cold, dark evenings, he would fuel his innate need to draw by working on more detailed sketches of Emma for his portrait. Too tired to begin work on the final canvas, he contented himself with filling his little sketchbooks with images of her—hands, feet, capturing the myriad of expressions that passed across her face, the way she crossed her legs, tilted her head, smiled… This became the most intimate and special memory for her of those war years, because when he was sketching her, Emma felt the connection that existed between them run through her like wildfire. It didn't matter that Rupert was there. Somehow, when Patrick drew her so intimately, when he was focused on her, it was as if no one else was in the room. Night after night, as if he were both sated and exhausted, he would go to bed early, leaving the younger Rupert and Emma sitting up alone.

In the depths of the freezing winter, she and Rupert sat night after night in the small sitting room. Emma couldn't help but notice how his blue eyes were splashed with telltale red train tracks due to lack of proper sleep, and his blond hair was tousled and growing longer each week. He rested his head in his hands and remained quiet.

Snow lay about outside the window, a thin, cold layer of white, freezing underfoot and wet enough to soak the wood they needed to burn for warmth in the house. Emma knew that the only way to survive Patrick's infatuation with Rupert was for her to become intimate friends with him. She'd made every effort to do so, because she knew if she kept Rupert near to her, Patrick would also be close. She was a little unsure of him, though, and of the veracity of his love for Patrick. Rupert had enjoyed several affairs with women back in London, and she worried that Patrick was more in love with the handsome, younger blond man than Rupert was with Patrick.

She turned to the weak flame that tried and failed to crackle in the fireplace. They'd placed the only cuts of wood that had any potential to light up properly in Calum's room.

"There is one way we could warm ourselves." Rupert's voice cut into the candlelit room. He moved closer to her. The scent of strong woodsmoke mingled with the sweaty smell of Rupert's hard-worked body.

Instinctively, Emma moved away from him on the pale sofa. She'd made a new cover for it, printing woodblocks on cheap calico that she'd brought from London.

He went on, his voice low and silklike. "It would be impossible to imagine that tension could not exist between you and me given we are closeted here for the duration of the war, both loving Patrick as we do. Surely, Em, were we to sleep together, it would break any difficulties between us. I've been wanting to say this for weeks. Please, give me a chance, Em."

Rupert was too close.

"Rupert, that would be impossible. We could never hide it from Patrick. And it would upset him so."

Rupert's usually pale cheeks were flecked with bright red, and his nose was swollen from the cold.

Emma tucked her hands into the sleeves of her cardigan. "Come on, Rupe, you know that won't work."

He traced his fingers along the patterns in the sofa. "You, me, Patrick. Patrick and I lovers, you in the middle between us. I know how you feel about Patrick. But you know that I love women too. It would make sense, you and I. Why not?"

Emma stood up. She made her way through the relentless biting air toward the scant sliver of warmth that resonated from the fireplace.

"Don't tell Patrick about this conversation, for heaven's sake," she said, her words seeming to cut in the freezing air. She pressed her fingers into the white-painted mantelpiece until they left a wet impression on the cold wood.

"I've been seeing a woman up in London—" he began.

She whipped around. "Patrick is in love with you. He adores you, Rupe." She ground the words out. She would not see Patrick hurt. She would not.

"He's in love with you." Rupert's words swirled in the room.

Emma lifted her eyes up to the ceiling. She'd painted that too. Would she spend her entire life trying to make something out of nothing? She lifted her hand to cover her eyes.

"Well, that's your subjective viewpoint," she said, gathering herself with all the strength she could find. "And one I do not entirely agree with. Love chooses us, just as birth chooses us, just as death chooses us. These things are entirely random. The more I think about it—and perhaps my thoughts are intensified because of this stupid, infantile war—the more I realize how random everything is in this world. I just cannot see any meaning in it. Me, Patrick, you." She softened her voice. "I know that three of us here is not ideal, Rupe. But he's not in any way in love with me. He loves me, yes, but there's a difference in the way he loves me and the manner in which he loves you. And I am also very fond of you. Please, don't let's complicate things any further. I am unable to sleep with anyone without an emotional connection to them."

"Oh, why are you so damned *good*?" He was up and standing next to her before she could take a step away. "Why do you lock yourself up with all these theories rather than allowing yourself to be with someone who can love you like I can? You don't *live*, Em. Can't you see that other men desire you?" He reached out and stroked her icy cheek.

Emma jolted. Her cheek was cold, that was true, but she had not realized how cold until he stroked it with his freezing finger. "Rupert." Her voice was dangerous and low. "I will not have Patrick hurt. You misinterpret my friendship and exploit it."

He remained close to her. "You are a sexual woman. More so than many women I know." He growled the words. "What is wrong with men who are not homosexual? You surround yourself with them. You stick, hopelessly, to being in love with Patrick. Why?"

"You are being irrational. You just told me that Patrick loves me. And as for the way I choose to live—is there something wrong with a woman wanting to live life on her own terms? I acknowledge that love is beyond our control, that so much in this world is random, but I insist on the dignity of being able to run the aspects of my own life that I can run myself. And that includes saying no to love affairs that will ultimately go nowhere."

"I don't want in any way to change what you have, Em."

"That may be the case. But you want both Patrick and me, and we both know who would be devastated!" The air from her nostrils was thick with frost. "Please, don't raise this again."

But he was behind her. "Nothing is going to stop my wanting you, Emma. You need someone who can love you properly. He can't. I can."

Emma closed her eyes. "All I can repeat to you is that I want you to never, ever raise this again," she said. Her teeth were gritted now.

He reached out and ran his hand around her waist.

"No!"

"It would make things so much simpler between us. You need satisfying." His voice was silken now.

"Rupert. Stop." She pulled away from him and rested her hand on the biting-cold, round brass handle of the door. "I want us to be friends. You must never speak of this again."

"You deserve to be properly loved."

Emma closed her eyes. "I cannot in any way hurt Patrick, and I will never do so."

"And yet you let him hurt you," he said.

"You are being ridiculous." She let out a short laugh.

"He holds you on an elastic band, reeling you in when you appear to have any doubts. But you can't see it. You continue blindly, like a little mole in a dark tunnel. Em—"

"That is not the truth. Stop it." Emma's voice seared into the candlelit room. She faced him, her body freezing, almost rigid with cold. "I am going to bed."

"Take me with you." He slumped down on the sofa, throwing his face into his hands.

Silently, Emma picked up a candle and walked out of the room. But once she was at the top of the staircase, she stopped. Emma looked at Patrick's closed bedroom door, stood there a moment, only to move back to her own single bedroom, where she hovered briefly, her hand on the door handle, before letting herself in and locking the door.

Emma threw herself into a frenzy of gardening throughout the spring, exhausting herself as if mirroring Patrick's and Rupert's constant physical hardship. She taught Calum to read, to draw, shared with him the beauty of nature that was resplendent at Summerfield, allowed him to run wild and free as much as she could, showered him with love. During the hours when she had any time on her hands, she decorated the walls in every room, painting murals for Patrick in his bedroom as he worked outside day after day.

His weight dropped until he was a shadow of his usual self. While Em fought to provide him with the vegetables he needed to survive, baking bread and trying to make do with the limited supplies that they shared with their landlord, in the evenings she sat upstairs in her attic studio designing cushions, pots, anything for Lawrence's studio. She sent her patterns up to Lawrence in London at every chance she could.

Emma used darker colors as the war drew on—the murky turmoil inside her at how she felt about the world, the tenuous and delicate balance she was trying to maintain with Patrick and Rupert while dealing with Rupert's growing irritation with her coming out in her work. No matter how hard they all strove to create beauty and peace, she rationalized that Rupert's intense reactions toward her were also a reaction on his part to all the death in the world. In wartime, everyone wanted to grab life and bottle it every second they could, but at the same time, horrifying reality loomed around them, a terrifying, brewing nightmare.

Danger frightened them into behaving in ways they would never contemplate in peacetime. Emma forced herself to tolerate the way Rupert would hardly speak to her when they were alone, brushing past her as if his emotions controlled her, letting his fingers touch hers if she passed him the salt. He put on an act in front of Patrick. Emma willed that Patrick must never know how Rupert tormented her.

Emma kept silent except when she retreated to the place where she could not hide from anything: her studio. She threw out her frustrations on the canvas; her clouds were the color of gunpowder, and the humans she painted were faceless. The faceless victims of war. Were they all that, in the end?

She would neither fight with Rupert nor give in to his silences. Emma simply pressed on.

"Perhaps," she said to Patrick as they stood one evening by the lake when Rupert was in London in the late spring, "relationships mirror everything there is in this world. True relationships involve everything—love, peace, happiness, duty, terror, family, sadness, grief. I wonder if we expect too much of each other. As nations, individuals—is that the problem? Is that why we fight? Because we don't understand that life involves the whole darned gamut of experience? We expect it to be all good."

Patrick looked out at the water next to her. "I'm sure that we deny others the humanity that we allow in ourselves. But cruelty, bigotry, hatred of others—these things are not in any way part of your make-up, Em. You go to great lengths to get inside other people's heads. For you, to know others is to understand them. You see their points of view. Some people, like Rupert, I'm afraid, struggle with your generosity of spirit."

Emma startled a little. But she remained quiet. Because this was part of her relationship with Patrick. There would always be things that would remain unsaid.

As she stood in silence next to him, the sound of gunfire raged in the distance across the sea.

But no matter how Emma tried to instill peace into her homelife, by 1918 fighting spread its insidious wings directly into Summerfield. When Rupert told Patrick in rage and frustration and anger that he had fallen in love with the woman he'd been seeing in London and that he wanted to marry her, the two men's fights became long, howling, yelling, screaming wrangles. Every night. Night after night.

Emma's heart was locked in her throat. She stood in the middle of her bedroom. She'd been pacing for long enough. The short bursts of shouting rang through the house like bullets. Emma had no idea where each agonized roar was going to fall next, who was going to get hit, which voice was which, whether things would ricochet out further to hurt her, Calum?

She'd become nervous and gotten into the habit of checking on Calum like a mother who worried about her cub being attacked by some fox while he slept, determining that he was resting peacefully now that the house had taken on this mad, demon-like force. Summerfield pulsated with the two men's own crazed civil war. But Calum, always, was oblivious when she went to him, his face flush with pink, his dark eyelashes splayed across his cheeks, sleeping soundly from days spent playing freely outside, drawing with Em, making cubbyhouses under the dining room table, and walking with his nanny or Em on the path that wound below the South Downs.

Now Emma stood alone, wringing her hands in her nightgown, her hair falling in loose waves around her shoulders. She felt like a madwoman, both helpless and locked out. She'd decided at the beginning of all this to keep well out of it. She knew she was sensitive to men's tempers. How could she not be after living with her father, and now this, this was bringing it all back.

They were trying to keep their voices down—having realized, Emma supposed, that they'd hit some dreadful crescendo, a peak that needed to be tempered before someone got seriously hurt. But the tight, deep growls that snaked across the landing, seeming to seep under her bedroom door like wisps of foul-scented smoke, felt far more ominous than any honest yelling ever could.

She ran a hand over her tired, sleep-deprived eyes and took a step toward the doorway, letting her fingers linger on the smooth wooden handle—it was a mantra, this hovering, that she had taken up in war. The wood was bare of decorations—a rare surface that had escaped her artistic touch. Sometimes she wondered why she persisted with trying to make everything here beautiful when all around her the world seemed a bloody mess.

Patrick's bedroom door slammed. Emma jumped. She closed her eyes, distress spinning through her system, physical pain jerking at her insides. They'd hit a final note for the night.

Pounding footsteps resounded down the staircase. The front door slammed. And all Emma could think was that things had traveled in some dark, insidious full circle. Rupert had behaved in a way that was unacceptable toward her, and he, in turn, had been kicked out without Patrick even knowing that had happened. She had tried so hard not to let him ruffle, and now, this.

Emma closed her eyes at the sound of Rupert's little car revving up. Her fingers stroked the door handle now; breath quickening, she opened the door. The landing was cold, alien, lost—she wanted it back the way it used to be. Wanted to return to that hope and potential and promise that she'd felt when she first came here. Summerfield had started to feel as if all the homeliness had deserted it these past weeks. It was as if the spirit and love had been sucked out of it by all the fighting that was going on.

Emma clenched and unclenched her own fists and hovered outside Patrick's room.

It was open, just a chink. She took a step forward. Candlelight tapered, flickering through the tiny crack between door and frame. Emma reached out, pushing the door open, standing there in her nightgown, feeling the quiver of the candle on her face. She fixed on him. Her eyes wouldn't budge once they rested there, as if at home.

He lay on his back, hands behind his handsome head. And yet, when he saw her, he sat up, his eyes dark and yet clear and so visible, only to her, in the dim light. She stood there, hovering like some lost bird; when he reached out to her, both arms drawn open, she went to him.

She stood beside him, her hands halting a moment before landing like some great full stop in his palms, touch to touch. She felt the beat of her chest, rising and falling as he held his palms up, face-to-face with hers, almost an alluring lover's kiss.

He took her hands and grasped her fingers tight. The candle, burning bright on the bedside table, sat between them. The silence was so clear and perfect that Emma could have rolled a marble across the floor and it would have sounded like a thundercrack.

He held her gaze. His own dark gaze was locked, alive and honest and painful and loving and everything—oh, everything at once.

She reached out one hand and rested it on his cheek. He leaned into it, pulling her other hand toward him, bringing it up to his mouth, his lips, bow lips that she'd painted so very many times before.

She took one step closer, and he pulled her closer again, and slowly, and yet fast, she seemed to float down toward him, on top of him, her body lying in her thin nightgown against his. And he kissed her, tentatively at first, butterfly touches on her lips, dancing and touching and tender and warm all at once.

And she kissed him back. And she gave in to it, knowing that he would too. Knowing with dead certainty that, if she didn't do so, she'd regret it for the rest of her life.

Chapter Thirteen

London, 1980

If anyone had asked what had caused the dramatic change that had swept Laura into some strange new state of being, she would have found it impossible to pinpoint any answer. All she knew was that she had morphed from being stuck in some dark, dreaded place, disconnected from her music, to wanting to play in a way she'd never, ever done before. Her job and her teaching—anything else—was a mundane distraction from her need to express everything she felt with her music. It overwhelmed her now.

Perhaps it was fear that propelled her—fear of losing that which she loved causing her to want to cling to it in a way she'd never done before. And she wondered if that was one of the brutal things about life, that we did not appreciate how much something meant to us until we were under serious threat of losing it for good, and only then did we panic, only then did we understand the full implications of what loss actually was.

Laura placed her foot on the top step that led to the stage in the Amaryllis Fleming Concert Hall to rehearse in front of her fellow students.

As soon as she lifted her bow, Laura felt it, that new strange force that gripped her. While she had been swept into a panic at first by Ewan's statement, all she wanted to do now was to cling to what she had, even while knowing it might all go away. The passion of the music took over as she forgot about rules and technicalities, the wide leaps, the multiple stops, the trills and the tremolos, and just played from her heart. She swept into the opening movement, the Hungarian folk melodies coming out from inside her in a swirl. Laura closed her eyes.

As she progressed through each movement, the staccato, pulsating fugue, then the lyrical melody in the third through to the fast bumblebee-like fourth movement, all the time, throughout every mood, it was as if she was always accessing some ultimate truth embedded in the music. And somehow, right then, all she could think was that she had to work through everything deep inside herself and in her past and in Em's, leaving nothing to rest in order to save herself, just as she had to reach into her deepest self if she were to play her music in the way it deserved to be played.

When, finally, she let her bow rest by her side, Laura felt a thin line of sweat blooming on her brow. A moment of stillness hung over the auditorium before her fellow students stamped their feet on the ground. As Laura stood there, her bow hanging in her hand, she spotted her teacher alone off to the side. When he looked up, caught Laura's eye, and nodded, just a slight inclination, Laura felt her entire body sag with relief.

She made to leave the stage, exhausted, satiated, replete and still half panicking about what the future would hold. But as she moved to exit the stage, a man stood in the periphery of her vision.

Laura raised her hand to her eyes. As a hesitant smile slipped across Ewan Buchanan's features, an almost imperceptible movement, she frowned, some new wave of feeling sweeping over her while her eyes remained locked on to his.

She made her way down the stage stairs to the auditorium, and he walked straight toward her up the aisle. The next soloist appeared from the wings, and people were waiting for Laura to take her seat. An acute silence lingered in the auditorium.

Laura felt every one of her peers' eyes watching her while she placed one foot in front of the other until she finally stopped dead when she stood opposite Ewan in the aisle.

"That was wonderful," he whispered.

She looked up at him, her eyes narrowing.

A cough sounded. Her teacher. Laura frowned.

Ewan stood there, waiting for her.

She ducked her head, moving past him toward the back of the concert hall. As she almost tiptoed on, the next student swept into Beethoven. Laura focused on the patterns on the carpet as she made her way to the swinging doors and the entrance foyer.

She marched toward the heavy double doors that led out to Prince Consort Road, pushing them open hard until they swung back and forth on their hinges. She wanted air. Now. Fresh air and normality and London. She'd spooked herself with her playing, and now the person who had infiltrated her world was standing right behind her and she did not know what to think.

But as she turned to face Ewan, she fought with the realization that he had also caused her to play like she had. He was the person who'd forced her to have to fight, to plumb the depths of everything she had inside her in order to save everything that was under threat. Because of this, her essence, her music, was speaking to her in some new way that it had never done before, and there was no turning back to the way she'd always played.

"Laura." Ewan reached out and touched her arm before drawing it away as she flicked her elbow from him, an involuntary, fast jerk of a movement. "Your violin," he said.

"Excuse me?"

"I just thought you might like to go back inside and get your violin case. That was amazing. Incredible. I've been feeling so guilty, Laura."

She let out a wry laugh.

"Can we go somewhere and talk?"

Laura took a fast step back.

"I know how angry you are, and understandably so. I want to talk to you. That was astonishing—"

"Have you any idea what music means to me?"

"You have no idea how much I understand it."

She lifted her hand up to her eyes to shield them from the bright sun. The sky was blue and radiant. "Art and beauty and truth and music? Your actions tell me the extreme opposite of what you've just said. Do not come in here and pretend to be something you're not. Because, frankly, if this is some stupid attempt at making amends, then please, just go away."

"Laura." He took her shoulders and held them, his dark eyes intense on her face. "I ask that you let me show you something. I want to show you something. If you will let me."

"You need to retract your stupid statement, Ewan. There's nothing else to say."

"There is a lot to say. I wish I could help you understand." He looked straight at her. "If we are going to sort this out—"

"What are you trying to say?" She didn't even attempt to hide the fire in her voice. It was a flickering, dangerous storm.

"One hour. I want one hour of your time." He beat each word out as if with a metronome.

"And I want you to retract your statement."

"Can you go back in and get your violin case before someone knocks that beautiful instrument out of your hands? I'll wait right here. I'm not going anywhere. I promise."

People marched past them, stopping to admire the grand Royal College of Music.

Laura watched them, and all she felt was sadness that she was going to lose it all.

"Against my better judgment, I'll come with you and hear what it is you have to say. But if you're trying to convince me that your theory about my grandmother's portrait is correct, then I don't want—"

"Please go and get your violin case. I'll be right here."

Laura made her way back into the college and picked up the leather case from her practice room. She laid her treasured instrument down inside the dark-blue nest of silk with the reverence she would give to a rare piece of jewelry. Laura clipped the case shut and stood up, wiping a shaking hand over her face.

Once she was back outside, she walked in silence alongside him toward Kensington Road, making her way along the very route that Emma took when she was a young woman, trapped.

They skirted Kensington Gardens and Hyde Park in silence, Laura sadly taking in everyone they passed as if their very presence validated her complex feelings for the whole neighborhood. Nannies pushing ridiculously expensive prams; wealthy, well-dressed women; businesspeople who made livings out of exploitation. Did any of them understand the first thing about the emotive quality of music or art? Or were they just collectors of experience, saying they had heard such and such a musician, as if it were just another thing they could own?

The desire to put all her hard work to good use, now, in 1980, might be different from the battle Emma faced when trying to be herself in 1912, but by goodness, Laura's feelings about the way she wanted to live her life and the career she wanted to have were just as honest and real.

Ewan reverted away from the park once they were in Knightsbridge, taking her up a narrow street lined with tall, classy buildings, their pillars a testament to wealth, until they crossed Brompton Road toward Harrods, while Laura wondered idly if this was where he did his grocery shopping, spending ten pounds on a banana or a pear—perhaps twenty on a razor for his chin? But he led her on toward a lane of mews cottages just behind Harrods. He stopped outside one whose front door was painted red.

"Shouldn't it be black?"

His face twisted into a grimace.

She shrugged. "Sorry. It's a joke. Doors in this part of London always seem to be black."

"Please," he murmured, turning the key in the lock. "Could you give me a chance?"

"Why?" she asked. "Tell me why." She softened her voice.

He leaned his blond head on the doorframe and loosened his tie. "Look."

Laura folded her arms.

"Please, Laura."

"I should be taking legal action. But you know I can't afford that. I'm sorry, but I can't help seeing all this as a game for you. Sales, money—a lovely little circle that only the privileged can enter. As for the rest of us, it doesn't matter. We don't matter."

"Stop." He growled the word.

Laura gazed at the renovated mews houses, all gorgeously tasteful. Even the cobblestones on the road looked freshly swept. And somewhere inside her, a treacherous voice accused her of envying the people who lived here… only, of course, because of their proximity to the park.

He opened the door and stepped aside for her to enter. A small entrance hall, with polished floorboards that gleamed, led to a set of open doors and then into a large living room.

Striking, stunning twentieth-century artworks hung on the walls. Ewan flicked on the lights. The effect was breathtaking.

So he had taste—that didn't mean anything at all.

Laura's eyes swept past the pair of deep-navy velvet sofas laden with bright modern cushions to the opposite wall. A cobalt blue square sat against a white background with a black frame. Simple, perfect. Underneath the painting were bookshelves filled with books on art.

Ewan moved toward the back of the house. All-glass walls led to a small courtyard, and he opened the rectangular doors wide, flooding the room with warmth from the sun. He moved into his kitchen. Laura couldn't help but think that if the white kitchen were any more up to the minute, it would still be on the delivery truck.

"Coffee? Or would you like tea?"

"Coffee," Laura said. "Thank you."

Each piece was given a chance to show off its beauty here on Ewan's walls. Laura simply had to wander around the room, taking her time to look. The art was too beautiful to be scanned or dismissed, no matter who the owner was.

Once he came to stand next to her, she reached out for the coffee and took a sip.

She faced him, but as she did so, her eye caught at something. An easel. And on it was a painting, a beautiful, clear rendition in the same cobalt blue as the box painting she'd been drawn to the moment she walked in the door, but this one was of lines, clear blue lines reaching, Laura thought, into eternity.

He put his hands in his pockets and looked at the floor. "Graduating from art school and announcing I was going to take the leap straightaway and paint didn't seem like such a sensible plan to me."

Laura glared at the easel.

"Hang on," she said. She put the coffee down on a side table. "Where did you train?"

"Slade School," he said.

Laura hugged her violin tight against her chest.

"Let me help you," he said.

"What?"

"I should pay your tuition. I can't sit by and watch you lose everything. Not after hearing you play Bartók—"

"At least you know who he is."

"I know who he is." Ewan leaned against the kitchen bench.

"Of course you do," she murmured. "I can't accept your offer to fund the huge amounts of money that I need for my college tuition, Ewan. But I do need to ensure the legacy from my grandmother's relationship with Patrick."

"And I should have known."

She waited, looking up at him in the still, quiet room.

"I should have known that any granddaughter of Emma Temple's would be incredibly special. Her fire and talent are within you. Laura, you must keep going with your music."

Slowly, she moved over to the kitchen. She placed her empty coffee cup down on the bench. "I'll see myself out," she said, coming back to pick up her violin. "You know what I want you to do, what I need you to do. I've told you why."

"Would you have told Emma to give up her art if she were in your circumstances, Laura? Didn't Patrick rely on Emma to help him financially?" His voice came from behind her.

She didn't turn around. "That was different."

"How?"

"If you don't know the answer to that," she said, "then you know nothing at all about the way they were with each other." She closed her eyes at the sound of his sigh. "You know what I need you to do. I can't accept your money. But I think you knew that already. The answer… what has to be done is simple. You just need to understand the truth about Patrick. You might know a lot about art, but you see, I know the truth about Patrick and Emma, and that's why I also know that what you're saying is false. You just need to realize that too, and when you do, I'll be waiting to hear it."

Laura walked out.

Chapter Fourteen

London, 1923

Emma and Patrick returned to London as a couple. With Lawrence's considerable support their careers flourished, but it was Patrick's flamboyant genius that was becoming famous, while Emma continued with her daily practice by his side. He'd had three shows in the capital entirely devoted to his work, and his name was beginning to be starred in catalogs when he contributed to other exhibitions. His collaborative, decorative work carried out with Emma and sold through Lawrence's workshop became wildly fashionable; *Vogue* picked up their screens and lampshades, and their modernist style was so popular that at one showing, all their pieces sold out in a great crush in one hour, with the profits going to Lawrence's cooperative and the thirty artists all sharing in a little of the margins. Meanwhile, Emma remained of the acute opinion that Patrick's talent was far superior to her own. And she kept on producing her quiet, reflective pieces that were picked up by the occasional collector. She was content to work for her work's sake and because there was nothing she would rather do.

She saw Patrick as more inventive and more imaginative than she would ever be, and she remained fascinated with his love of conceits in both art and life—by the way he made her laugh and was always the center of attention at any party. Mostly, she was in constant admiration of the way he could draw up a miracle directly with his brush.

When Lawrence told her one afternoon in Gordon Square that he felt her work had deeper feeling and integrity to it than Patrick's did, that her art held a steadiness that was missing in the frivolity of Patrick's work, Emma turned away and shook her head.

But Lawrence was insistent. "Underneath that calm luminescent surface we all see, I worry that you are not happy," he said. "Your depth of feeling and the sadness I can see in you shows in your work. I worry that it's become part of you. Something you're living with. Something you've accepted as your lot."

Emma glanced across at him—the man she'd found comfort with, briefly, when her marriage was falling apart. But Patrick had so eclipsed him since then in her head that she'd not given Lawrence a second thought romantically. Now he was working for both her and Patrick, tirelessly organizing exhibitions, promoting their decorative work, while his other career as a London art exhibition reviewer went from strength to strength.

He remained close in the inner Circle, but he was out of the circle that was Emma and Patrick's tight-knit orb by a mile. She created a bubble, and she saw this as her core and her reason for living. While she and Patrick were sometimes lovers, she would never be everything to him. To love him was to accept him as he was. It was beautiful, heartbreaking, and a means of complete contentment all at the same time.

It was, in a word, life.

But why her circles always had to sharpen into triangles was the constant rub.

And at the same time, here was Lawrence. She could not be dishonest with him. She could not lead him ever to believe that she was in love with him when she wasn't. While guilt sometimes plagued her about Lawrence loving her and while she worried that Patrick might feel about her the way she did toward Lawrence, only one thing remained clear: she was in love with Patrick.

So she went on. Since the war, she'd gained several devotees in Patrick's strings of lovers. Because she reached out the hand of friendship to them, Patrick's lovers, in turn, felt safe in her presence.

Patrick's affairs came and went, sometimes more than one at a time: there had been an artist with eyes the color of wintergreen moss; a shy, sensitive musician who lived with his sister and mother; and a displaced Russian aristocrat. In the turmoil of all this, Patrick always reassured Emma that she was the one constant he adored in his life.

Meanwhile, London society viewed Emma and Patrick as an undeniably bohemian couple, gossip about his homosexuality and speculation about their relationship lending a thrilling air to how they were seen. But Emma viewed her love for Patrick as final, and she drew her circle of old friends close around her after the war. She became adept at creating her own safety net.

"I am thinking of going to France for the summer," she said, glancing up at Lawrence. "But before that, I'm going to Italy with Oscar and Calum for a short holiday. I find myself in need of a break from London for a while." She and Oscar kept in touch over their son and the practicalities of Oscar's help funding Summerfield and the Bloomsbury house. She'd managed to keep his friendship, making it clear that she accepted his relationship with Mrs. Townsend. She'd even started decorating a bedroom for him so he could stay occasionally out at Summerfield, scouring local markets to pick up old books and small comforts, things she knew that he liked.

Lawrence lit a cigarette, holding it in his pale, tapering hand. He pulled the sleeve of his light tweed jacket up to his elbow and regarded her through the smoke. "Taking Patrick to France? Having him all to yourself in the very country where he won't be illegal? And yet, will he have reason to be jealous if you go away with Oscar?"

Emma reached out and took the cigarette from Lawrence. "Italy's only about sun. And I want to live an entirely antisocial existence in France so that I can paint."

"Come on, you want Patrick to yourself."

Emma couldn't help but smile. "I've found a villa to rent in the middle of a vineyard in Provence. Don't bring that little friend down with you, will you, if you come?"

"If you mean Coco, then I'm afraid I can't grant your request. You can hardly expect me to—"

"It upsets the balance entirely when someone is wrong, Lawrence," she said, staring out at the square.

"Coco is a wonderful distraction. Couldn't you find the same thing for yourself?"

Emma blew out a smoke ring.

"I'm thinking of marrying her. Unless you want to change your mind about me instead?"

The room was filled with haze.

"Very well, then," Lawrence said. "I could take a separate house down in Provence for myself and dear Coco," he went on, "and we will not intrude our vulgarities into your… art."

Emma sighed. "Oh, do shut up, Lawrence. You are welcome to stay with us."

"Your life could be so much simpler, darling, beautiful Em. Why not be with me rather than in love with a man who is 'that way'? I do worry that you are destined for a long agony of unrequited passion. It's a cruel way to live, you know."

Emma put out the cigarette, rubbing it into the ashtray until there was only a tiny stub left. "As I get older, I'm coming to believe that being in love is less and less important, but loving people is more so. Friendship is the thing. Loving one's friends. And accepting them as they are."

Lawrence removed his glasses, his eyes taking on a startled expression for a moment. But then, he took in a breath. "You know, the view is that you are giving up far too much of yourself for him."

"Fortunately, I don't believe in the 'view.'" Emma rolled her eyes.

Lawrence was silent.

"I have far too much respect for you than to treat you with anything other than the utmost of honesty," Emma said.

"And that is why I'm in love with you."

"So we go round and round. I am fond of you. You know that, my dear friend."

He was silent.

Lawrence was starting to grate.

Oscar and Italy, then France and Patrick were just what she needed.

"Mas d'Aurore is in a field of wildflowers," she said. "Anemones and marigolds among groves of olives. When I went down there to inspect it, the almond trees were in blossom." She faced him, her expression serious. "Work is the only thing that is constant, Lawrence; what a mercy we both have that passion in our lives."

Lawrence reached his hand out to her, and she let him hold it for one brief moment before she stood up and walked over to the window, where she looked out at the verdant square, the emerald-green of it seeming rich and delicious with possibility.

It was another two months before Emma, Calum, Patrick, Oscar, Lawrence, and Coco traveled on the famous Blue Train from Calais to Saint-Raphael. Patrick had wanted to remain in London for a month to complete a series of paintings for an autumn exhibition. After the ferry ride across the Channel, during which both Calum and Emma were ill, Emma was glad that she'd booked a little luxury for them all on the well-known train to the South of France.

"You have outdone yourself once again," Oscar said. "Your genius for organization shines, as always."

Emma rested her head on the velvet seat, trying to take in the elegant walnut that lined the interior, the plush cushions scattered on blue velvet headrests, the waiters who brought around canapés that Emma could hardly look at, let alone eat. She attempted to push aside the nausea that hung over her like an unwelcome mist. Emma had only returned from her short break to Italy with Oscar two weeks earlier, and she felt they had reached an even deeper understanding of each other; their regard and respect would, she felt certain, always remain strong—a friendship that was based on shared memories and one boy. She knew she was lucky to have such an easy, if unconventional, marriage.

Normandy's green fields flew past outside the carriage, lush pastures that would soon give way to dramatic hilltop villages, where valleys carved by wide-flowing rivers would, in turn, unfold into the south, with its olive groves, grapevines, and sunshine.

She was thankful right now for two things: the first was that Patrick had no tricky young men on the boil, and the second was the addition of the young Lydia to their household, as companion for Calum, help for Emma, and general housekeeper as well.

Lydia had arrived breathless for her interview back in London with a story about how affected she'd been by the sight of an ex-serviceman with his tiny son begging on the streets of Hampstead. The boy's legs, Lydia told Emma, were like a pair of twigs. Lydia announced in no uncertain terms that she was not interested in giving up her own employment should she ever marry anyone and had no problems with Emma's aspiration to work all her life. What was more, Lydia did not bat an eyelid at Emma's unusual household and her bohemian choice of friends.

"Are you really going to be a recluse, Em?" Lawrence asked as he brought his glass of champagne up to his lips and the train rattled on.

"Oh, absolutely," Emma said, eyeing them all: Lawrence with his sketchbook on his knee, Oscar smoking his pipe and gazing out the window, Coco reading a little red novel that she'd produced from her bag... and Patrick staring out the windows at the changing landscape... What was he seeing through those eyes? "I have everything I need right here in this carriage," she said.

But the run-down train from Saint-Raphael to Mas d'Aurore was as hot and crowded as the Blue Train had been serene. Jagged cracks ran across the windowpanes, and the old green seats were tattered and torn. By the time they arrived at the station, taking several minutes to alight with their odd collection of easels, a gramophone, and Roorkee chairs, Emma thought she might faint. Calum had been sick twice on the journey, and even the formidable Lydia was swaying and looking green.

"I think I should take Em, Lydia, and Calum to sit down," Oscar said.

"We'll sort the luggage and find a cab." Patrick rolled up his sleeves and smiled at Emma, his eyes brightening below his shock of dark hair that had curled in the heat.

She reached out a hand, and he took it, holding it for one moment. "Go and sit down. You are exhausted," he murmured. "Sip lemonade, preferably pink, darling." He wandered off with Lawrence and Coco, whose eyes glittered with excitement. She'd not been sick in the least.

Once they drew up outside Mas d'Aurore, a small farmhouse set among the vines of its famous neighboring chateaux, Emma stepped out of the hansom cab, threw her head back, and took in an enormous breath. A range of hills overlooked the vineyards, which glowed green in the heat. It was Summerfield out in France.

Patrick stood behind her, wrapping his arms around her waist. "This is perfect. Well done. Although I'm not surprised. I have no idea what we'd all do without you."

Emma leaned back into him. "I want to sleep for a week. But I suspect I'll be up at dawn tomorrow. The light down here fascinates me, and the colors are as striking as ever. I can't wait to get my paints out and begin."

Oscar and Lawrence stood around, both men with their hats off, wiping their foreheads in the searing Provençal sun. Calum started kicking a ball around on the lawn, his lanky, youthful movements almost elegant in the sun, while the young Lydia, with the determination of a saint, wiped her perspiring forehead and joined in.

"I don't want any guests at all," Emma murmured. "This is heaven."

"In that case, don't look at six o'clock," Patrick said. He let go of her, and Emma made an about-face, her heart sinking as a rotund gentleman made his way toward the farmhouse.

"British," Emma muttered. "Wonderful."

"It's our neighbor—the famous Colonel Bird!" Oscar took great struts toward him and held out his hand.

The man approached and removed his hat, revealing a bald head and a face that was dappled with drips of sweat. His shirt hung loose over his trousers, and his tan shoes, while clearly smart and new, were dusty from the dry soil on the roadway. "My dear friends, you will be exhausted," he said. "I am your neighbor, Colonel William Bird."

Lawrence and Patrick made their way over to shake his hand.

When the colonel looked directly at Emma, his face lit up in genuine delight. "And the famous Mrs. Temple," he said. "Enchanted…"

"Delighted to meet you," Emma murmured, taking his warm outstretched hand and staring at the hard ground beneath her feet.

"Dolly and I will leave you to…" He stopped. "Settle in. And then get on with your art and… whatever else you do…" He coughed.

Emma had to turn away to stop herself from laughing out loud.

"We are a motley lot of expats here," the colonel went on. "Most of us have abandoned England for one reason or another…" He looked at the hills a moment.

Emma looked at him with more interest now.

"Dolly, you see, my dear companion, is not socially acceptable back at home. We are free to live as we choose in France, no matter what side of the blanket we are from."

Emma sighed. "I assure you, being acceptable in society doesn't concern us one bit. But yes, I do understand how limiting social restrictions can be."

The colonel cleared his throat. "Well, I hope you will all find yourselves most welcome in France, and you are, of course, utterly acceptable to us."

"I'm afraid we might be terribly dull," Emma said. "I've come here to paint."

The sound of Calum's youthful whoops resonated around the valley, and Lydia's and Coco's high-pitched giggles provided a joyous, birdlike accompaniment.

"Oh, I adore you already, Mrs. Temple," the colonel said. "And I know you are not going to be dull."

She ran a weary hand across her forehead. "Do you know, I think I want a bath and to sleep forever just now."

A week later, Emma was both settled into her farmhouse among the vines and more unsettled than she'd ever been in her life. In being here, where she had sought escape, she only found herself confronted with the full force of her own intense feelings. Perhaps it was the warmth, perhaps it was the beauty that was France, or maybe it was because she was back in Provence, where she had first laid eyes on Patrick and fallen in love.

She forced herself to attend to practical matters. When she wasn't painting, she kept herself occupied by going down into Cassis, making a valiant effort to be charmed by the bay and the winding cobbled streets. It was exquisite, not as tiresomely fashionable as Saint-Tropez... and yet still, she felt no desire to mix with society here. As she walked through the town, she was aware of the locals' acute gazes. Oscar, Lawrence, Coco, and Patrick were making regular forays into town in the evenings, sitting outside the *tabacs* and smoking, making friends with the men of the town. But Emma felt every eye on her when she wandered through the cobbled streets. Gossip, it seemed, was a universal occupation, no matter how liberal a country's views.

It was amusing, she supposed, or scandalous—she, the charming Coco, and a houseful of men. She supposed it was a consolation, the fact that no one would ever get to see beyond the facade she presented. Sometimes in life, there were no answers, there were just feelings, and one had to get on with things as best one could.

On the surface, Emma's life would seem one perfect, serene painting, hardly a complicated book. She spent her days working on the veranda alongside Patrick. She arranged for Lydia and Calum to have French lessons in the mornings and to spend the afternoons exploring Cassis and swimming at the local beaches. Having seen them off in a donkey cart after lunch each day, Emma would return to her work.

As the summer drew on, their world began to expand. Oscar's friend Roger Dalton arrived for a visit, quite crowding up the house, to be followed by Freya and Henry, who took up residence in a cottage nearby, and Emma began to feel more relaxed. Until a newcomer arrived, who caused Emma's heart to sink like a stone down to the bottom of a murky pond.

Chapter Fifteen

London, 1980

The phone pealed. Laura rushed toward it, leaving her front door open wide as she fumbled to pull her key out of the lock on her return from Ewan's house. Outside, rain pelted a strange beat, an accompaniment to the people on the footpath who rushed from the train station to wherever they intended to go.

"Hello, Laura."

In spite of everything, a sudden irrational hope swelled inside her at the sound of Ivan's voice, only to be laced with despair. The bank had become a shadow looming, a threatening, brewing sky.

"Is this a good time to talk?" he asked.

Laura twirled the phone cord around in her fingers until she'd fashioned a series of tight knots. "I'm on my way to a… rehearsal."

"Very well; I'll be brief. I have spoken to my superiors about your matter."

Laura closed her eyes.

"And unfortunately, given the doubt that has been thrown onto the provenance of the painting, they have advised me that we will definitely be recalling fifty percent of the principal of the loan in a week now. I am sorry. I thought I should do you the courtesy of confirming our position."

The rain was relentless, heavy. All she could see outside her door was an impenetrable sheet.

"I have no way of coming up with fifty thousand pounds. And Emma—"

"I understand. But we all knew the risks entering the agreement."

"Emma guaranteed the loan because she knew there was no chance of any doubt about the provenance of the portrait. You accepted that as fact when we signed the documentation. Emma has been a long-term, loyal, and sensible client of your bank for decades."

"Once again, I'm sorry."

Laura clutched the handle of her violin case until her fingers, damp from the rain, were wet with sweat instead.

"I will work longer hours to pay you back as fast as I can. I cannot have Emma lose everything. I can't let that happen."

There was a silence before Ivan spoke. "With all due respect, have you considered that it might be time to move Emma into a nursing home?"

Laura closed her eyes at his blunt approach. "No."

Ivan sighed down the line.

Laura added, "Given the history, the artistic heritage of the painting, the personal implications, and Emma's age, can I have a little more time?"

"We can't loan out such a large sum of money with no guarantee."

Laura wiped the back of her hand across her face. "Well, I wonder if there's any point in my going to string quartet rehearsal right now…"

Ivan was quiet for a moment. "I'm sorry, Laura. I honestly am. I wanted to let you know…"

Silently, Laura hung up the phone. Still clinging on to the handle of her violin case, feeling as if it could slip out of the palm of her hand, she stood up, hardly aware of what she was doing, where she was going. And she walked out, raising her umbrella against the pelting rain.

They say in life, she thought as she walked the few hundred yards to Russell Square Station, *the most important things are love and work*. A few weeks ago, Laura had been buoyant with both; she knew she loved Jasper, and she'd regarded him as a model inspired by Em's relationship with Patrick. She'd been flying at the Royal College of Music.

She was quiet as she unpacked her violin at Marguerite's house; she hardly spoke to the others until she rested the Guadagnini under her chin. Aware of Jasper's eyes on her, knowing full well that he'd never ask what was wrong in front of the others, she'd have to avoid him, make up an excuse to get out of here after they were done.

Laura had lost control of her own destiny. It was as if something or someone had picked her up and put her on a different course. She felt her way through the melancholy Beethoven string quartet. When the Beethoven finished, beautiful, sad, and endlessly mournful, even Ed sat in silence, holding on to his cello, his expression serious.

"I hope the audience won't mind such a melancholy choice," he said, sending a sidelong glance to Marguerite. "I do wonder if we should have chosen Schubert rather than late Beethoven for a concert in a church."

"The church," Marguerite said, "is perfect for Beethoven." She stood up as if the conversation was dismissed.

Laura looked up at her. Marguerite had such a way of doing that, finishing things, having the last word.

"Laura?"

She jumped at the sound of Jasper's voice, hadn't even realized that he'd stood up and had packed up his viola while waiting for her to move. The others were in Marguerite's small kitchen, having a rowdy discussion about London traffic. Laura sank against the back of her chair.

"Surely you know I'm not going to have you sitting there like that without talking to me. You look very strange. Tell me."

Laura started to pack up her violin.

"Okay..." Jasper said. "Let's get out of here. Together."

Laura clipped her violin case shut. She focused on the neat, black smoothness of it.

Laura stood up. She regarded Jasper. "I'm fine."

"Laura and I are going," Jasper called to Marguerite and Ed.

Once they were outside on the sidewalk, Laura started to walk away.

"No, you don't," Jasper said. He kept pace with her as she marched up the street, ripe with bright post-rain sunshine now. It glared in her eyes, illuminating every speck on the pavement, rendering the sky almost too searing to look at.

Jasper grasped her elbow and swung her to face him. And tenderly, he reached out. He stroked her face, tracing one finger down her cheek.

"I know what you're going through. But don't shut me out. Laura, I'm your friend. I'm always here. It really is simple, you know."

Laura shook her head.

His grip on her arm tightened. Roughly, he pulled her into his shoulder.

Her face might be pressed into his shirt, but she was as rigid as a steel plank.

"We just need to take this step-by-step. And whatever you do, don't give up. To start with, you need to get Ewan to talk. Properly. And now."

"Ewan thought it was acceptable to offer to pay my college tuition, as if that would fix everything."

"But Laura, Ewan *is* the only person who can fix this. Not me, not Em. And to be honest, why can't you accept his offer of money to stop Em from being kicked out of her house?"

She looked down at her violin.

"If that's something you need to sort out with him, then go back and do so."

Laura swallowed.

He seemed to struggle a little. "You're not Emma, with her luxury of being able to afford to live and support herself on allowances in order to pay her rent and bills. I'm not Patrick, but you need to save everything good in your life, and you deserve… everything."

He waited.

Silently, she made her decision. Quietly, as if some new stillness had taken over her, she reached out and touched Jasper's arm; then she made her way to the station.

Laura gathered her light trench coat around her as she made her way toward the gate that led to the street full of mews houses where Ewan lived. The sound of her footsteps echoed on the cobblestones in the otherwise silent old lane. She stopped at his red front door, and she reached up to knock with the brass knocker.

The sound of brass knocking on wood rang through the small circle of old converted stables, ringing around the tall houses that rose behind them. The preserves of the rich might always dwarf these little buildings where the carriages had once been kept, but the lives that went on here were just as important, just as full of stories and love and loss, as any of the grand houses that surrounded them.

No one came to the door.

Laura switched her gaze back to the little street. The large window that had been converted out of the stable door in the little house opposite caught her eye. A woman sat at a desk in the window, a lamp shining on her bent head. The woman raised her head, as if impulsively, and smiled at Laura.

Laura, hesitant, smiled back and felt some connection to the old past now. The woman almost reminded her of an artisan in a medieval lane.

"Hello." Laura jumped at the sound of Ewan's voice.

Ewan held an art catalog; his keys and his suit coat were slung over one forearm, while his sleeves were rolled up to his elbows. He searched her eyes.

"Look…" she began.

"Come in." As he reached for the lock in the door, his shoulder brushed hers. His hands shook a little as he turned the key.

"Sorry about the mess," he said, striding into the middle of his living room. He stood a moment, as if bewildered by the fact that a couple of books lay on the sofas: the professor's biography of Patrick and the catalog of the retrospective exhibition held after he died.

Laura felt a smile play around her lips at the sight of the two stray books that were not quite in line with the rest of the house. Ewan moved toward his small kitchen. He turned on a couple of lights and opened the fridge. Pulled out a bottle of wine.

He opened a cupboard in the kitchen and reached for two wineglasses. "White okay?" He paused, watching her, his head tilted to one side.

She nodded, her whole body feeling wound so tight it would burst if anyone touched it. She could not walk away without a resolution.

Ewan continued moving about in the kitchen.

He brought her drink over to her, holding it out to her for a moment, his eyes meeting hers.

"Let's sit down," he said, his voice gentle.

Laura perched on the edge of the deep-blue velvet seat.

"How was your day?" he asked, like some partner at the beginning of an evening and after the end of a normal day.

"Fine. Thanks." Laura gulped her wine.

Ewan sat back in his seat, resting his head against the cushions and regarding her.

"You can't lose your music career, Laura. I won't stand by and let that happen." He looked off to the side, a strange expression passing across his face. "I will help you get back on your feet."

"No. I need to do this myself." She heaved out a sigh. "I can't let you fix it. Thank you for your offer, but I was wondering, could you come out to Summerfield with me and look at the portrait? Would you do that?"

Ewan's handsome features sharpened in concentration. "Look, Laura—"

"Have you got a bike?" She could not take no for an answer. She had to get him in front of Emma's portrait and talk to him. Now.

"A bike?" A smile danced around his lips.

"A bike." Laura stood up, taking her wineglass with her and placing it back on his pristine kitchen bench. No crumbs on the white marble. No telltale bits of paper, pens, loose change. "We'll ride from Lewes Station to Summerfield. It's what Emma always did."

"A *bike*?"

Laura nodded. "Of course."

"You are adorable."

Laura felt herself smile—was she actually having fun? "You can ride Emma's old bike, then. I kept it."

He laughed and looked up at her, his tanned hand twirling the stem of his wineglass.

"It's rusty, and you'll have to deal with the cobwebs. It has no gears, of course. But I think it will suit you very well."

He stood up and moved toward her. "I suppose I could swap a couple of meetings. But, I'm sorry, I don't think it will help—"

But Laura held up a hand. She needed to get him out of his London comfort zone, out to Summerfield, where the Circle and everything that mattered to Em would surround him. Laura picked up her coat and started to pull it on, moving toward his front door.

"I live three doors up from Russell Square Station, on Bernard Street. You won't miss it. The house has an emerald-green front door. Except I'm in the basement. That means you have to go *down* the stairs—"

"I understand about basements."

"We'll wheel the bikes up to the train station. Eight thirty? I really have to go. Abject poverty calls me, along with a debt I'll never pay off and the prospect of working at least three jobs so I can support my grandmother. Who will have to come and live with me in my basement flat. I thought we'd get ten cats." Laura grabbed her handbag. She pulled out a notepad and jotted down her phone number and address on the first page before tearing it off and handing it to Ewan. "In case my instructions weren't clear enough."

"Laura—"

"Bye," she said. "Oh, and don't be late."

"Hang on. Stop." He was next to her in a few strides as she held his front door open. He took hold of the front door at the top and stood there. "Let me know if you want help feeding the cats."

"I'm not borrowing money from you," she said softly.

"Why not?" His voice was equally intimate now.

"Would you do that if you were me?"

He raised a brow.

"Until tomorrow." Laura wheeled around and marched off up the cobblestoned mews. She nodded at the woman who worked in her window.

Game, but not, in any way, set and match.

Chapter Sixteen

London, 1980

An hour later, Laura waited for Jasper in the local pub. He'd called her for an update the moment she walked through her front door. She'd filled him in on her meeting with Ewan and their plans to go to Summerfield the next day. Nonetheless, he'd insisted on meeting her at the pub. But as soon as she saw him arrive at the Lamb, framed by the paneled walls that must hold all the secrets in the world, since the Circle used to come here as their local spot—in fact, perhaps she could simply ask the walls if they knew whether Patrick had painted *The Things We Don't Say* and she'd get her answer—Laura's brow knitted. She pushed away the bowl of salted nuts that she'd been playing with.

Jasper's long cardigan was wrapped around his body. He was swathed in navy cashmere. Even in the dim interior of the pub, Laura could see well beyond the strikingly handsome facade that caused half the students, both male and female, at the college to swoon whenever he appeared. His face was the color of parchment. Jasper scoured the room for her, and she lifted her hand to signal him over.

He slumped down opposite her, bent his dark head down on the small wooden table, and reached a hand out to Laura. She held it. His hair stuck up on end.

"I'm dying," Jasper said.

"You can't. That won't work."

"Mark isn't moving to London."

Outside the pub's mullioned window, the blurred shapes of people walking by were only just visible. Indistinct shadows in the dark.

Jasper had been obsessed with Mark for years. Hadn't she dreamed of Jasper not being obsessed with Mark for just as long?

"I'm sorry," she said. Maybe it was just Mark being Mark. He often let Jasper down at the last minute when they'd organized a date; Mark demanded commitment, then refused any such thing for his own part, playing Jasper as if he were his personal instrument, Laura always thought.

Jasper met Laura's eyes. "I've had enough."

"Oh."

"Take me with you to Summerfield tomorrow. I want to get out of London. I can't stand being here alone for a minute."

Laura didn't answer right away.

"I'll practice in the garden," he said. "I'm sick of stupid boys distracting me. He has no concept that I have my performance exam next week. I'm going to get us drinks."

Laura watched him march across to the bar.

He was back in three minutes, holding two glasses of bubbles and handing one to her. "When everything goes wrong, one may as well drink champagne."

Laura took a sip.

"Anyway," he said. "Back to your stuff."

"We should talk about Mark."

"Later. You're urgent."

Laura resisted the urge to slump her head on the table.

"What if you seduced Ewan? Then he'd confess."

"Shut up." But Laura moved away, her face flushed with red.

"You're too much of a romantic to think like I would, darling."

"You have to be joking."

"Nope."

"Oh, come on—"

"You wish you could do Emma's free-love thing, but you never could. It's not in your nature."

Laura pushed away her glass. Right now, the thought of bubbles in her stomach wasn't sitting so well. "Stop it."

"You've said he's handsome…"

"Jasper…" Laura spoke through gritted teeth.

"Listen to me."

She crossed her legs and folded her arms as if they were a brace.

Jasper reached out. Gently he took her hand. "Putting aside the ghastly financial scenario for a moment—you've tried, religiously, to adopt Emma's tolerant, accepting views… and let's face it, we both adore each other, but Emma applied the Circle's theories to her situation because it suited her to do so. That was her reasoning. She rejected her parents' traditional views of love, and you have, in turn, rejected your parents' functional approach to it as well."

She shot her head up.

But he went on. "Right now, my heart is breaking; I need a romantic distraction—I really want to talk about this and about you, Laura. I think you're attracted to Ewan, interested. In some ways, you've met your match, and I think from what you've told me, he's starting to care about you, which is seriously good."

"Jasper…" she whispered. "I just don't need that right now. It's way too complicated. Crazy."

"I just don't want you sacrificing your own life like Emma did. Over Patrick."

Was that what Emma had done? And yet, Jasper was her safe boat, her harbor. But was he also her way of avoiding risk? He had always been adept at voicing the things she hardly understood about herself.

"Music puts you in touch with Emma too; it gets you away from what you see as your mother's way of life. It brings you closer to that magic that you saw in the generation before your mother's, in the Circle. Bach's music, our favorite, is divine, and I cannot

wait to perform the Double Violin Concerto with you at the end
of your exam. But so, darling, is letting go and loving a man."

She usually adored this about Jasper—his ability to take a
conversation somewhere she never expected it to go, along with
his caring approach and the mutual, genuine affection between
them that was part of what kept things so entrancing for her. But
right now, he was hitting notes that she didn't want him to play.

Jasper reached out his hand and covered her own.

"Playing music is the only way I can achieve anything that feels
real apart from when I'm with you." Her words were raw, honest.
She looked up at him.

"But what's stopping you from being open about being with
someone else properly? You will always have me; you have to fight
for your music and... someone who can love you the way you
deserve to be loved. I don't know if it's going to be Ewan, but it
needs to be someone. And I have not seen you affected like this
before. Not by a mile. Don't push Ewan away if he wants to help
you. Honestly, I don't think the poor guy had any idea what he
was getting into. And you did say he is an artist..."

"But he's not offering me anything."

"He's dropping everything to get on Emma's old bike and ride
through Sussex with you tomorrow. He's offered to pay off your
loan. Come on, Laura."

"Isn't that only guilt?"

"The guy might be an art dealer. But I don't think he's evil."

Laura bit her lip. She needed to change tack, and fast. "Are
you going to try and work things out with Mark?" she asked, her
voice barely audible.

She smiled at the thought that somewhere, deep down, she still
half hoped he'd say no.

"I'll give it one last try."

She nodded. "Well then."

"I believe love exists, Laura. And the reason I know it does is that I've found it with you."

"But no one else is you," she said.

"No. Nothing wrong with that."

"And he's wrecking my life."

"He's also challenging you. It doesn't have to be wreckage."

Laura couldn't help the short laugh that escaped from her throat. "Oh, come on."

"Are you attracted to him?"

Laura rolled her eyes.

"Do you think he's attracted to you?"

"I don't know!"

"All you have to do is convince him that the love that existed between Patrick and Emma cannot ever be broken—that Patrick's memory can't be broken for her. You need to make him see that Patrick and Emma were ultimately about something purer and better than so many people ever get... and that he would not have lied to her. But I think the two of you need to sort out what's also going on right now. Between you as well. He's not behaving in the way I thought some dealer out for a quick gain would."

Laura let go of his hand. "I want my old life back."

"No, you don't. You can't go back."

"I don't know why I invited him to Summerfield!" Laura stared at Jasper, her eyes feeling huge.

Jasper stood up. "I'll be at your place at eight thirty," he said. "You know I love you, darling. Consider me backup, a place to rest your weary head, as Patrick told Emma. But you *have* to live your life, you know."

Laura smiled at his quotation of Patrick's famous declaration to Emma.

The pub had filled around them, and yet she hadn't noticed people arriving. Jasper, as usual, had gotten under her skin. But that gave her no answers as to how she was supposed to convince Ewan that it was enough, that Emma's and Patrick's honest love for each other and their relationship, something intangible, was enough reason to explain that the portrait of Emma couldn't be anyone else's work.

Chapter Seventeen

Provence, 1922

Jerome Douglas moved into Mas d'Aurore on precisely the same day that Patrick began working on the canvas of Emma. He'd chosen it with care, bringing it all the way from London, rolled up and tucked under his arm. He would not allow it to travel with the rest of their luggage. He told everyone that even blank, it was too precious to pack away. And yet in Emma's mind, the day that he started to put his brush to it would always be far more linked with Jerome than with any memory of Patrick starting her portrait. Jerome's arrival was etched into her as if rendered in dark ink.

The sound of his footsteps coming up the driveway to the house was what started it. Emma sat, sketching alone at her easel under the vines. The first thing that struck her as odd was that the person approaching seemed to be stopping over and over again—his movements erratic, stilted, as if he was distracted at every turn.

She looked up once the footsteps came closer, thinking this must be someone from the village who was looking for Colonel Bird but had taken a wrong turn instead. But Emma felt a frown ripening across her features at the sight of the man in front of her. She laid down her brush and did not move from underneath the cool protection of the vines. For some reason, she wanted to be able to observe the newcomer before he saw her.

Because Emma had a slow, ghastly sense that she knew exactly who he was.

He looked to be somewhat younger than Patrick and Emma—a fine figure of a man, stunningly handsome. The young man stopped just before he reached the vine-clad terrace, removing his hat and waving it in front of his face like a fan. Emma narrowed her eyes, her artist's gaze taking in the detail of him. He was at least six feet tall, well proportioned, chocolate-colored hair and eyes, tanned skin. And it struck her that he looked as if he could be Patrick's brother. Except he definitely was not.

Emma laid down her brush and ran a hand through her too-far-gone hair. She stood up, straightening out her painting smock. The man's lazy smile morphed into an inscrutable expression as she moved toward him. If Emma were pressed, she'd say that she detected insolence in his look.

"Bonjour," he said, drawing out the last syllable as if he were a Frenchman, but Emma could tell he was not. She didn't have to dig very far into his accent to tell that he sounded, most definitely, American.

"Hello," Emma said, fighting with irritation at his interruption of her work. She'd come here to paint, not to entertain what she was certain was one of Patrick's lovers.

She cast about for Lydia or Elise, knowing full well that Lydia was out with Calum and the local French girl, Elise, tended to sing while she cooked in the kitchen, so there was no chance she would have heard such a thing as footsteps on gravel out here.

Emma glanced back at her easel and heaved out a sigh.

"Can I help you?" she asked.

"Up for a gate-crasher, Mrs. Grundy?" His accent was pure New York. "I am ab-so-lute-ly certain that my crush is sitting pretty here."

Emma gasped.

"Patty told me he was sitting pretty with some swanky folk in the sun." The man smirked. "I was a bit grummy up in Paris. Whole place empties out in August, did you know that? Pat told me I'd be welcome here anytime. So I took him up on it."

"I think he's working… I'm Emma Temple."

"He mentioned some dame."

Emma's heart sank as he put down his suitcase.

"Who do I have the pleasure of meeting?" she asked.

She gathered the sides of her skirt in her fists.

"Hasn't he told you?" the man said, something unpleasant creeping into his voice again. "What a darned double-crosser. We studied art together in Paris. Among other things." Another smirk ran across his face.

Emma closed her eyes. Right now, she'd give her left arm for blond, bearded, insufferable Rupert to appear out of the past and declare his unbound affection for Patrick if it meant she never had to have a conversation with this guy again.

"Do you have a name?" she asked.

"I can't believe Pat hasn't told you about me!" He laughed, throwing back his head, impressed enough with his own joke. There was no need for congratulations from anyone else.

Emma heaved out a sigh.

"Name's Jerome Douglas, Emma," he said, languishing on her name.

The screen door clattered open behind her. Patrick brought his hand up to shade his face, his pale-blue cotton shirt hanging loose over his trousers. He ran his other hand through his shock of curly hair in a sexy, slow sort of way. A broad grin spread across his face as his eyes alighted on Jerome.

Emma switched her gaze, hawklike, to the other man.

But Jerome was too quick. He strode straight on past her and embraced Patrick, kissing him on the cheek, his lithe arm lingering too long on Patrick's shoulders.

Emma's breathing quickened, and she focused on the flagstones under her feet. Her shoes, her smock, her hair, everything about her seemed dowdy now. She wished she'd dressed in some wildly fashionable way today.

It was as if Jerome had changed the dynamics of everything in one second flat, thrown out and threatened the contentment that she and Patrick had been enjoying since they'd arrived in France.

Emma hovered like the third wheel in an unbalanced cart.

"Patrick, old boy. You look like a ragamuffin." He punched Patrick on the shoulder. "Come on, I'm only razzing you."

A bashful grin spread across Patrick's face.

"But seriously, how can you stand it out here? I reckon I've arrived just at the right time. You and I need to go on the toot down in Cassis. Get you away from these live wires around here."

Emma clutched at her smock.

"Jem, Emma is a very dear friend."

"Yeah, we've met already," Jerome said.

Emma simply did not have the words.

"Tell you what," Patrick said. "Why don't you leave your suitcase here, and we will go down to Cassis for the morning? That way, Em, you can get on with your work uninterrupted." Patrick placed a hand on the other man's shoulder now, and they moved away into the house.

Emma stood there, alone on the terrace, trying to fight her own revulsion and failing hard.

"Em."

She jumped at the sound of Patrick's voice again right behind her. She didn't turn around when the screen door opened again.

"I told Jerome before we came here that if he was getting sick of Paris in the heat and needed a change of scene…" His voice trailed off. "The point is, I assumed he'd let me know if he'd accepted my vague invitation. Sorry. I didn't think for a moment he'd come all the way down here. Okay with you, Em?"

Emma nodded. "Of course," she said. "Yes, I'm delighted."

She returned to her easel, picked up her brush, and got back to work. And fought the dreaded certainty that this man was going to be different from all the rest.

*

Two weeks later, Emma wandered down the stairs at Mas d'Aurore and out onto the veranda, her eyes drawn to the green vines that glistened in the early morning sun. She stopped, taking in the serene hills that sat beyond the vineyards. They were already shimmering in the heat.

She'd woken in a sweat, nausea pulsing through her system. For two weeks she'd known, and now, the knowledge seemed to spread through her until she was taken over by it entirely.

But unlike her previous pregnancy, when she had been ecstatically in lust both with Oscar and the idea of their marriage, the joy that she should feel at this new life stirring inside her was eclipsed entirely by the irrational yet constant fear that Patrick would leave her for Jerome. She'd tried talking to herself firmly, admonishing herself that it was only pregnancy making her feel so unsure. But at three o'clock in the morning, when she'd woken and been sick, the idea of Patrick's leaving her for a carefree existence with his lover did not seem so unlikely at all. Patrick was besotted with Jerome, and he, in turn, was magnetic, charming, amusing—everything Emma was not capable of being in any way right now.

The local doctor in Cassis expressed no emotion as he told her that everything appeared to be in order while Emma carried on a normal conversation with him about returning to London to give birth. Inside, panic ripped through her, while she focused hard on the joy she should feel and did not.

Emma padded back through the cool, silent house, diverting her eyes as she passed the bedroom that Patrick shared with Jerome. Patrick used the interconnecting room to his bedroom as a studio, where he was working on his portrait of Emma while Jerome flounced down to Cassis most days, going on excursions to the cinema, often bringing a troupe of bewildered locals home for drinks, where he entertained them on the veranda, painting, wildly, only when he felt like it and when his muse struck—which seemed rare.

Emma worked alone in her bedroom when Jerome was about, and on the veranda when he was out, missing the company of Patrick painting alongside her now that his secretive work on her portrait had begun. The portrait seemed like the only link she shared with him while he was in the full flush of his relationship with Jerome. As if it were some lifeboat, Emma clung to the idea of it, to the fact that he was still doing it, to the way she caught him watching her sometimes.

She made her way into the cool, early morning, silent farmhouse kitchen and hovered a moment by the door. She should try and eat something, for the sake of the baby—as secret from Patrick as the portrait seemed to be from her—but even the sight of the bowl of crisp red apples on the scrubbed table caused her stomach to turn. If she were to step in any farther and smell food, she knew she would be sick. Elise would be here in a couple of hours with fresh baguettes and croissants. That thought, and imagining the smell of buttery pastries, made Emma want to retch.

She wrapped her shawl tight around her still slim body and went back out to the blessed relief of the veranda, where her easel was set up under the vines. Emma retrieved her latest painting from the stack of canvases that rested inside the dining room doors, sat down on her stool, sorted her paints, and looked after herself in the way she knew best. She started to paint.

"Good morning, Mrs. Emma."

Emma smiled at the sound of Lydia's voice. The teenage girl had become indispensable to the running of the household since they'd arrived in France. She'd taken the youthful Calum in hand, accompanying him to French classes and to the beach with either Jerome and Patrick or some of the other young people he'd met at French school. Lydia was adept at allowing Emma to work. The understanding sat like some unspoken knowledge between the two women. What was more, Lydia ran everything, upset nobody, and was entirely devoid of any oddities of character that would make things awkward given the delicate balance under which Emma's "family" usually worked.

"Lydia." Emma smiled. She looked up from her easel, placing her paintbrush on its ledge. "Are you planning on going with Calum to the beach today?"

"Oh, yes." Lydia nodded. "Mr. Patrick and Mr. Jerome are thinking of coming with us later on. Calum adores Mr. Patrick. He is full of antics. I think he views him as an older brother these days."

Emma gazed at her work in progress, a view of the veranda with a woman on a wicker chair under the wisteria that would have been so verdant and beautiful in the spring…

"I'll get to work," Lydia said.

Emma stood up and wandered out to the lawn to stand in the sun for a moment.

The creak of Jerome and Patrick's shutter sounded in the still air. Jerome leaned out of the window, his bare torso glistening in the sun. Emma slipped back to the shelter of the veranda.

She picked up a piece of sketching paper and fanned her sweating face, forcing herself to think of practical matters: she'd heard Lawrence rising early for his walk down into Cassis; Oscar took ages to appear in the mornings, as he insisted on taking a daily morning grooming ritual without which he was absolutely no use; Coco would not be up until noon.

Emma ran a hand across her still flat belly, trying to find some consolation at the tiny secret she was keeping, but the sound of Jerome and Patrick thumping down the stairs obliterated her determined calm thoughts. She picked up her brush, her eyebrows raising by only the merest sliver when she heard the sound of Patrick clowning around with Lydia.

When Jerome announced in a loud voice that he was going down to Cassis, Emma reached uselessly for her paintbrushes. Just as she sat back down again, Patrick appeared. He grinned at her in that lopsided way she adored and rolled the sleeves of his blue shirt up around his elbows.

"Good morning, darling. I don't want to interrupt you, but you couldn't think I'd mooch off to my studio without saying hello. Even if I'm going to work on what we both know is closest to my heart, my portrait, darling, of you."

Emma winced at Patrick's usage of Jerome talk, but she reached her hand back as Patrick came closer behind her. He stroked her fingers as if smoothing over any worries that might trouble her, but the feel of his fingers entwined in hers only caused her breathing to quicken.

"How is it coming along?" she asked.

"Well, I think. But I can't discuss it with you. You know that. I can't wait to see your reaction to the end result."

Emma bit her lip.

He crouched down next to her after a moment. "She looks sad," he said, scanning the painting on her easel.

"I worry that she lacks... vitality." Emma knew she sounded tired. And boring. Oh, she did not tolerate bores so very well herself. But right now, the last thing she felt was in any way attractive or enticing.

"I think she has gentle strength, like you. But she doesn't look happy, Em."

Emma swallowed hard. The urge to tell Patrick about the baby overwhelmed her. But it was also the last thing she wanted to do.

"You've been looking pale lately," he said. "Different." In a split second, he stood up and walked back into the house.

Emma picked up her paintbrush and ran her finger down the smooth wood toward the brush.

Within five minutes, he was back, holding a wooden tray with a plate of sliced baguette and a glass of water. The relief that tempered her at the sight of him returning was like a salve. He placed the tray on the long stone table behind her easel and swung his legs around one of the two long benches that sat at its side.

Gently, he reached forward and handed her a piece of baguette. Salt scattered across its crust. Emma took it, examining it before taking a small bite, letting the salt rest on her tongue a moment.

"Tell me what's wrong."

The words were a tempting slide...

She knew his eyes were on her as she struggled to eat the bread. "I'm fine," she said.

"I know Jerome can be challenging."

Emma opened her mouth.

"He wants to go to Paris," Patrick said, staring out at the vines.

She knew that. They all knew that. Emma drew in a sharp breath. She placed the baguette back on the plate, putting it near the rest of the crusty slice so that it sat almost next to the large piece but a little separate.

"How wonderful," she said. And reached out her hand across the table.

Patrick did the same thing, his hand melding with hers. She would not tell him. Not now. Were she to do so, he might feel obliged to stay here, and he wanted to go to Paris. With Jerome. She would not hold him back, nor would she expect him in any way to feel a responsibility to be here right now. Silence held between them, both the most uncomfortable and easiest thing in the world.

"It's been beautiful here," he whispered.

Emma nodded. She directed her gaze to the side, focusing on the vines that flickered in the sun. But instead of seeming full of freedom and color and light, as they had when she first arrived here, all they seemed to do was to hem her in to their dense wall of invidious green.

Chapter Eighteen

London, 1980

Emma hit the table beside her sofa, her old hand shaking with fury. Her memories were like a series of streetlamps in an opaque fog! All she could recall was what she'd wanted to see at the time, perhaps all she could recall was what she felt with the most intensity. Or maybe now. Trying to capture answers out of the nothings that had slipped away was like trying to find a teardrop in the ocean. She was never going to get the answers she sought.

How could she prove anything concrete when Patrick was dead and when Lydia had never seen him pick up his paintbrush? As for Emma, she'd played into the mystery of his painting her just as she'd fallen into Patrick's beautiful heart.

Fear underlined what she did remember of that summer in France. Her own thoughts and feelings ran like a dark thread beneath every memory she had of that time with Jerome. Sometimes, though, she found herself wondering whether it was uncertainty that had kept her relationship with Patrick alive. There had always been some version of unresolvedness between them, a sense of unknown possibilities lingering and dancing around their relationship for their entire adult lives—never quite certain, they had not slipped into predictable routine or the banality of a conventional life.

Nothing had dulled her feelings for him, nor taken away the sheen of what seemed to her to be the perfect relationship. Unanswered questions always hung over them, and Emma had wanted answers the whole time. But in the end, had not knowing been better than knowing?

Emma knew only too well that everyone put untold effort into trying to fix unresolved tensions in this life, but perhaps it was the very state of unresolvedness that gave us hope. That kept us striving on, after all.

She eased herself out of the sofa, leaning heavily on the armrest as she stood up. Unresolved questions might be a normal state in life, but for now, she'd had enough. A few answers would be more than welcome. She reached for her cane. Was her relationship with Patrick too deep to fathom even now? She'd never had the stalwart of religion to back her up during her formative years, had lacked the certainty of so many—to be honest, most—of her contemporaries because of her father's atheism.

In the end, she always came back to one ultimate question: What possible motive could Patrick have had for lying to her and telling her he painted that portrait out of love if he did not? Was he capable of such momentous deception? For momentous it would be if the young Mr. Buchanan was correct. No matter how hard she tried to convince Laura that her main concern was her granddaughter's education—and it was—Emma could not push aside the looming worry that Patrick might have lied to her, that he'd let her believe a complete falsehood. Emma thought she had known the man she loved, but the idea that she had failed in such a crucial matter sat in her like some dark menace.

But who else could have painted the portrait? The thought that Lawrence had painted her was ridiculous. Jerome was around and Patrick did paint the portrait in their shared studio that was next to their bedroom, but the painting screamed of Patrick's style rather than Jerome's flamboyant, almost rough use of stroke and color. In any case, Emma was certain that she was the last person Jerome would have ever wanted to paint in a sympathetic way.

Yes, Patrick liked jokes, and yes, Jerome would have been capable of taking on some trick to annoy Emma, but still. For Patrick to then declare that he'd painted the portrait for Emma and lie about it? Emma refused to believe that.

She took a couple of small, difficult steps with the aid of her cane. She was being ridiculous. Rationality was the only way to solve this.

And yet, she could not deny that the times which held magic in her life were the least rational of all, and they all centered around Patrick. He was every one of those lamplights shining out of the fog. And trying to recall what happened without him being here anymore was like trying to touch one of those yellow flares without getting her fingers burned. She could not bear the thought that this investigation could put out for good all that had glowed in her life.

Chapter Nineteen

London, 1980

Laura tipped Emma's old bike upside down and inspected it. The tires were pumped up, the chain worked, and while of course there were no gears, the ride from Lewes Station to Summerfield was made up of only gentle, undulating slopes. Ewan should be fine on Em's bicycle. Emma had ridden the journey hundreds of times. And the thought of Ewan perched on this very bike gave Laura cause to smile…

She glanced at the mess on her bed. This morning she'd tried on everything she owned, opting, after a frenzy of indecision, for a pair of jeans and a white shirt. She'd tied her hair back in a ponytail to avoid the breeze whipping tendrils into her face as they rode along the country roads toward Summerfield.

Laura placed her hands on her hips. Emma wouldn't have cared a twig about what to wear on a trip to the countryside—Laura knew her vacillations were not making sense. While ridiculousness fluttered around in her insides, she started to pick up her discarded clothes, piece by piece.

It was hard to pinpoint the exact time in her life that she'd started to view Emma as a role model. Laura's relationship with her own mother had seemed safe and fine and mundane throughout her childhood years, but the moment she had picked up a violin, it had been Emma who had recognized her granddaughter's passion and Clover who had done whatever she could to put Laura off. A new, fledgling flame had burned between Laura and her grandmother, firing and strengthening their relationship, something that ran deep. Throughout her teenage years, Laura had found that the more she came to know Emma, the more she was drawn toward and fascinated by her grandmother's extraordinary way of life.

What was more, as Laura now struggled with her own reactions to things that she could not control, the more she came to admire Emma's calm acceptance and tolerance of life. Laura respected the fact that Emma had been true to herself, to her art, to her values. Conversely, she was confounded by the fact that her own mother, Emma's daughter, had not only refused to look through the old sketchbooks she'd made as a child but had thrown out all the equipment she used to own when she was considering, for a brief time, becoming a ceramicist. Clover would not speak about any of it. Why had her mother so dramatically recoiled from her Bohemian upbringing and lived the most conventional of lives that anyone could endure?

Was it natural, then, Laura's own breaking away from Clover, in turn? She had become entirely entranced with Jasper once she'd started at the Royal College of Music. Here was someone who, like Emma, was trying to forge a life despite society's rules telling him he didn't fit in. Jasper and Emma were undoubtedly the most important people in Laura's world. Her mother's light had dimmed in Laura's life. Laura hadn't even thought to turn to Clover as all this drama had played out. But lately, being tangled up in the two strong personalities of Jasper and Emma had left Laura feeling a little unsure, still, about where exactly she fit in herself.

Laura was floundering, trying to search for answers about her grandmother's past while having absolutely no idea where the future was taking her. As for the present, that was unfolding like a roller coaster that had flown off its rails. Jasper suggesting that Ewan cared for her seemed like madness. She wanted him to see what the problem was and knew that the only way she was going to appeal to Ewan was to get to his heart. But honestly, somewhere, she was starting to become intrigued by him too. Laura sighed. She busied herself with putting away her clothes. Nothing seemed certain anymore.

When the last piece of clothing was put away, Laura shut the cupboard door with a gentle push. It was beautiful, decorated by Patrick and Emma, an old piece of furniture they'd found at a market and revived. And yet, this wardrobe was the last thing Clover would ever have in her pristine house, and so Laura had it in hers.

Laura wanted, so very much, to create an extraordinary life rather than something prosaic.

She jumped when there was a knock at the door and whizzed a glance around her small studio. Her half-eaten bowl of Weetabix still sat on the table. As swift as a cat, she slipped across the room and tipped the soggy remains in the bin, took in a deep breath, and went to answer the door.

Jasper propped his bike up against the outside wall. Laura gaped as she took in his outfit.

He looked down at his burnt-orange jacket and green jeans and shrugged. "Trying to stir up the art guy," he said. "I'm ready to step up if he plays for the other team," Jasper went on.

"Oh, for goodness' sake. You'll blend with the marigolds as it is," Laura said, brushing an imaginary piece of dust off the front of his jacket.

He swiped a playful arm her way.

Laura shut the door. Jasper lounged against the kitchen bench. She couldn't help but smile at the thought that he would have fitted in oh so very perfectly with the Circle.

"Jokes aside, are you okay?" he asked, regarding her.

"I feel like today is—"

"Don't pressure yourself too hard," he said. "Let Summerfield work its magic on him."

"You haven't alleviated my concerns saying that." Laura ran her fingers along the back of one of Emma's old wooden chairs.

"I have every faith in you and Summerfield, and Patrick's integrity, and Em."

"I wish I had your confidence."

"Well, this is all super tidy, sweetheart." Jasper chuckled. "Don't tell me you've been up since five in the morning cleaning to impress him."

Laura glared. "Of course not." She darted a glance at the front door.

"So I hate to lump you with this. I mean today of all days." Jasper slumped down on one of her kitchen chairs. "But I finally broke up with Mark for good."

Laura found the involuntary impulse that was something— joy?—inside her and crossed her arms instead.

"We both know it was hopeless, darling. Don't suppose you want to turn into a man?"

Laura moved over to the window and glared at the dusty windowpane. She gathered her thoughts. Sometimes they seemed like wasps ready to sting. "I'm so sorry."

"I think it just filtered out into something with no life anymore."

"Talk about it with me." She watched the legs that walked up and down the sidewalk.

When a knock sounded at the door, she startled. "I'm so sorry about Mark," she whispered. "Please talk to me later. This is hardly good timing for you!"

"Oh, I'll be fine, honey," Jasper said. "And I'm around all day if you need me. Go get the door, darling. One step at a time, for heaven's sake." He rolled his eyes.

Laura's palm was slick on the unpainted handle.

Ewan stood on the doorstep, running a hand through his blond hair. He wore a pair of jeans and a blue-and-white-striped shirt. He smiled tentatively, his dimple showing up.

"Hi," he said, his head to one side. "Sorry I'm a few minutes late. I love Bloomsbury."

Laura bit her lip. She had to admit that she'd worried that he might never have ventured beyond the periphery of Hyde Park. He'd told her his mother lived in Edinburgh, and he'd been in London a few years now.

"I often spend Sundays out here, you know," he went on, as if this was the most natural conversation in the world. "I like sitting in the squares and reading in the sun. But the Tube let me down this morning, it turns out…"

Jasper appeared right behind her, placing his arm high on the doorframe above her head. "I'm Jasper. Joining you guys for the train ride, I'm afraid. Come in," he said.

Laura stood aside in a rush just as Jasper leaned forward to shake Ewan's outstretched hand. She nearly fell into them both before retreating deeper into the room on her own.

"So here's your bike…" Jasper brought his hand up to his chin and frowned.

Laura glanced at them under her eyelashes.

Jasper grinned.

Ewan ran a hand over the ancient bike. It was still upside down on the floor. "Fair enough. I know I'm not the flavor of the day, but you don't have anything a little less antique, I suppose, Laura?"

Jasper chuckled, caught Laura's eye, and raised a brow.

Oh yes, she understood that look. Jasper approved of Ewan. Perfect. She did not want Jasper fawning all over him like some puppy dog. Laura reached for her green coat, but it slipped from her fingers to the ground when she touched it, landing in a soft pool on the floor.

Ewan picked it up for her, holding it out. Her arms became tangled in the lining. She glanced at Jasper, whose eyes were lighting up now, two sparks catching on kindling that she didn't want to light. Finally, at last, she was wearing her coat.

Jasper kept up a steady banter throughout the short walk to the station. Laura marched along in silence. And reminded herself that she had to make a breakthrough, or she was done. But Ewan and Jasper both chatted away like a pair of friends at a party as the train moved through the outskirts of London, leaving, in some unspoken agreement, Laura to brood alone in her own thoughts. Their conversation was both soothing and unsettling.

As the scenery widened into the deep fields of Sussex, Laura occupied herself by staring at the landscape outside the train window. Everything was vivid green and blooming and verdant and beautifully unfair—plants cascaded down the sides of the steep embankments that lined the railway tracks.

Spring and the countryside seemed to mock her. She placed her chin in her hand and took in the familiar picture-perfect church spires hovering over treetops in the distance. Smoke curled out of windows of the houses that lined the track. Everything seemed settled. It was as if all was in the right place. Was Laura trying to realize some impossible, crazy, artistic dream in a world that was too neat and too organized to handle her aspirations? Had her mother been right to lock all her passion away? Or was Emma correct—was an artistic life the only one to pursue if you had the desire?

When the train pulled into Lewes Station, nerves fluttered like tiny moths in Laura's stomach.

Emma, of course, would say nothing. Clover would button up, too, and hold it all in. Maybe they were more alike than Laura gave them credit for... even though their views were polar opposites on life. But Laura's emotions turned and turned like the wheels on her bike. She glanced at the small row of shops opposite the station—two general stores, a post office, a taxi service—this was *her* place.

"Stick behind me," she called to both the men. She took off, pedaling furiously, as she suspected Emma always did.

After a couple of wobbles, Ewan was beside her on the road that led through the quiet town, looking ludicrously handsome and at the same time oddly in place on the seat of Emma's old bike.

Laura focused on the road ahead. She knew every bend, because she'd often ridden to the village as a child. She wound her way out of Lewes, past the grand old manor house that sat behind a long stone fence, until they were out on the open roads that led to the isolated farmhouse that was Summerfield.

Once they turned left, up the old dirt lane that led to Summerfield, Laura had to draw on all her strength to fight the urge to scream at the impossibility of the task ahead. She allowed herself only a brief glance at the house closest to Summerfield, Ambrose's house, where he and his ballerina wife had spent their weekends once he married. They had been Emma and Patrick's closest neighbors for miles, and Laura used to go there as a child, enchanted by the tales of the Russian ballerina whom the famous economist had shared his life with after a brief affair with Patrick when he was young.

The sight of Ambrose's house usually lit up her insides with anticipation whenever she came to Summerfield. But instead of being a beacon that meant they were drawing close to the place Laura loved most in the world, the neighboring house seemed like a grim reminder today that she was not here to see Emma's artistic friends and that they were all gone now, for good. She was here to strike a match to their mounting funeral pyre.

As they approached Summerfield, Laura hardly looked at the dear pond—Emma's lake—on the right, nor did she allow herself to be sidetracked by the beloved garden, where she knew flowers would float, their colorful spring faces shining above the green lawn as if everything were perfectly all right.

She felt ludicrously protective of Summerfield and of Emma and Patrick. Ewan and Jasper pulled their bikes to a standstill in front of the house. Laura moved away from them. This was a sanctuary. There should be rules about who could come here.

And Ewan was not a person who should be allowed to pass the front gate.

Laura could not help but realize that she was letting the whole Circle down, that she was going to be the one to lose everything they'd worked so hard to build up. What if she couldn't save it? Because Summerfield seemed like a very dear casualty right now.

Determined not to allow her feelings to boil over, she parked her bike. Jasper and Ewan seemed to have given up altogether on talking to her, as if in some complicit understanding that she was not able to carry on any intelligent discussion at all. Laura fought the absurd thought that if she reached out a finger to touch the walls of the old house, the whole place would tumble in a pile of rocks at her feet.

"Everything is so clear out here," Jasper said, stretching his arms high above his head. "The air. It's as if it's all imbued with new life somehow…"

Or certain death. Laura pulled the house key out of her pocket.

As she slid the old key in the lock, reveling in the way it didn't quite fit, finding the way she had to fiddle around with it charming, until it unlocked with that final, satisfying *click*, she stood for a moment on the doorstep, breathing in the particular smell that she always associated with Emma's house. It was a mixture of the scent of a library blended with oil paints and heady spring flowers drifting in from outside. If she closed her eyes, she could almost convince herself that it was Emma's perfume that lent one final note to the air.

Summerfield was, in the end, not Laura's legacy to lose. It was a place and a time that the world needed, art needed, and—goodness knew—people needed in this modern age.

The two men stopped to look at the paintings in the entrance hall. She waited while they wandered into the dining room on the left, Ewan having to bend his head as he passed through the low doorway that led into Patrick's wildly decorated room.

Laura followed them, pulling open Patrick's decorative curtains and flooding the room and its stunning black and silver bold geometric wallpaper with light. Patrick had chosen black for the wallpaper; he'd adorned the paper with tiny silver squares, which he'd applied to the black base by hand. The round table in the middle of the room sat as if waiting for them all to come back. Emma's circles and flowers decorated it, the chalky paint showing charming signs of wear. An uneven stain splotched the spot at the table where Emma had always sat, and the door that ran to Lydia's kitchen hovered slightly open, as if she were about to appear with a delicious farm-cooked meal. Or a plate of Em's freshly baked afternoon scones.

Laura went out to the hallway.

Next, they moved into the sitting room. Laura remained mute, allowing Jasper and Ewan to wander and take it all in. The sight of Emma and Patrick's absurd little electric heater from the 1940s still sitting in front of the fireplace moved Laura yet again. She had to turn away. Laura remembered how Emma had told her that it was freezing out here before they enjoyed such a luxury as a small electric heater. Patrick had developed muscles of steel chopping wood for the fireplaces during their first winter here in the First World War.

Ewan took in the art on the walls, fine examples of Emma's work, along with several of Lawrence's paintings. Ewan was shaking his head as he moved around the room.

Jasper saucily caught Laura's eye, but Laura didn't respond. She wanted to get this done.

"It's wonderful," Ewan whispered. "I'm even more astounded than when I came here last time. And I didn't get to study these works. We were so focused on *The Things We Don't Say*…" His voice trailed off.

Laura moved toward the painted panels on the living room door. Patrick's circus men leaped and pranced on the wood.

But the little paintings that adorned the walls, charming as they were, were not gold mines. They were examples of decorative work from the Circle. Emma's paintings only ever fetched around a hundred pounds at auction. The only painting of any real monetary value in here was *The Things We Don't Say*.

Laura held her head up and led them farther into the house.

She paused at the closed door to Emma's bedroom, her fingers resting on the door handle. Jasper laid a hand on Laura's shoulder, and she closed her eyes.

"I'm going to leave you and Ewan to look at the painting together," he murmured. "I'll be out in the garden. Going to find a spot to practice." He slid his viola case off his back.

She nodded, her eyes fixed on the door. But she waited until the sound of his footsteps retreated down the passage.

The silence that surrounded her and Ewan was loaded, impregnated with far more than the old stories from the past.

She opened Emma's bedroom door.

Ewan's shoulder brushed hers as he moved past her into the room. He made his way straight over to Emma's bed. Laura stood poleaxed in the entrance to the room. Her hands felt cold. Everything seemed cold.

He took in the portrait in silence.

The sound of Jasper tuning up filtered in from the garden. As he flew into the viola part in Mozart's lively Fifth Violin Concerto, Ewan faced her.

"Laura," he said, "I'm so sorry. Nothing's different from what it was before."

Jasper went on with the Mozart—happy, content music. Laura heaved out a sigh.

"Sorry?" she asked.

He looked at her, his eyes genuinely, if she were not mistaken, sad. "Yes," he whispered. "I can't tell you what you want to hear. I wish I could, believe me. I just…"

Laura moved toward the French windows. "Why did you come here with me today?"

His tread was solid on the wooden floor until he stood and looked out at the window next to her.

"I wanted to see it again. And to see it with you."

Jasper moved on with the delicate, sweet Mozart. In spite of everything, Laura found herself taking it all in. Mozart moved in patterns. If only life would do the same thing.

"I can't lie and tell you it's Patrick's work. And I honestly am sorry," he said.

Laura found herself facing Emma's writing desk. A portrait of Emma's late mother still sat on its top, staring out, serene, beautiful, so like Emma... yet only in looks. Laura picked it up and turned it over in her hands, taking in the woman who had been her great-grandmother—part of her, Emma, and Clover—as if for the very first time. How did this work—four women with such different personalities, all cut from the same cloth, and yet trying to figure life out in a way that would work for them? Had her mother, grandmother, and great-grandmother really succeeded in making sense of this world?

"We both know you owe me an explanation," she said. "Surely you can tell me what you are talking about, because from where I'm standing, that portrait is clearly the work of the man who loved my grandmother for most of their lives. How can you possibly say it's not?"

Laura placed the photograph back down, but her hands shook.

"Listen," he said, his voice coming out low and solid and warm behind her.

Laura didn't turn to face him.

"I can't do what you want me to," he said. "But believe me, I do want to."

"You could talk if you wanted to. You could, at the very least, explain. You just choose not to. You choose to stay silent." She leaned on Emma's small desk.

He came and crouched down next to her. "I am offering to make amends, to put things right, so that you and Emma can both live in the way you deserve, so that you can have your career—surely you can see that. I'm trying to buy you time, to let you get your finances in order."

"No. Not good enough, Ewan." Laura jolted in surprise at the way she'd said that.

Jasper stopped playing.

Outside the window, the silence seemed to hover. Emma's once well-tended plants were starting to turn wild—no one was going to love and care for this place like Emma had.

"I can't—"

"What can't you tell me?" she whispered. "How could telling me be more harmful than not talking to me? If you really love art, think of Emma, at least. And what about her loyal companion and housekeeper, Lydia? Don't you realize that she'll be unemployed and homeless after all this?"

Laura tried, but she could not fight the tears that brewed up in her.

He drew her into a rough embrace. In spite of herself, for some untold reason, she did not pull away, but she knew she should do so. This was dangerous, dangerous ground. And yet, some part of her told her that Jasper never held her like this…

"You're not fixing it by handing out money," she murmured. "That's what you don't understand."

Jasper began the second movement, the viola singing a strange, lonesome, mournful song, as if it were a lost bird. The orchestra would only support it, Laura knew, with the odd quiet chord.

"You have no idea," he murmured, leaning his chin on her head, "how much I understand."

She sprang back. "Talk to me, then!"

He looked at her, his eyes holding such sadness that Laura fought the sudden instinct to move toward him again. She stood there while she swore she saw every emotion under the sun pass over his face.

Finally, he let out a loud sigh. "There is something I can tell you." His voice sounded rough.

He moved toward the painting as if he was resigned. And he pointed at it with his finger. "See this?"

Laura craned forward. Emma looked as if she'd been painted yesterday. But Ewan pointed at a tiny red mark on the bottom of the painting, almost invisible.

Laura's breathing seemed to ring in her ears.

The Mozart was a quiet, untold whisper filtering in from the garden.

Ewan took her hands and looked her straight in the eyes. "I am so sorry, but that mark tells me the work is not Patrick Adams's."

"What?" Laura whispered, the word hardly sounding more than a breath in the quiet room.

Jasper played a descending run of notes.

"What are you saying?"

He moved across to the French doors and stood looking out.

Laura stayed where she was.

Slowly, he swiveled around. "I have the most…" He leaned forward then and ran a hand across her face.

"What is going on?" she murmured, but her eyes were widening, and she knew with certainty that her senses were on full alert.

"Don't you feel this?" he growled. "I'm struggling here."

She took in a shaking breath. "I can't…"

He rested his forehead against hers. "I can't talk about it. But I can tell you the painting's a fake. I cannot stand here and lie about it. I just can't."

Laura, in spite of herself, in spite of everything, reached out and took his hand.

"I am right; that's the problem," he whispered. "I'm so sorry, Laura."

Laura reached up. She took his face in her hands. "You have to tell me why. You can't hold that back from me."

"I know," he said. "Do you think I don't understand what's at stake?" Gently, he took her shoulders and held her at arm's length again. "Don't think, Laura, that I don't understand. Don't think that I don't understand Bloomsbury and the Circle. Everything that they fought for is so very real to me. And I know exactly how you feel about your music. I promise you that I do."

Laura fought the cynical smile that appeared on her face. But then, there was his mews house, the easel, his collection of beautiful books. She'd tried to dismiss them all, fought so hard not to see what she knew was staring her in the face when she was there… but the fact was, being in his surroundings had made her feel both entranced and somehow at home.

"You have to talk to me," she whispered.

"I don't want you to lose your music."

"Ewan," she said, "Emma needs to get to the heart of what lay between her and Patrick. Was it truth and honesty or deception? Paying for my music tuition is putting a tiny bandage on a gashing war wound. It doesn't get to the heart of anything that matters. Surely you can see. You need to talk to us."

He was silent, his chest rising up and down. "There are things that I cannot say."

"You must tell me."

He was silent.

"Nothing you can say could be worse than anything she's experiencing right now."

His chest rose visibly, then fell again.

Laura knew he was so close—on the cusp of something. And by goodness, she would get it out of him if it killed her.

"Why don't you work as an artist?" she blurted out. "Why are you hiding your art away from the world?"

He let go of her.

Laura fought the slump that overcame her as he moved away from her. He stood, his back to her, staring out at the garden.

Jasper was quiet out there, too, now.

"You have the talent," Laura said, her words whisper quiet. "You can afford to support yourself. So why not do what you love?"

"After the Slade, I couldn't face being an artist."

Emma's neat, blank writing pad lay as if waiting on her little desk. Laura waited too, but Ewan seemed to have clammed up again. The sound of bees flirted around Em's hollyhocks outside the French doors.

"My mother, Clover," Laura said, "is talented. And yet she denied herself the one thing she loved because she did not want the lack of security that goes with it. So she gave it up. Hid it. I think she did so because it was too hard, too real. Something that she thinks turned Emma into an outcast who never made any money from her art. So my mother, Clover, hid her passion in neatness and conformity, following the rules that Emma never followed. My mother works in a library cataloging books. I think she was scared of that artistic side of herself. Scared of opening herself up like Emma had done or, sort of, didn't do."

Ewan twisted away from her.

"Patrick, on the other hand," Laura went on, "was famous for the fact that he didn't care about money at all. He was always penniless. He would put a price on the back of his paintings, and then when a collector wanted to buy one, he was ridiculously generous, reducing the cost until he got almost nothing."

"He had Emma." Ewan's voice cut into the silence. "She supported him."

"Yes. Emma was his home."

Ewan's voice was low. "For heaven's sake, let me help you, Laura."

"Not doing what you are born to do… it's not good for you, Ewan."

She watched him.

"What is it like, working at the gallery, constantly surrounded by other people's art, when you could be exhibiting your own work? You have the talent. I can see that," she whispered.

Ewan looked at the floor.

"I saw passion in your work."

Jasper started the slow movement up again. The long, tender notes wound their way through the air, lilting like mysteries.

"Emma's art was her expression, but in life, she kept things locked inside her. She didn't talk about things so much of the time, but that was because she had no choice with Patrick. You, Ewan, have a choice." She stopped. Jasper was soaring right now. "And life is short. Em's life is nearly over. But if you won't talk to me, if you won't trust Em and me with why you think that portrait is not Patrick's work, then what next? Because I'm getting to the point here that I don't want to report to anyone what you've just told me, not to an expert or to the media or even my grandmother. I want you to tell me, and me first, and that is probably—"

"Bad and wonderful at the same time?" he whispered, turning toward her.

Laura frowned up at him, but what she was feeling right now was too much to express in words.

He leaned down, and with the gentlest of caresses, he circled his arm around her waist, pulled her toward him, and kissed her, a feather-light touch.

Chapter Twenty

France, 1923

Lydia hovered on the veranda at Mas d'Aurore, her damp floral-print dress clinging to her shins. The cloche hat that she'd worn to the beach hung in her hand by her side, and the sound of Calum's laughter rang from the cool interior of the house.

Emma was painting three poppies—two red and the third one perfectly separate and white. She waited until Patrick was out to work on it because she knew only too well that he'd know exactly what had inspired her to paint them like this.

"I'm sorry to interrupt you." Lydia tilted her head to one side. "And that is a capital painting—but it makes me sad, I'm sorry to say."

Emma did not look up.

"Forgive me," Lydia said.

"That's perfectly all right, Lydia."

"I'm wondering if you are of a mind to return to Summerfield."

Emma blew out a breath. "Well, now that you mention it, yes, I am thinking that I would like to go home. My studio…" She clasped her skirt with her hands.

"At the top of the house, where no one can disturb you, Mrs. Emma—"

"A woman needs a place where she will not be disturbed by the constant demands on her time if she is to be able to work, Lydia. That is an inescapable fact. I don't know if it will ever change for us, but one day, I hope it will."

Lydia nodded and moved away.

But then Emma felt a sudden rush of sympathy and cursed herself for her own tactlessness at the same time. Lydia would not only never enjoy the luxury of having another person to do her own chores, but she was stuck carrying out all Emma's household duties as well. How that cycle was supposed to resolve itself was anybody's guess.

When Emma saw Patrick walking up the driveway toward the house, she picked up her poppy painting and took it inside, straight into the privacy of her bedroom, collecting another piece and bringing that out.

"Em!" Patrick appeared on the veranda, tucking his shirt into his cream trousers. A grand smile spread across his handsome face. Emma regarded him, her heart doing its usual flip-flop as he padded across to her.

He leaned forward and inspected her hastily brought out work. "That empty chair looks a little lonely," he murmured.

Emma smiled sadly. It was as if her life was playing out in a series of exquisite polarities, her love for him, the hopelessness of that. And the baby that was growing inside her that was in itself a source of odd comfort, laced with confusion and uncertainty.

"How about a party?"

A sudden breeze whispered through the vines.

"Jerome wants to throw one for his new friends down here, before we go to Paris."

Emma forced a tight smile. "Of course," she said, reaching her hand up to take his a moment. "A party is always such a good idea."

Jerome's farewell party was a soiree for more than one hundred guests. He invited every American and English expat he'd met in Paris, along with everyone else he'd encountered while in France, and it appeared that he'd become acquainted with half of Cassis.

Jerome seemed to have charmed everyone except Emma. Even the usually unflappable Lydia seemed to have fallen under his spell. While they prepared for the party that day, he name-dropped shamelessly—aristocrats, eminent business people, along with writers, artists, and intellectuals. He wafted around in loose white shirts with broad sleeves flapping around his tanned wrists, and he'd grown his hair out over the past few weeks so that it curled around his shoulders. His presence was commanding, and anyone could see that Patrick was besotted. Emma smiled and smiled and wished Jerome would disappear in a puff of smoke.

While she sat at her dressing table, ostensibly preparing for the night's revels, a letter from Oscar lay open in front of her. She had it close because it gave her solace, perhaps because the thought of her easy relationship with Oscar and her love for Calum gave her a little more perspective on the turn her life had taken since Jerome had arrived to stay.

Dearest Em,

> *I worry that you are miserable, that you are not happy, and that your present domicile puts you under great strain. Why not, I think, return home? Go to Summerfield, where you will be in your own surroundings and where at least you will have some control over your days. I hate knowing that you are unhappy, and I see the strain that this latest amour of P's puts onto your heart.*

> *I'm sorry that France did not work out the way you'd hoped. I understand that P was bored in London, and I, too, thought that France might inspire him to settle a little more. How trying for you.*

> *No, I think returning to England with Calum and Lydia would be best. If P wishes to carry on this dalliance—and a dalliance I do believe it is—why not let him miss you for*

a while? We both know he can't function for long without
you. Why not stretch things at your end and wait for him
to bounce right back? He always does.

I am of a mind to travel to Summerfield for a time once
you are there too. I will bring Calum his requisite treats…
As for the other situation, which I am honestly delighted
about, I have written to my parents, to ask them for their
support for him… or for her. I have a feeling this will be
a daughter to match our son, but once we have my family's
blessings, we can move forward and work things out.

Thinking of you, dear Em,

My love,
Oscar

Emma held a hand over her nonexistent bump. It would not
be long before things were obvious. If Oscar was going to tell his
family, then she had no excuses to keep the truth from Patrick.
But she would not have Patrick thinking that this pregnancy was
some desperate last resort on her part, and she knew only too well
that the baby would have to be seen as Oscar's if it were not to
be ridiculed, no matter how strident Emma's views were about
freedom in life.

Three hours later, the party was in full swing. Patrick wore a turban.
As usual, people flocked around him. Emma smiled to herself at
the charming way he was entertaining a London aristocrat with
bohemian leanings who had come down from Paris, where she'd
been on a shopping trip at the time she'd encountered the mercurial
Jerome. On her head she wore a spray of ostrich feathers that was
studded with jewels. She'd held out her hand to Emma, who had
taken it graciously, while the woman informed Emma that she

would be ordering more of her and Patrick's divine creations for her London house. Her friends were quite wild for their fabrics and designs.

Patrick insisted on taking only half the payment the woman wanted to give them to design bespoke curtain fabrics for her Parisian salon. No wonder he was always penniless, as was Jerome, but at least the American could wire his wealthy family back home for funds when he wanted them, living on transfers. As far as Emma could see, Jerome earned nothing himself.

"Darling." Patrick appeared behind her, wrapping his arms around her.

Emma leaned back into his body, the natural contours of their shapes fitting together as if they were made for each other. Or so it seemed to Emma.

"I've decided this is my last weekend in France too," she said. "I'm going home, Patrick." She maintained warmth in her voice.

"You know how much I hate not having you around," he murmured. "I'll miss you."

Emma closed her eyes. He'd had lovers before, but she'd always gotten on with them. But it was impossible to consider doing so with Jerome. He'd gotten under Emma's skin right from the start—she found him belligerent toward her when they were alone and dismissive of her whenever they were gathered together at mealtimes. As much as he could, Jerome put in every effort to pull Patrick out of Emma's orbit. Whenever he came near her, Emma felt herself gritting her teeth. And all she could hope, in the end, was that he was not going to be a permanent fixture in Patrick's life, while asking herself if she had any right to make such a wish for Patrick herself.

Chapter Twenty-One

London, 1980

Sometimes, it is only the most old-fashioned remedies that do the trick. Laura was in need of a cup of tea. Her grandmother and an English tearoom seemed the perfect plan. She took Emma to a tearoom on Marchmont Street, around the corner from Gordon Square. Emma eyed Laura as she poured the tea into two cups, balancing the strainer on the delicate rims in turn. Emma reached out and placed her ancient hand on Laura's.

"Dear," she said, "I'm going to make this easier for you."

"Don't," Laura whispered. "I can't bear it. I don't want you to do anything. None of this is your fault."

"Ivan called me. From the bank."

Laura reached for her cup of tea.

"Of course, my paintings are not worth anything like the price that Patrick's fetch, but I will sell them all, and I can find somewhere cheaper to live. Summerfield has to go—"

"No, Gran."

Emma leaned forward, her eyes holding that resolve that she was famous for displaying. "It's time, Laura. It's simply what needs to be done."

"Gran—"

"I've had my turn. It's your turn and your life that matters now. Soon I won't be around to even know whether Patrick painted me or not. It won't matter, but your future will."

"Yes, but Gran—"

"I can't see that Patrick would have lied to me. He was always a bit of a clown, but I'm certain he was an honest one. However, I'd prefer to fix this quietly and let you continue your studies. The more fuss we make about Ewan's pronouncements, the longer this whole process is going to take."

"No—"

"I took on the loan. I'm very happy to step aside. You know that material possessions mean nothing to me. But an education? That is a different matter. If I stop paying rent in Gordon Square and on Summerfield and sell everything I own, then I should be able to meet your loan requirements. I won't have it any other way."

Emma reached out a hand. "It's going to be impossible for me to prove that Patrick painted me in France. And I don't think you'll ever find out either. It's too late. That story is over. The past is gone. Memories are unreliable, and in any case, they depend entirely upon the person who is doing the reminiscing, and, my dear, the only person we have to do that is me. We simply need to bear up, face the consequences, and move on."

"Gran!"

But her grandmother simply reached forward to the plate in front of them, chose a cream-center shortbread, and took a bite of her biscuit.

Laura had no idea how Emma could stomach food.

France, 1923

Emma stood by the suitcases in the front hall of Mas d'Aurore. She'd spent a few moments lining up all the luggage with perfect precision. As if that would take care of things. Put the whole mess of a situation and her feelings toward Jerome straight. She slipped on her gloves and focused on the colors outside the window. She ran through a list in her head... emerald-green for the vines, dusky paler version for the grapes flecked with brown spots. There. Now which exact tubes of paint would she use? She switched her attention to the hall. Shadows seemed to linger here now that they were leaving. The house had lost its sheen.

Jerome and Patrick's chatter punctuated the otherwise quiet morning. If Emma were not so annoyed by Jerome, she'd be almost grateful for his endless talk right now. He and Patrick were planning to stay in Paris for some time, and after that, they'd continue "on the up and up" in London, as Jerome put it. Emma forced herself not to think that Jerome was riding on the back of Patrick's artistic contacts in the French capital because Jerome's contacts were more of the social kind. Jerome seemed thrilled about the prospect of being introduced to Picasso.

When Patrick shot concerned, knowing glances her way, Emma simply busied herself with putting on her gloves. Everything should roll forward as she'd planned. When the car she'd organized to convey them to the train station in Marseilles pulled up in the driveway at exactly the minute it was due, Emma whisked into the fresh air and called for Lydia and Calum to come straight out from the house. But Patrick was close behind her.

"I hate your being alone at Summerfield," he said, reaching out and drawing a loose strand of hair back under her hat. "You won't be terribly lonely out there?"

"Of course not. I'll have Calum. I'm looking forward to getting back home." Emma didn't meet his eyes as she picked up her own valise. She called to Calum and Lydia yet again. She wanted them here. Wanted to put things in motion.

"Ready to mooch off?" Jerome asked, coming up behind Patrick and leaning his chin on Patrick's shoulder. "Paris is going to be the bee's knees."

"Have you any particular plans?" Emma asked.

"Oh, mind your potatoes, Emma. I'd only be feeding you a line if I told you we were anything but spontaneous. None of your killjoy planning for us, Mrs. Temple."

"All right, old chap," Patrick said, reaching to take Emma's suitcase from where it sat next to her. But she almost tugged it away from him.

"I might not come to London, though, Jerome. After Paris, perhaps I'll go down to Summerfield and see Em," Patrick said.

For goodness' sake, Patrick, don't come and see me unless you want to, Emma fought the urge to shout. Dear God, the deepest humiliation would have to be the sense that someone wanted to see one only because they felt obliged!

"Oh, once we get you on the giggle water in Paris, you'll forget all about the damned countryside and old Em. Paris is gasping with my fellow countrymen on the fry. It's spiffing, and us Ethels are right on the edge of it. Paris is the cat's meow!"

Emma lifted her skirt and climbed into the car.

Three weeks later, she sat in her studio at Summerfield. She'd forced herself into a state of neutrality. Not happy, not miserable, but undoubtedly better being home than in France.

Ambrose brought his ballerina friend down to visit, but the young woman's antics and complete lack of understanding of art irritated Emma, and she'd gotten herself in a lather because in some ways, the girl reminded her of Jerome. Emma had been glad when they left, but she admonished herself for being unkind. If Ambrose liked a ballerina, just as Lawrence liked Coco, then she would respect them both for that.

But she found herself asking the unaskable—whether the idea of living by principles was a wonderful thing in theory, but in practice, was it impossible to do? Never in her life had she struggled so much with adhering to her beliefs on the one hand, while dealing with her feelings on the other. Jerome, Coco, that dancer—she wanted her intimate circle around her, not these distracting people who seemed only to upset the mood that they'd all fought so hard to create.

But she would never, ever breathe a word, because that went against her beliefs.

Now she held a letter in her hand from dear, brilliant Ambrose. He was marrying the ballerina and thinking of taking on the house nearest to Summerfield as a country residence. They'd be neighbors. Emma frowned at the thought that he'd picked up on her annoyance when they were visiting and felt he had to give up his room at Summerfield.

Unfortunately, because she sat at the center of the group, when the needle was sharp, it was Emma whose heart was pierced.

She'd busy herself with decorative projects, that was one means of escape. She threw herself into them—focusing on Oscar's bedroom for a full two weeks, painting the fireplace surrounds with a geometric pattern, before pouring yet more of her energy into working on the upstairs library, which was next door to his bedroom. That looked more like a traditional gentleman's room than any other part of the house and would do nicely for her husband now. She'd lined the space with her father's books, put down warm Turkish rugs given by Ambrose, and installed two comfortable chairs. She'd even procured a wooden reading stand for Oscar, allowing his books to be propped up while he read. She'd scoured that at a local market on a Sunday when things seemed particularly bleak.

But there was only so much she could do to distract herself from her thoughts before they returned like an invading army. Oscar's visit, like Ambrose's, had been a welcome distraction. But he'd brought Mrs. Townsend with him. So Emma had painted her and was going to send that portrait to Lawrence for his next London exhibition.

Once Oscar had informed his family of her pregnancy and they had agreed to give Emma some financial support, she'd broken the news to her friends. If they had probing questions, they kept them to themselves. And that suited Emma to a T.

But still, she had not written to Patrick…

When the crackle of bicycle tires on the gravel drive sounded through the open windows, Emma drew her shawl around herself and pulled aside the soft sheer curtain in her attic studio, startling slightly at the feel of her hard, pregnant belly against the wooden windowsill.

The bicycle stopped in front of the house. A boy with a gray cap perched on his head climbed off it. He took the cap off when Lydia answered the door. Instinctively, Lydia looked up at Emma in the window as if expecting to see Emma hovering there. Goodness, could the girl read her like a transparent book? Emma moved away from the window to stand at the top of the stairs.

A few moments later, Lydia appeared. "Mrs. Emma, it's the painting. Patrick's painting. Of you. The one he did in France." Lydia twisted her hands about until her apron was in a knot. "It's arrived."

"Oh?" she asked—feeling as if her voice were floating about in the ether. She couldn't tell whether the interior dancing that she felt was her own insides moving or the baby fluttering about.

"The painting's at the local post office. Would you like me to go down and pick it up in the car?"

The slow murmurs inside Emma became sharp pangs. She was an unwanted ghost in Patrick's life. He hadn't brought it himself…

"Please arrange for it to be sent here," Emma said.

She went to her studio.

The following day the painting sat unopened in the dining room near the French doors. It seemed to her a summation of her relationship with Patrick, and she wanted to open it when he was about. It was both an expression, she felt, of the greatest intimacy that they shared and, right now, a cruel reminder of the way Jerome made him so happy that he only sent her the portrait rather than delivering it himself.

Emma threw herself into the imaginary world of her art, where colors were alive and real to her and where she could express on the canvas the feelings that she couldn't speak. She completed a series of still life works, the colors bold, fearless, defiant. She forced herself to find solace in two things—her art and the fact that the people she loved were happy. Ambrose, Patrick, Lawrence, Calum…

By late September Emma focused her artistic eyes on the garden and the outside world. It had transformed into a riot of color. She spent hours trying to re-create the very colors that she picked up with her unwavering eye. Burnt oranges, deep reds, and bright yellows flooded the trees, while stunning golden light glistened every afternoon, and the sunsets were a glorious explosion of pinks. Emma took to working outside until dusk. It was as if she were trying to capture something indefinable. The last of fall perhaps, before winter set in and everything was laid to rest.

When, after what felt like a decade of silence, Lydia brought a letter from Patrick out to her as she sat painting by the lake one afternoon, she refrained from seizing it and tearing the envelope open. Instead, she eyed it for at least five minutes before wiping her hands on her cleaning cloth and slowly slitting open the seal.

Chapter Twenty-Two

London, 1980

Laura fought with every emotion and every complication under the sun. Juggling seemed to be the order of her limited days until the loan ran out. She needed to practice, should be practicing hours and hours every day, and she did so, melding that in with the time she had to spend working at the supermarket and teaching her students so that she did not let them down. And yet all the time, her mind whirred and her insides churned with the knowledge that she had only two choices, and neither of them helped Emma.

She could accept Ewan's offer. Leave all the questions surrounding the portrait and Patrick and Em hanging. Or she could go with Emma's plan to move out of Gordon Square, handing over Summerfield for some new tenant to paint over all her loving decorations. Either thought made Laura feel even more ill than she already did.

"Laura?" Jasper caught her hand and held it right as she went to knock on the office door of the dean of the Royal College of Music.

"Stop," he said. "Don't you dare."

Laura took in his unkempt appearance, the way his shirt hung untucked over his old jeans. He was unshaven, and he wore a baseball cap on backward. Mark's baseball cap.

Laura sighed and reached out to take it off his head. "You know, I have a bad relationship with that cap," she said. "And I never take advice from disheveled men. I'm worried about you. Are you okay?"

But Jasper only frowned at her in turn. "Why are you protecting Ewan?" he said, his eyes intent on her face. "I don't understand why you're not making him speak out."

Laura made her way back to the door.

"You're giving up."

"No."

"Yes," he said, taking her hand. "You are."

Slowly she crossed her arms.

"What are you going to say to the head of the school?" Jasper asked. "That you're going to stop playing your violin because Ewan makes sense? And because you've kissed him? Because if you don't mind my saying so, that's bloody ridiculous. Have you talked to him in the last couple of days? Come on, Laura, when I said to seduce him, it was all about getting the intel, not about getting between the sheets."

Laura took in the bulletin board on the opposite wall of the hallway. The usual things sat there: ads for concerts at the Royal Albert Hall, a sign-up sheet to audition for a new chamber group, notices that she usually scoured with her notepad in hand while planning how she could procure cheap tickets with a bunch of friends... but now there was no point.

"I broke up with Mark because I know I deserve more in a relationship than he was able to give. It's going to be hard for a while, but I'm not going to settle for half a life or half a relationship. And it seems to me that you are going to do exactly those two things."

Gently he took her shoulders in his hands. "I know how hard this is, but you must go back to Ewan, no matter what your feelings are, no matter how complicated things are, and get him to talk. What happens between the two of you, I don't know. But you can't run away, and from what I saw, the fireworks that were sparking were something else. I will lie across this door and attack anyone who walks into that office to tell the college you're quitting. Including you."

Laura folded her arms around her waist.

His hair stuck straight up like a scrubbing brush. "Don't worry about my breakup. I'm always here for you, and I know you're here for me," he whispered. "But it's time to take things head-on, Laura," he said, sticking his hands in his pockets. "Emma hung on to unrequited love, but she had a choice not to do that. She could have been with someone else. And you deserve everything."

"But Emma's determined to move out of her house. I can't let that happen. Surely you can see that. I have to take responsibility."

"I understand about Emma. But in the end, perhaps it's about turning all this adversity into something worthwhile, even beautiful," he said. "I think it's time you stopped emulating Emma and started being Laura."

"What?"

"I'm serious," he whispered, taking the hat and placing it back on his head.

She hovered on the spot. Jasper reached up a hand and leaned on the wall next to them. "The way Emma dealt with things was her choice. Isn't it time to create your own way of living? I know the way your mother lives her life is difficult to watch. It's hard to understand. I get that. But you and I aren't going to do that, my friend. We're going for the full deal—passion for our career and passion in our relationships. Nothing less.

"And I understand that Emma's sense of freedom and respect and tolerance for others looks almost divine to us, but you're Laura, and if Emma believes in anything, I think she knows that everyone is unique. Your grandmother accepts that. She chose her path; surely you can choose yours. Couldn't you talk to Ewan rather than simply being tolerant, like Emma would be?"

Laura reached up and ran her hand across the contours of his cheek. "Jasper, can you promise me that you'll find someone who treats you well next time? Someone who doesn't let you down over and over again?"

"Only if you promise me you will not walk in there and quit." He held her gaze. "The only reason I'm able to walk away when things aren't right is because of the heart-to-hearts I've had with you. Your uncompromising pursuit of the best in your playing and in your life so far has inspired me to no end. But I will not see you give up on yourself. I won't let you walk away from everything you deserve."

"But the bank is requisitioning the loan," Laura whispered. "I agree that sometimes we can be our own worst enemies, and I realize that my life is completely different from Em's, no matter how much I admire her. But what about the forces that run against us in the outside world? Because they seem pretty insurmountable to me right now… It's not only about Emma and Ewan and whatever's going on in my head. There is the problem that the bank needs to be paid back. And I should be the one to do that because the loan is mine, not Em's."

"And giving up your music is in your best interests? What about *you*? Self-sacrifice is a measure of desperation sometimes; it's not a show of strength when you have such a choice as you do. You're running away from the man you're attracted to. He's running away from his passion for painting. Emma ran away from society, and your mother ran away from being the artist she could have been. Fear is a pretty big de-motivator, Laura. Avoidance won't fix this; it will only make you angry down the track."

Laura looked away.

"What do you want to do? Forget what everyone else wants. Forget all their issues. You've been caught up in those for too long."

When she spoke, her voice was so soft she could hardly hear it, but it was there. "I want to play music. I think I want Ewan, and I know I want you in my life no matter what."

Jasper pulled her to him roughly, and she rested her head on his shoulder and closed her eyes. But comforting as Jasper was, it was one thing to know what you wanted but quite another to know how to get there.

Summerfield, 1923

Emma held Patrick's letter. She sat at her desk in the late afternoon, and with her free hand, she sipped at Lydia's strong coffee. She couldn't help but ask herself one question: Could the landscape that love roamed over ever truly be accompanied by her beliefs in rationality?

She read his note for the ten thousandth time. And if the feelings that were growing in her rapidly swelling body were borne out of any reality at all, then she was going to run with them.

When it came to Patrick, she'd never had any choice.

> *Dearest Em,*
>
> *I miss you, and I find that things are not the same without you around. I have been wanting to ask you to come to Paris. But I want to come home to you and to Summerfield even more than I want you here. I'm going to catch a train down to Lewes on Sunday. Can I come home? It will just be me, darling. Jerome is returning to America. He's decided New York is a better place for him.*
>
> *Thank goodness for you,*
> *P*

When he appeared in the front garden, throwing his suitcase down on the driveway in front of the house, Emma went to him with her hands held out, but instead, he enfolded her in his arms.

"By God, I've missed you," he murmured, ruffling her hair with his mouth. "And look at you!" He held her out in front of him. Gently, he ran a hand down her distended belly.

Emma felt herself blush. She had ended up rushing off a telegram to him in London, telling him it was fine to come home, while adding a quick aside about the baby. She'd reverted back to her painting in a frenzy of energy afterward.

"Oh, Em," he said.

Emma stepped back a little, but he drew her to him again.

As they wandered toward the open front door, the porch scattered with late autumn leaves, Emma fought a sudden stab in her insides. Once they stepped into the entrance hall, her eyes flickered to the dining room and the parcel that still sat, unopened, against the wall. She hated to admit, even to herself, that opening it seemed too much while Patrick was traveling with Jerome. She shot a glance toward him, starting a little at the way he frowned when he saw it sitting there untouched.

He moved toward her.

She knew she didn't need to say a thing.

"Shall we open it together?" she asked.

He nodded, reaching out and tucking a strand of her hair behind her cheek. Silently, he reached down to pick it up, carrying it to the dining room table and laying the flat parcel on it with great care. His artist's fingers prized open the brown wrapping paper that hid the portrait, and as he revealed his work, Emma leaned over his shoulder and drank in the colors, the sight of what he'd done for her.

Her face. He'd rendered it as if he knew everything she never said; her eyes seemed to stare away into the distance. It was hard to tell her age—was she thirty-three as she was now or that girl in her early twenties as she was when they first met in France? It was as if he'd captured all the Emmas he'd known over the years—the long war years with Rupert by their sides, the time spent working in London with Lawrence, the painting and traveling in France… the turmoil that had accompanied his relationship with Jerome. Every expression she'd ever known, every feeling she'd ever had seemed to stare out at her from his portrait of her. Because he knew her, and that was all she needed right now. If we are defined by those whom we love, then it was also true that the man she loved undoubtedly knew how to define her. For him, she was not a closed book. And for her part, she knew she'd learned to love Patrick as he was, which in the end was all she could do.

Emma rested her hand on the table, her eyes scanning his exquisite taste in color—the way her green skirt shimmered in the sunlight, while the pearl buttons on her blouse shone, each one with a lustrous light.

There were no empty chairs in this portrait, no melancholy scenes on desolate verandas. He'd chosen a backdrop that was perfect: a painting she'd done of a bunch of oranges and lemons he'd brought her once in London as a gift. Bright colors, her looks honest. She was in love with the painting, and it reassured her that everything was all right.

"I adore it," she whispered, her fingers itching to reach out and touch it, bottle it. Instead, she ran her hand over the simple wooden frame.

"You know, I've worked out what is so unique about my relationship with you," he said. "It is never possible to be lonely or to feel alone whether we are together or not, because I know you are always with me."

Emma reached out her hand to him. It seemed clear now that sometimes in life, one had to sit out the bad times, because what made life bearable was the knowledge that some feelings never changed.

London, 1980

Laura reached for the phone in the common room at the Royal College of Music, only to place it back down on the receiver. She glanced around the empty common room. Everyone was closeted away practicing. With such a short time to performance exams, no one was lounging around in here. They say doubt is the preserve of the intelligent. Right now, Laura could do with a barrage of decisiveness instead. When Jasper appeared next to her, she arched her brows at him.

"You should go and practice," she said, reaching out an arm.

"Have you called him?"

"Nope."

"You're worried that he could tell you a truth you don't want to hear."

"Exactly!" Laura leaped away from the phone. "I'll just go back to plan A." She turned toward the dean's office.

Jasper caught her. He took her hand in his and held it, his fingers intertwined with her own. "Isn't it better to find out—better out than in?"

She regarded him.

"So." Gently, he took the piece of paper with Ewan's phone number written on it out of her hand. "You call him. And you go and sort this out. This is very unlike you, by the way," he said.

She shrugged.

Jasper scanned the number. "Are you going to call him or am I?"

"I will. But you stay here while I'm talking to him."

Jasper rolled his eyes. "Goodness, what are we? Twelve?"

Laura picked up the handset. She kept her tone businesslike. Arranged to meet Ewan at the sunken garden in Kensington Gardens.

"Happy?"

He grinned at her. "I don't know what I'm going to do with you," he said.

Laura held up her head. "How are you going with your… stuff?"

"I am actually okay." He smiled. "I'll be fine. It just wasn't meant to be with Mark. That's all. Let's focus on your… *stuff* for now."

"Go and practice, Jasper. And you know I'm here if you need to talk to me."

He picked up his viola. And waved to her as he made his way out into the corridor.

*

Half an hour later, she stood overlooking the spring flowers in the sunken garden outside Kensington Palace. Laura tried to take in the sea of color in front of her, but she turned when she heard the sound of footsteps coming along the path. She took a step back as Ewan approached, reaching out her hand to hold on to the low stone wall that surrounded the gardens.

He stopped a few feet away from her, a darkness across his handsome features. He wasn't dressed in a suit, nor did he look in any way like he'd come from work on this weekday. Instead, he wore a pair of faded jeans, with a white shirt hanging, untucked, above it. His hands were stained with paint.

His eyes softened as he looked at her. "I'm taking a week off. A painting retreat, you could call it. First time I've done so in… well, ever." He smiled, that dimple showing up. He placed his hands in his jeans pockets and hovered. "It was good to hear from you," he said.

"Can we go for a walk and have a chat?"

He nodded, stepping aside so that she could come out from under the canopy of wisteria that edged the perfect spring garden.

"You know, Emma never comes here anymore," she said. "She grew up around the corner, but she's avoided this part of London for years—it doesn't fit in with how she lives her life."

"No."

She stopped. They'd passed the Round Pond and were heading up one of the wide paths that led into the wilder part of the park, where old English trees were dotted like beautiful green havens, canopies over the stretching lawns.

He looked out over the landscape. "Let's go this way," he said, choosing one of the narrow, quieter paths. Dogs scampered in the grass.

"But this was her old stomping ground. It was where everything began," Laura said. "Her imagination developed in these gardens, you know." She took a glance over at Ewan.

He kept walking. "Go on."

"Kensington Gardens was a retreat from the rigors of her life. The colors in nature inspired her to paint, and I think it must have shown her what a man-made construct society was. How things were made to seem important that were… not so important. An appreciation of beauty and nature—no one can ever take that away from you no matter what is going on in the world. That was the philosophy of the Circle. She's offered to move out of her house for me, you know. She's insisting on selling everything she owns so that I can continue at music school. She says she doesn't need any of it."

Ewan stayed quiet.

Laura fought with the dreaded knowledge that this was unplanned. Her meticulous, strategized career, hours of practice, a position in an orchestra somewhere, was being floored by feelings she'd never had before—but somewhere, a new force was emerging, a willingness to throw away her safety net, to simply go with the flow, to head down a path she knew she had never taken before. Even her love for Jasper was slipping into some cool, safe abyss of a place, replaced in turn by this strong need, this wanting to get to know Ewan better, to see his truth now, while knowing at the same time that she would not settle for anything less than she deserved in either love or what she wanted to do with her own life.

The colors in the garden—greens and flowers and the blue of the sky—had become merged into one beautiful swirl.

Ewan ran a hand over her shoulder.

After they'd wandered awhile, they came to a garden bench. "Shall we sit down?" he asked.

Behind them was a dense hedge that protected a thick garden filled with low shrubs and trees. The sound of traffic along Kensington Road was the only background hum to break up the silence.

"I could never be the person who took your music away, Laura," he said.

She sat down next to him, turning to face him. "And you must know that I can't accept you paying out my loan in the same way that I can't accept Emma's offer to sell all her belongings," she said. She searched his face. "You have to trust me with the truth. You have to tell me the things you don't want to say. No holding it in," she whispered. "Tell me everything. I *want* you to tell me everything. And I want you to know you can trust me."

But he hunched forward on the seat, staring at the gravel path. A squirrel appeared, a quick-witted little thing, darting between the legs of the bench before scurrying back into the bushes.

"Do you understand that some things cannot be spoken of, no matter how much we may want to do so?"

"Ewan." She heard her voice coming out as some firm, new, and strong version of itself. "That's what this is about, isn't it, ultimately? Trust? Because I'm telling you, I could never do anything to hurt you. Whatever it is, we'll work it out together. Because something's shifted. I was angry with you at first, then… confused about my feelings."

He looked up at her sharply.

She had to plow on. "I was confused about my feelings for you. They came on when I least expected them. It seemed all wrong, so I tried to push them away. But now, now, I think that they are right. That, perhaps, you are right… but I cannot sit by and let you just hold on to this, whatever reason you have for not talking to me. Ewan, I've seen what that did to my mother. And I've gotten to the point where I don't want that happening to you."

Laura frowned at the misty scene in front of her. "I think that not talking, not opening up to other people and the world, can cause more problems than taking a risk and dealing with things and, ultimately, living your life properly rather than getting stuck in some immovable place."

He sighed heavily. "Weren't Emma and the Circle about avoiding confrontation, war, all those things, in order to allow others to live their lives in turn? They were intelligent people, Laura."

"Yes, but Em's philosophies were also what she had to cling on to because her situation in love and in life was impossible. Her ideas gave her a blueprint, and they were good ideas, for her, but I've come to the conclusion that we all have to live in our own way, to do what we know deep down is best for us. I want to live from my heart when it comes to love, but I also want to live in that place where my heart and mind converge. That, ultimately, I think, is where the truth lies."

He reached out and stroked her cheek. "I want to talk about it." His words held an urgency but also, right at their base note, there was sadness. "Don't think I don't. There are other people whom I'd hurt, whom I care about, so what then?"

Laura took his hand. "I promise I will do everything to respect those people you don't want to hurt. You can trust me, Ewan. You honestly can."

His face paled, and there was silence for a moment before he spoke. "My father painted the portrait at Summerfield."

Laura pressed the fingers of her free hand into the wooden bench.

"I can't tell you any more," he muttered. "All I can do is offer to make financial amends for the entire ghastly mess."

"Ewan."

But he was up. He stood and moved right away from the bench.

"Sorry," he said, bringing his hand up to shield his face. "I should not have spoken. I don't know what I was thinking." And he disappeared into the park.

Chapter Twenty-Three

Summerfield, 1924

Emma gave birth to her daughter on a relentless, blustering spring night. The trees whipped in the wind outside Emma's bedroom—taking on a new life force of their own, the branches twisting into confounding, distorted shapes. She stood at the French doors during the quiet times in her long labor, looking helplessly at the hollyhocks that heaved on their spindly stalks, their delicate petals flurrying around the walled garden while the sky took on an enigmatic coral blush.

Emma leaned on the doorframe when it was bad, pain rending her body, splitting it in two halves. After fourteen hours, the next morning, she sat up in her freshly made-up bed, Lydia next to her in a rocking chair, holding the tiny, perfect little girl in her arms. The midwife was making notes by the window, and the now thirteen-year-old Calum had already been in to visit his little sister, appearing delighted although, Emma suspected, struggling to hide his disappointment that the baby was not a boy.

When Patrick appeared at the doorway, Emma turned her tired face to him, her heart opening at the sight of him. He walked toward her, eyes on her, before they moved toward his daughter.

"She is adorable," he whispered. "A miracle. You are a miracle, Em."

And she rested her hands, her exhausted, strained hands, on the sheets, and she sat back and closed her exhausted eyes.

Summerfield, 1937

If Emma could replay one time in her life, she would choose those years between the wars. But her mistake was thinking that the feeling of contentment that she'd felt during her thirties and forties was ever going to be a permanent state in her life. Her mistake was in thinking that finally, she had found what everyone sought in one way or another. She thought she'd found stability.

Patrick spent most of his time at Summerfield during those years, keeping any lovers down in London tactfully separate from his relationship with Emma and their daughter, Clover, and from Calum as he grew into a young man. Patrick's presence in the children's lives was all Emma could have hoped for from any man. His delight in Clover as she grew up, the way he taught her to paint, encouraged her burgeoning interest in playing the violin, sat listening to her tentative concerts out on the lawns at Summerfield, and provided the gentle, sheltered upbringing for her, based on love and kindness that both he and Emma wished they had enjoyed, turned the years into a golden era, lacking any of the turbulence of her twenties and that awful time during the last war.

What was more, she and Patrick settled into both a working partnership and a sensible friendship that was the touchstone of Emma's life. Ambrose was on the nearest farm, and Lawrence still came by to stay during the summer, as did Oscar, who enjoyed a room of his own in the house.

If falling wildly in love with Patrick in her twenties had been deliriously exciting, then loving him as a dear friend with a slow, steady burn had mellowed her into feeling she knew both herself and him inside out. The sense that her life was going to span out in some beautiful pattern based on kindness and friendship seemed certain. Nothing could have prepared her for the explosion that happened as they both slipped into middle age.

It was in 1937 that Calum announced he wanted to contribute to the Spanish Civil War. He'd become passionate about politics as he grew up, and he'd worked for the government after he'd graduated from Cambridge. It had been Ambrose, Oscar, and Lawrence who further fueled and deepened Calum's interest and understanding of the far left-right divide in Europe as the thirties wore on.

Calum passionately supported the republicans in Spain and wanted to do something to stop conservative nationalistic politics taking control in that country. The long conversations Emma's friends had enjoyed as young men did not falter or lessen in intensity as they moved into middle age, and Emma could only watch while the youthful Calum took his own slant on the older men's ideas. With the rise of fascism in Germany, things were brewing to a head, but Emma was horrified when her only son announced that he wanted to go and help fight the republican cause in Spain.

She made desperate calls to Ambrose and Oscar, conflicted as to whether she should hide her panic or simply give it full rein; after all, there was nothing she could really do to try and stop Calum from following his own convictions. In the end, instead of trying to convince her adult son not to go, instead of trying to impose the Circle's philosophy of pacifism onto a young man who already understood exactly what those philosophies were, Emma forced herself again to take the sensible, balanced view she believed in and to respect her son's need to do something in the way she and her friends never could. Reluctantly, she did not try to hold Calum back in any way when he announced he wanted to go overseas to the Spanish Civil War, but there was a compromise. He agreed to go as an ambulance driver, thus avoiding any direct combat while helping look after the wounded.

Calum had always been a heartbreaking mixture of sweetness, almost to the point of naïveté, and passionate intellectual intensity. He was going to seek adventure no matter what; Emma was wise enough to know that. She sent him off with a tiny miniature painting of Summerfield in his kit bag that she'd done for him especially. Oh, how that little painting would haunt her in later years.

Calum was blown up three weeks after he arrived in Spain by a direct strike on his ambulance truck as he drove a wounded soldier through a lonely, isolated road in the south of that country.

Emma took to her bed. She stayed there for months. She aged overnight, becoming a shadowed skeleton of herself, unable to paint, to move, almost to breathe. Her hair became gray in the month after the news was relayed to Summerfield—a telegram, that dreaded, awful envelope, came with the news. After the funeral, at which there was no body for her to weep over, because there was nothing of her adored son left, Emma remained unable to work for a year. She could only sit and stare out at her garden. It took a monumental effort to walk to the lake.

It was Freya, in the end, who calmly stepped in and stayed by Em's side through that dark, awful time. Freya bicycled over most days from the house she and Henry had taken on in a local village after their house in the woods had become too isolated for Freya's disposition. Freya read aloud—poetry, Jane Austen, anything that was nothing to do with war and all to do with the beauty and wit of the human spirit and its ability to survive.

Even though twice during Emma's own peaceful years, Freya had descended into a great melancholy out of which Emma had helped her to escape, there remained a close understanding and bond between the sisters that nothing would ever tear apart. Sisters got each other through the hardest of times.

But once the Second World War had settled over Europe again, by 1942 when the thirties turned into the new, terrifying forties, guilt at her own relative safety out at Summerfield and dark thoughts plagued Emma. She could not ignore that most people's lives reverted once again into a raging torrent of terror as Hitler's armies marched on and on in their relentless quest for power. But still, she stuck to her principles, avoiding newspapers and painting her grief onto the canvas.

While Emma worked on steadily at her painting with little recognition, it was Freya who garnered huge attention for her literary brilliance. She'd turned novel writing on its head by writing about the minutiae of the inner world, where thoughts were random and scattered across the page. Although Freya was viewed as odd, singular, and buried deep in that elite group that was the Circle, Emma suspected her sister was going to be remembered as a great literary force.

As another long war became inevitable, she stockpiled food, knowing from past experience that eventually they could be entirely self-sustaining with the vegetables they grew on the farm. This time, they had heating in the house, and the true sense of longevity they had built up at Summerfield rendered them ready for whatever might come during another period of darkness in the world. The old house and garden remained a stalwart haven. Its isolated location was once again a blessing, even with the guilt of its safety.

But remaining still lost in the pale fog of her own grief for Calum, Emma did not recognize the signs of depression in her sister. And when Freya drowned herself in a local river as the war rolled on, Emma went under all over again, stunned at the brutal, random cruelty the world could inflict on all, no matter who or where.

And all the while, Clover had been trying to grow up with a mother who'd become absent with grief for Calum and who seemed unable to connect with anything beyond her personal torment. Emma, in turn, failed to recognize that Clover needed her at this most crucial time, as she became a young woman.

Emma knew she'd protected Clover as a child. She'd shaded her from society, from schools, and from the harsh structures of London's upper classes. But when Clover, like Calum, wanted to dip her toes into the waters of that real world, Emma never suspected that her little girl would dive right into her own shark-infested lake.

Emma had been gardening, one of her few recent happinesses, when the smart London car pulled up on Summerfield's gravel driveway. She would never forget the sight of her daughter, the new eighteen-year-old and somewhat harder version of the Clover she'd watched grow with such joy, arriving back from a brief trip to London on her own, her dark hair bobbed like a young boy's and her cream cashmere cardigan buttoned up to show off her newly formed figure. "Mother," Clover said, appearing from the car and adopting a new scathing tone that cut Emma to the core.

Emma drew her hands up to the neck of her blouse and made her way across the gravel to kiss her daughter, this oh-so-familiar stranger, on the cheek. Emma winced a little at the scent of Clover's strong perfume. She couldn't help staring at the way her fingernails were painted into a row of neat little orange orbs.

"How was your journey, dear?"

"Fine." Clover's eyes darted to the right. "I may as well tell you," Clover said. "Not that you're in the habit of talking about things—"

The sting of her daughter's barb pierced Em like some ill-fated needle. She'd become resigned to it, this stinging sensation. Pain.

"We thought we'd give you a few moments to say hello to me first." Clover giggled.

Emma followed her daughter toward the metallic-blue-painted car. The circular headlights that shone in Emma's eyes even though the sun had not yet gone down rendered it impossible to make out the features of the person who sat in the driver's seat.

Until he climbed out.

Emma staggered back. For some reason, the sound of his footsteps on the gravel, the way they crunched in that particular uneven way, only served to take her back twenty years or so to that double-edged morning when she was supposed to be reveling in the fact that Patrick had taken his brush to canvas to start painting her portrait in France.

She found herself focusing, for some reason, on his shoes, on his pointed, still-smart shoes. He still stood with one foot turned out wide. He walked toward her, Clover hopping along behind him like some schoolgirl following a pied piper whom she'd conjured up. Emma tried to gather herself and failed.

Jerome strode forward and took off his hat. His eyes still held the allure of chocolate, and yet Emma burned against the deceit in them the moment he caught her gaze. He wore a clean, smart linen suit, and his tie was knotted just so. No longer did the smell of turpentine waft around him, nor were his fingers stained from any momentary dalliances with paint.

"Emma," he said, that voice rich with the whatever-it-was that had always gotten under her skin.

Emma held out her paint-stained hand. Goodness knew, she'd managed to take up painting again only in the last year or so…

She felt like either throwing her easel in the pond or running to the studio that she and Patrick had built onto the back of Summerfield. The temptation was to lock herself in there, just as she'd hidden herself away upstairs in her old studio when Patrick had traveled in London and Paris all those years ago with…

"Jerome." Patrick's voice came somewhere into this nightmare scenario. He ran his hand over her arm as he stopped next to her. She saw the way he took in Clover's appearance and winced.

Patrick reached out to shake Jerome's outstretched hand.

"Long time, no see," Jerome said, as if he'd been there last week.

"Indeed." Patrick regarded Clover, who still held her chin aloft.

Clover wasn't going to budge; Emma could see that. Stunned at her daughter's defiance—Clover knew very well who Jerome was—Emma fought between admiration for her daughter's determination, something she recognized oh so well, and horror at her feeling of complete hopelessness. She wondered if this was things turning full circle in some torturous way…

They walked into the house—the four of them, an odd blend of past, present, and an uncertain future. It felt like a reckoning to Emma. As they stepped over the slate front step, Patrick took hold, suddenly, of Emma's hand. When she felt him clinging on to it as if he, too, were lost, she squeezed his fingers, but she saw nothing in front of her now.

Silence hung over the sitting room after dinner. Lydia cleared the table, her gaze focused downward. Goodness knew she must have seen enough during her time working for Emma to know when to remain quiet. Clover, on the other hand, chatted away as if she were the toast of a party.

"Jerome will be sleeping in my room," Clover announced the moment Lydia had gone back through the corridor to the kitchen.

Jerome placed his napkin on the table, then reached out and took a sip of his wine. "Real McCoy red you've got here, Patrick. Did you source it back in France? At least Provence was keen for *something*, old boy." He raised one long leg to cross it over the other.

Emma fought the feeling that right now, she was more and more like an ancient mother figure, while Jerome held on to his potency. His dark hair was thick and lustrous, while Patrick, who was, to be fair, a few years older, was starting to turn gray.

But why on this earth, other than for the one obvious reason, had Jerome fixed on Clover? She had no money and she would hardly be some repository of sexual experience. Above all things, she was hardly male.

Patrick rested his hand on her daughter's small white fingers. "Clover, would you mind very much if Mama and I spoke with Jerome alone?"

Clover rolled her eyes to the ceiling. She threw her napkin down on the table and pushed back her chair with a loud clatter on the hardwood floor. "Oh for heaven's sake, don't try and do the harsh grown-up thing, Emma and Patrick. We all know that's the last thing you are. If you've got something to say, then say it. Don't be so darned polite. I'm sick of the way you skirt around things."

Patrick stayed quiet. Clover flounced out the door. When the sound of her bedroom door slamming upstairs rang through the room, Patrick regarded his old lover.

"I don't know where to start, Jem."

Jerome remained still, his gaze not shifting from Patrick.

All Emma could hear was the sound of her own breath.

"What exactly are your intentions?" Patrick asked. His voice held that endless politeness, that old-school charm that Emma suspected was not long for this modern world, then winced at her own middle-aged use of that term.

There was a brief, awful silence. Until Jerome threw back his head and laughed. "You haven't even told her, have you, you pair of saps?" He threw out his comeback as if it were the winning dice in a board game. "Screw you, Pat. The bloody skirt still thinks her father is damned Oscar."

Patrick pulled back his chair until it crashed to the ground, lying on the floorboards with its legs straight up in the air. He glared at Jerome for one monstrous moment before he strode out of the room.

Emma excused herself immediately. She went to Patrick's room, where he stood, silent, by the window. Emma moved over to him, delighting, oddly, in the way the moonlight threw a straight golden dart, dividing the lake into two glimmering halves.

He swiveled to face her, helplessness creasing his worn face. "I'm so sorry," he whispered. "I could never have predicted this."

"If Clover wants to take a lover, then that is her choice—" Emma started.

"He is the last person she needs." Patrick shot out the words. "He's unstable. Highly unstable, and he's twice her age."

Emma reached out. She laid her hand on his arm. "We will get through it," she murmured. "We get through everything."

But Patrick leaned against the windowsill, his beautiful features murderous in the dark.

Chapter Twenty-Four

London, 1980

Emma ached with the fact that she had kept such a secret from Clover for years, but she'd never thought that Patrick would ever hold a secret, in turn, from her. She looked out the front window into Gordon Square, watching Laura trot up the front steps to the house. Emma was aware that in some way, her relationship with Laura had compensated for the breakdown in her relationship with Clover. And she'd learned the hard way that the loss of a child's trust is one of the most heartbreaking pills to have to swallow in this life. There was no chance that Emma was going to risk losing Laura's faith in her as well.

"Darling," she said when Laura appeared, all long legs and opaque tights.

Laura set her violin down on the floor. Her face was flushed. Emma took in the way her granddaughter seemed agitated rather than pale and wan, as she had been these past couple of weeks.

"Gran?" Laura folded her arms around her slim frame.

Emma forced out her own words. She knew what had to be said. "I think you should open up to your mother. I don't think we should leave Clover out of this." The words hung silent in the quiet space.

Emma saw the way Laura's chest rose up and down.

"I think—I am sure—Clover will understand. And maybe she can help."

Laura rested her hand on the windowsill, her long fingers tapering over the painted edge.

Emma continued. "I think at this point, we need to have everyone, and I mean everyone, around us."

Laura remained still, and Emma worried that her granddaughter regretted involving her to the extent she had.

"I worry that when I am gone, you will be alone." Emma's voice was a chipped version of itself. "I have been thinking about the one time in my life that I was alone, Laura. It was at Summerfield, just after we'd been in France, when I was pregnant with your mother. All the people I loved were gone and happy. I had Calum, my sweet boy, but you see, the thing is, I had my art. I had my painting. Without my work, at those lonely times in my life, I don't know what I would have done. You have to fight for it. And your mother will help you."

"She is the last person who will understand. How can you think that she would ever come around?" Laura's voice was low and rich and rough. "She gave it up. Art. Gave everything that is passionate away. I love my father, you know that. But he is hardly a Patrick, and the way Mother views love? She has locked her true passions away. All of them. I try not to judge her, but I struggle to understand."

"You should understand, darling. Believe me, you should try."

Laura kept her gaze out the window. "Patrick stayed with you after your brief spell alone at Summerfield, and you and he raised my mother together. You worked together as companions." Laura focused downward on the old coal grate, with its intricate inlaid curlicue of patterns. "Certain people are with us, others are not. Isn't it simple?"

Emma's voice sounded close. "Don't leave any stone unturned to save your own life."

Laura's fingers slipped on the windowsill's shiny white paint.

"Clover should be aware of this. We owe it to her, darling."

Laura swung around to face Emma.

"Go to her. Talk to her. I want you to have support."

"From my *mother?*"

"Perhaps," Emma said, her voice gentle, "you might be able to find some sympathy for her. You've told me that Ewan hides who he truly is from the world. I think it's time to understand that your mother is doing exactly the same thing. Clearly they both have their reasons."

Both of them had caused Laura such consternation. But even after trying to see Ewan's point of view, even after the tiny foray he'd allowed her to take inside the pages of what was clearly his own closed book, even after that, Laura was having a hard time understanding him. Because he had shut *her* out. He could have told her at the beginning that his father painted Emma's portrait, but instead, he'd sat by while she was at risk of losing everything, and Clover, well, she could have been here for Laura and for Emma during these past tumultuous weeks. After all, Clover read the papers. She might have closeted herself away, but she was still, after all, part of this world…

In a quiet voice, Laura told her grandmother that Ewan's father had painted the portrait that was hanging above her bed.

Emma held up a hand. "But, Laura, all this is getting somewhere!"

"He wouldn't tell me any more. I pressed him—"

"If Ewan is starting to open up to you, you need to get him to come right out with it and tell you what he's hiding. Keep going, Laura—he needs to talk to you, and clearly, he wants to. Once people start a thing, most times they want to reach the end."

"But your portrait?" Laura choked on the words.

Emma glanced out over the still square. "Get him to talk. I know that's ironic coming from me."

Laura let out a sigh at Emma's grace in the face of her revelation from Ewan.

"This weekend I have to go to Bath to play with the string quartet. I cannot let them down. Ewan wouldn't budge any further; believe me, I tried. And I cannot deal with the fact that he kept it from me, while pretending, in some false way, that he cared."

"No. Don't think like that."

Laura looked at Emma incredulously.

"Laura, you must keep going." Emma's old eyes remained firm and resolute. "Rise above all that. Never, ever give up. Get to the heart of a thing."

But Laura simply had to focus on the string quartet all weekend. Her playing required total concentration. She had to push everything else out of her head all day on Saturday while they rehearsed, knowing that on Sunday, if she allowed any of this disaster to affect her during the performance, she'd let down every other member of the quartet.

Laura rested her bow on her lap and took in the church in Bath that Marguerite had secured for this, their first proper performance. Little did everyone else know it was also going to be Laura's last time with them.

"Laura?" Jasper said, his voice coming as if from some distant place.

The others were packing up their instruments in one of the pews a little farther down the church.

Laura felt bad, so bad, that she hadn't supported him during his breakup with Mark in the way she'd wanted to. She had become a terrible friend on top of everything else.

"I agree with Em," he said.

Laura ran a hand over her gritty, tired eyes. She'd told him of Emma's advice on the drive out here. And now, she looked down at her violin and fought the sinking feeling that she was spending the last few days she had left with her Guadagnini before the inevitable happened. And she had no doubt that it would.

"Not every story in this world has a happy ending, Jasper," she whispered.

But Jasper looked at his watch. "Clover lives nearby. We should definitely go there tomorrow. After the concert. Then, you go back to London and push on with Ewan."

Laura shook her head at the music on her stand. Dots, dancing around on a page. It was only when you knew how to read, to play them with all your heart, that they meant anything. Then, they produced something so beautiful that it hurt. Why was everything that was beautiful also laced with pain? She closed the old music book that Marguerite had lent her. Laura traced her fingers over the gold filigree on the title. She looked across at Jasper, her dear, dear friend. She held her hand out. And he took it. They sat in silence in the timeless old church.

On Sunday, Laura stood in her mother's kitchen. Clover poured tea into four delicate teacups made of porcelain. Tiny rosebuds decorated them. There was one cup for Laura, one for Laura's father, one for Jasper, and one for Clover. It was all precise and measured as usual, about as far away from Emma's blowsy afternoon teas in the warm kitchen at Summerfield, with her misshapen scones and thick, mismatched mugs, as anyone could get. Laura gazed at the shining Formica benches, the sterile familiarity of the stainless steel sink, the drab gray cleaning cloth that hung over the hot tap to dry.

"I worried from the start about you using the painting as collateral for the loan," Clover said. She held out biscuits arranged in a fan shape on a pink plate. Her voice held a slight catch, which Laura, for some reason, found irritating.

Laura declined the neat little biscuits.

Her father spoke quietly. "How did your concert go, dear?"

"Fine. Thank you, Dad. I just… It will be the last time I get to play with the quartet."

Her father reached out and placed his hand on top of hers. Laura took in his squared-off fingernails, the way his shirtsleeves were rolled back so that each sat symmetrical to the other. She fought back a laugh at the thought that perhaps her mother was right. Maybe perfection, neatness, and the hiding away of any dangerous passions was the only way to survive in this harsh world, and all that lay underneath in us was best avoided after all.

Laura pushed back her chair, sending a raucous clatter through the otherwise quiet space. She'd always felt like a gawky intrusion when it came to Clover's pristine life. Laura moved toward the kitchen window, her forehead creasing into a frown as she took in the frilled lace curtains.

"You can work with me in the butcher's shop, love." Her father's gentle voice cut in. "It'll take you a while to pay off your loan, but we'll get you there—"

The path of least resistance. Laura clenched her fists into two tight knots.

"We can't afford to employ anyone in the shop." Clover's itchy tone rang through the kitchen. "No man would want to marry a woman who wields a cleaver for a living. Your father is near retirement age. We can't be taking on new employees; much as we'd like to help, Laura, it would be impractical. You're going to have to be realistic about this, dear."

Laura leaned on the window ledge. How could Emma have borne such an antifeminist daughter? It was a mistake to come here. For once, Em was wrong.

"I think we should go," Laura said, her words coming out as tight, mean little things. She hated herself for saying them, but self-preservation had to kick in sometimes, and when family were shutting you down, self-preservation seemed like the only thing you had left. She moved across the room, dropping a kiss on her father's head. He pushed back his chair while Clover stayed rigid, holding her cup of tea in both hands.

When Jasper spoke, Laura reeled around.

"Clover," he said, "can you think of any evidence that might point toward Ewan Buchanan being wrong?"

Clover sniffed. "My childhood and youth were a time in my life that I prefer to forget."

Clover's neat bob swung as she folded her thin arms.

"Jasper, let's go." It was too hard. The past was a complicated web that none of them was going to be able to unravel now. Apportioning blame would not help, but trying to forge answers out of a time that no longer existed and from people who had changed so much that their past selves had all but disappeared was going to be impossible. Anyone could see that. Laura held her head up and waited while Jasper shook her father's hand.

As they stood at the gate that led from the immaculate front garden to the street, Laura took one last look at the semidetached house where she'd grown up. She pushed the little gate open and stopped at the cusp of the narrow street she'd walked down every single day for years. How well did she know every bump on this neat sidewalk? How little, if ever, did she want to return?

She started moving up the street.

"First, I need to go to the bank," she said while Jasper kept pace beside her. "I'm going to commit to paying off the loan and try to reach an agreement with them about a more reasonable time frame. I'll get a full-time job, drop out of the Royal College, and over my dead body will Emma have to move out of her home to cheaper accommodations. I don't want her selling any one of her paintings. The bank will not be touching any of her things. I'll move out of Bloomsbury and find somewhere less expensive to live. It's the way it is."

"You're giving up."

"There are some brick walls that no amount of bashing can knock down. Maybe one day I'll save enough to be able to pay my own way through the Royal College of Music. I will not rely on anyone else."

Jasper pulled her to a stop.

"No, Jasper. I'm capable of taking care of my own life. If Ewan knew his father did that painting and didn't trust me enough to tell me the truth, then how can I trust any offer of his to help in a way that only makes me beholden to him? And if Mother is happy to stand by and let me lose my music, then let her go right on. I'm going to take my life into my own hands here. I'll fix this. I got myself into the Royal College. I'll get myself out of it. I'm done."

She marched down the familiar route to the local train station.

Jasper walked beside her, the feel of his arm around her shoulder blades giving her poor relief.

Summerfield, 1942

Emma lay awake through the entire night, her darkest thoughts tumbling like impenetrable shadows over and over themselves, round and round again. She thought she'd gotten away from the past and from everything Jerome represented in her life—jealousy... There, she admitted her fear that everything could fall apart.

She thought she'd escaped. Goodness knew, she couldn't have delved much deeper into the countryside than this. She'd surrounded herself with her closest friends, thought she had created something complete. A circle? Now, she saw that it was only a thin safety net. She and Patrick were strong, but were they strong enough to stop the world from pulling everything they'd built up in the last decades away from under their feet?

The fear of losing another child was worse than any fear she'd ever confronted in her life. Mothers and fathers were losing children left, right, and center during the two foul wars she'd seen in her lifetime. Goodness knew, it had been impossible losing her sweet son. And yet, it seemed ironic that all that was going to do her in this time was one man's jealousy. Whatever the causes of all this, one thing was clear: she had never hoped to hurt Jerome so deliberately as he had set out to hurt her.

It was only when the sun shone through her bedroom windows that she gained a strange new sense of clarity; a sense of knowing what to do crept over her in that old, familiar way. She would not let her feelings override her tolerance for Clover or for Jerome. While Clover's coldness toward her not only hurt Emma, it frightened her—she would do everything she could to treat her daughter with respect.

Emma stopped at the top of the stairs. As the sounds of Clover's girlish laughter tempered with Jerome's deeper chuckles rang across the landing from her daughter's bedroom—the bedroom that held two single beds, one for Clover and one for the girlfriends she used to have stay—Emma fought back bile in her stomach.

Change had come too fast this time. But she had become used to the fact that nothing was permanent in this life. She'd learned that if one did not accept change or if you fought it when it came, then it had the capacity to fight right back and destroy everything in its path.

Emma would carve something positive out of this. Clover was, by all accounts, almost an adult, and if Emma were to in any way stop her from pursuing this affair, she would only be walking down the same path that Emma's father had trodden.

Emma knocked on Patrick's bedroom door, opening it an inch when he called her to come inside. He lay on his bed in the morning sun, his long legs stretched out in front of him, crossed at the ankles.

"Come and lie with me," he said, his voice honey-soft.

And she did; she went over to him and settled herself next to him, resting her head on his shoulder as if it were the most natural thing in the world.

"You know what they say about us." She smiled.

"Oh, God, yes. Degenerate, strange, weird, cut-off… Clover's completely conservative in comparison, you know."

"Good." She ran her hand over his familiar chest.

He caught it and brought it up to his lips. "Things might seem like they're ending sometimes, but you know that means they're beginning as well."

"Do you think she's in love with Jerome?" she asked.

"God, no. She's only doing it to annoy you. And me…"

Emma closed her tired eyes.

Once again, she would not create a mess.

Patrick went for a walk toward the South Downs with Jerome on the second morning after his arrival. Emma watched them wandering up the old lane toward the still, silent hills that had protected the farmlands around Summerfield for centuries, that had provided some protection from all the battles that had gone on over the channel during Emma's life so far.

It was a familiar sight, those two going off together, and yet it was something, heaven knew, Emma thought she'd never have to witness again. If she closed her eyes, she could imagine that twenty years had not passed at all. Except that now her daughter sat on a deck chair next to her by the lake, staring at an upside-down book. Her legs were splayed out in front of her as if she were a child.

Emma came to a swift decision right then, right there. She had to do it sometime. If Jerome were to tell her the truth that had been too hard to share with her… then heaven help them all.

"Clover," she said, "there is something you ought to know."

Clover's wide brown eyes were luminous with youth.

"Darling."

Clover rolled her eyes.

Emma fought every voice inside her that told her that this was not a good idea. Banishing them, she went right on.

"You know that while I loved Oscar for a time, there has been another love in my life that I'm unable to switch off. It's a love so strong that it's bigger than me. I would like to be able to explain it, but, well, perhaps the best explanation I can give for its existence is sitting right here beside me by the lake. Our lake."

Clover's head darted up like a rocket.

"What are you saying, Mother?" she whispered.

Just then, everything flashed before Emma. Uncertainty bit at her. She should have done this with Patrick. What was she thinking?

"Oscar, darling, is not your father. It's Patrick…" She'd thought about telling Clover so many times, and yet, so many times, fear of her daughter becoming some outcast had stopped her from saying what needed to be said.

Clover's hands moved, flailing, independent of her body, finally resting rigid by her side. The hands Emma had held so many times… Oh, how she wanted to reach out to her child.

But instead, as if overcome with the saying, with the speaking of what she'd held secret, with everything that had happened in the past few years and, were she honest, over the past few days, Emma stood up and went into the house. She spent the rest of the evening alone in her studio. She painted with the vigor of a woman on the run. From what, she had no idea. Her years of silence had wrought things that were felt so intensely that she was not sure she could broach any understanding of why she hadn't spoken out herself.

Had she, by not speaking, implied that Clover was not worthy of her trust? Was keeping the truth, veiled under the cloak of protectionism, a way of not giving those people we protected the benefit of the doubt? Of course it was. But she had held off telling Clover because Emma knew that, while she might have succeeded in getting away from a judgmental society, the fact was that society still existed beyond the walls of Summerfield. And if a girl was to venture into it, war or no war, she would be judged and shunned by other families, by those who still saw themselves as more respectable than Emma and Patrick, through no fault of Clover's in the least.

Emma rested her head in her hands on her painting stool, only to leap forward and rip the painting she'd started right off her easel.

What was more, Emma herself had been raised in a world where certain things were accepted but not spoken of. In the Victorian era, it was the way one operated. No one would trust a child with information that might ruin their chances of acceptance in society! Neither of her parents had ever trusted Emma with confidences about their personal lives until Emma was a young woman, and her father had expected her to remain silent about their financial situation.

The sound of footsteps, hard and heavy, thundered up the hallway as she sat there in the glorious, light-filled studio. A voice resonated through the house. Jerome was back from the walk with Patrick. Clover's voice was high, hysterical. Childish. And above all, angry.

Emma leaned her head on her empty easel.

Patrick appeared in the doorway. She stood up, helpless with grief.

Chapter Twenty-Five

London, 1980

Laura sat with the dean in his office at the Royal College of Music. The room's high ceiling and large windows seemed to hold the promise of beauty, of the beautiful music that was created between these lofty walls, while the everyday matters of finance and budgeting and running a university department were obvious in the piles of documents and letters that were scattered on his desk.

"As you know, my grandmother is the artist Emma Temple," she said.

He pulled his glasses down onto his nose and regarded her over the frames.

"Of course," he said. "I adore the Circle's work, and it is a delightful honor for us to have any relation of hers studying here."

Laura knotted her hands in her lap. "Well, you see, her dear friend Patrick Adams…"

"Yes."

"Painted her to the best of our knowledge during the summer of 1923. In France, and, unfortunately…" Her words faded off again. She looked away.

"Laura, I read *The Times*."

Laura took in a breath. "I took out a loan to fund my music tuition."

"Many students do."

"Yes, but my grandmother allowed me to use her portrait as collateral for the loan. Emma was—is—the guarantor. Now that the painting's provenance is under question, the bank has rescinded the loan. There's nothing I can do. And as far as I can see, the painting isn't... what we thought after all. The bank is going to acquire all Gran's assets." Something stopped her from mentioning Ewan.

The dean, who had charmed her with his gentle approach on the day she'd auditioned for the college, took off his glasses and laid them on the table between them.

"I'm going to have to drop out of the Royal College."

"We can't have that."

Laura had sat up all night.

A shadow passed across the dean's face. He stood up, his back to her, leaning on the windowsill and staring out at the Royal Albert Hall opposite the college.

"I'm sorry," Laura said. She stood up, too, hovering a moment in the quiet space. The dean's sigh was heavy in the silence.

He lifted an arm as if in a distracted acknowledgment of her decision. Laura turned, feeling a tight grimace gripping her features. She made her way back out into the corridor, out through the building that had held so many promises and yet now seemed like an empty shell of itself.

The phone rang by Laura's bed in the very early hours of the next morning. Like some crazed train that arrived at the wrong station day in and day out, she'd woken up as usual in the pitch darkness, her thoughts diving to their most panic-stricken place. She'd thrown off her sheets in a hot sweat. Her arm seemed to move of its own accord, picking up the handset.

"Laura."

Laura sat up and ran her hand through her messed-up hair. "Gran?" she whispered. "Are you okay?"

"Of course." Emma sounded matter-of-fact.

Laura lay back, hitting her pillow with a thud.

"Sleep becomes a useless activity as one gets older. When I close my eyes, I can't help thinking that I won't wake up."

Laura drew her quilt around her body. "I was awake."

"Yes. You've been looking dreadful lately. I can't begin to imagine."

"Gran, can I tell you something?"

"Of course."

"I want you to listen to me. While I can't pay the bank half their loan immediately, I'll negotiate with them and convince them I'll pay it off as fast as I can. I will move to cheaper housing, and I could even try to take out a personal loan from another bank to pay off this one, while I work full-time-plus. I'll take on fifty violin students as well if I need to. It will be fine. I love you."

"No."

Laura ran a hand over her sweaty forehead. Her furniture took on unfamiliar shapes in the darkness.

"I think there is someone who can help," Emma said. "It's a long shot, I grant you."

"What?"

"Jerome Douglas." Emma pronounced the name as if it were a triumph.

All Laura knew was that when Em mentioned that name, she usually accompanied it with a derisive sniff.

"I admit that I resisted the idea of involving him in this from the start," Emma went on. "But I'm afraid I'm desperate, and… you see, dear, if there was one person who was privy to what went on, it was Jerome. He was there the entire summer that Patrick painted me in France. He was close to Patrick, and, I hate to admit it, he was closer than I was at that time, and then, well, he was also important to Clover later on."

"*To Mum?*"

Emma was quiet a moment. "Jerome appeared twice in my life. Twice, I admit, dear, he got under my skin. He's the last person I want back, believe me. But, ironically, he is the person we need. How strange life is sometimes, but in some ways, I… Never mind," she said.

Laura frowned. "But is he still—"

"Alive?" Emma sounded as quick as a whip now. "He's not only alive, I've found him. I thought he was probably dead or in New York. But it turns out he stayed in London after he met Clover in 1942. He should, with any luck, be able to prove that Patrick painted me. He's our only chance."

Laura couldn't help thinking that this was going to be too little, too late.

"I have his phone number, dear."

Laura sat up and flicked on her bedside light. She reached for the pen and paper that she always kept by her bed.

"I suggest you ring him first thing in the morning."

"Won't you call him?"

There was a silence.

"I think it's best you do that, not me." Emma could be such a curious mix of throw-it-all-away confidence and deep sensitivity all at once.

"You should go to sleep, Gran."

"Bollocks to that," Emma said. "I'll be having a very long sleep soon."

The street outside was silent. Laura shivered now in the stark light from her lamp that flooded her bed in the otherwise darkened room. "Please, Gran."

Emma's voice cracked when she spoke. "I don't want to look down on you and see that you are not playing the violin. It was what you were born to do, and I won't stand for you giving it up."

The breath that Laura took in was ragged. "Gran—"

"You will not give it up."

"I'm going back to sleep now, Gran," Laura murmured. "Thank you, but…"

"Call him. Don't let him fob you off. And get back to Ewan as well."

Laura opened and shut her mouth.

Emma hung up the phone.

Laura lay awake until dawn crept through the curtains. She reached for the phone the moment the clock hand moved around to eight.

When she introduced herself, he came straight to the point.

"Emma's granddaughter?" he said without preamble. "Pinch me now!"

"Is there any way we could meet somewhere and talk?" Laura asked.

"Don't suppose you guys still haunt Bloomsbury by any chance?"

"How could you possibly think not?"

The sound of a chuckle came down the phone. "Why don't we meet at the fountain in Russell Square at eleven o'clock?" he said. "And, Laura, this sure is a bit grummy for you."

Laura hung up and shook her head.

At ten to eleven, she stood by the fountain in Russell Square. Fine sprays of water floated into the spring air. When an upright old man walked toward her, she scanned his features first: eyebrows that remained defined, dark eyes. He looked around ten years younger than Em, so eighty or so perhaps, but then Laura found her gaze drawn down to his shoes. The soft lace-ups he wore seemed to speak to her more than anything else about him. They were the sort of shoes that only the elderly wore. For some odd reason, Laura felt herself softening a little toward this man whom Em seemed to dismiss until now.

He'd seen her and was making his way straight over.

"Laura?" he said.

She held out her hand.

Some long-ago expression passed across his face. "You have to be Clover's daughter, and yet you have so many of Em's features too. God, that woman drove me insane. Can't help feeling this is a moment of reckoning," he said.

Laura took in the deep furrows around his chocolate-colored eyes, the way he gripped and relaxed his hands at his sides.

"Shall we sit down?" she asked.

Jerome Douglas eased himself down on the nearest bench.

"How is the old fire extinguisher Em?" he asked, taking a sidelong glance toward Laura.

It was hard to know whether to be consternated or amused by his odd expressions. Fire extinguisher? That was one way to describe Em. Laura focused on the children who ran in and out of the sparkling mist near the fountain.

"She's well. Fine. Amazing."

"Of course she is," he said.

"What was it like?" Laura asked suddenly. "If you don't mind my asking, being an outsider of sorts but knowing them all?"

Jerome was quiet for a moment. "I can't tell you how wild it made me feel being on the outer edge of their group! Only a week after my arrival in France that first summer, Ambrose, Lawrence, and Oscar all left the place, along with their dolled-up partners. It made me pretty balled up. I know I took my beef out on Em. Blamed her. But you see, she was such a hard-boiled egg—a toughie, Laura. You couldn't break her shell no matter how hard you bashed at it. And I bashed as hard as I could." He was silent a moment.

"She saw straight through me from the moment we met. Sensed that I was only dabbling in art. Saw me as full of hooey. And the fact was, I wasn't serious about art like she was. But I thought she looked down on me for that. For my part, I wanted to thumb my nose at my family back home, not go into the finance industry. I was having none of that. As for Em, I decided she could be the one left holding the bag, not me. I put on the live-wire act to foil her and set my cap to get Patrick and a career in art. Tried everything I could to be a bohemian, but I ended up training as an accountant instead." He chuckled and crossed his legs. "My family cut me loose in the end, too, you see."

"Oh."

He sat back on the bench.

Laura shook her head. She grimaced as she pushed on with her next question. "What about my mother?" Clover had never spoken about Jerome in her life. Sometimes it seemed as if Laura held only a little kaleidoscope of disjointed patterns when it came to her family's past. If she tried to turn the handle in order to dig in deeper, the few pictures she could see never became a pattern that made sense.

Jerome crossed his legs back. "I met your mother in a nightclub in London during the war. To be honest, after my family became killjoys, I'd come back here in the thirties with some pathetic hopes to get back with Patty again. When I met Clover later on, well... the old flame of resentment was still not dead. Need I say more? I'd heard on the grapevine that Pat had ended up shacked up with Em for decades. And that riled me."

"But my mother would have been, what, seventeen?" She knew she had to get to the point, but somehow she had to put small pieces back together before she could tackle the central thing.

Something akin to a smile passed across his face. "Clover was eighteen, by goodness! And, well, my dear, I thought that if I appeared at their wretched Summerfield, then Patrick would lay off stalling, realize he'd messed up by dumping me, and all that jazz. But he told me to mooch off and to lay off his daughter. Emma just thought I was even more of a sap. Hardly talked to me, as usual."

Laura tried to absorb it all.

"So you want me to verify the portrait," he said. "It's such a crazy thing."

"I don't know if you can."

It was his turn to listen while she told him a potted version of Ewan's story and her disaster with the loan.

"Did you see Patrick paint Emma in France? You apparently were the one who had access to the studio."

He was quiet a moment. "I can confirm that he painted every last damned stroke, my dear."

Laura resisted the urge to leap off the bench. Jerome might be Em's nemesis, but at this point, he was Laura's dearest friend.

"Not only was I in France, not only did I wake up every damned morning to see him standing at that bloody easel looking at her in a way he never looked at me, but I was with him in Paris and London afterward. That was when he was finishing the work. Even though, I admit, I'd safely gotten rid of Emma and I thought I had Patrick to myself, the wretched portrait hung between us like some spooky reminder of her in every hotel where we laid our heads. What was worse, it became clear to me that she was the one Patrick was really stuck on. I wasn't swell enough by a mile. No matter how many great people I tried to introduce him to, no matter how many parties I took him to, no matter how stuck on him I was, he was never going to treat me with the tenderness he showed her. So, like an unwanted dog, I went back to New York. And got short shrift from my family as well."

Laura stayed quiet.

"I made the mistake of trying to outshine Emma, you see, Laura. But in all the struggle, I realized too late that in order to be close to Patrick, the person I had to impress was not him… it was Em."

"Well, you know when you haven't impressed Em." Laura chuckled. "In spite of all her silences, she's no good at hiding the things that matter to her."

"Quite. As for the painting, Patrick sent it up to Summerfield from London as soon as it was done, and then he, too, went back to Summerfield and Em. He went back to her, and he never left her. My affair with Patrick was done. As for Clover, she was a much easier nut to crack than her mother, and the fact that she was in the midst of a rebellion against Emma… can you see how that suited us both?"

"So you seduced her?"

Crinkles appeared at the corners of his eyes. "Oh, you slay me, darling. Nope. Your mother seduced me! It was she who took me for a wicked ride."

Laura felt her eyes widen.

"Clover wanted to razz up Em. I thought I'd win my revenge. But it was your mother who won that round. But one thing I can tell you is that I'll be in love with the memory of Patrick until the very day I die."

Laura heaved out a shuddering sigh.

"The painting, done by Patrick, was delivered to Summerfield from London. It's simple, Laura. Don't you think it's funny now—that they all took me for a useless sap?"

"Thank you for talking with me," she said.

He placed his old hand down between them on the bench. "Well, you see, I did learn, finally, not to alienate any woman who is linked with Patrick!"

In spite of everything, Laura felt herself grinning at him. But still, the largest piece in her puzzle—Ewan's story—would not, in any way, fit.

Summerfield, 1944

The affair between Clover and Jerome seemed as interminable and impossible as the war that rolled on in Europe. A military unit was stationed in the fields next to Summerfield. Anyone who was staying in the house had to present their identity card to get through the front gate. Patrick lost his on several occasions, but he always charmed his way past the guards.

But the worst of it was that Patrick's studio in Bloomsbury had taken a direct hit, and everything he'd stored there was lost, his preliminary sketches for *The Things We Don't Say*, along with some of Emma's early works. But still, when Lawrence wanted to take *The Things We Don't Say* up to London to show it at a small wartime exhibition of works from the Circle that he was organizing in Hampstead, Emma and Patrick agreed to let him borrow it just this once, as long as it was stored safely in his cellar at night.

"I feel wretched," Patrick said, sitting with his head in his hands in the sitting room. "What I am going through is nothing compared with those on the front line. Again. And yet, I am lost as to what to do about Jerome and Clover. I'm so sorry, Em."

Emma stood close to the tiny electric heater. The small light that hung from the center of the room did little to relieve the resolute darkness from the blackout curtains.

"It's not your fault," Emma said. Desperate, she'd taken to writing to Jerome in London, admitting that she knew she got on her daughter's nerves, knowing that the way she'd raised Clover away from the reality of the world had restricted her ability to deal with certain things. He'd returned the letters unopened. She was at her wits' end with him.

She felt, irrationally, as if he'd stolen her child. He had cut her off and was refusing to communicate with her at all. All the while, Emma found it hard to grasp that Clover had a part to play in this ghastly scenario too.

No matter that she'd filled Summerfield to the brimming point with decorations, the house seemed strange and empty. Summerfield had lost its spirit now that Clover had gone under such dramatic circumstances.

"I have been a gloomy companion for her these past years since Calum's death," Emma said. "She's made me realize that I must not ignore what is in the palm of my hand, no matter how overcome by grief I might be."

Patrick looked up at her, his expression fierce. "Keep writing to her. The problem is…" Emma waited.

"Jerome plays games with people," Patrick said. "He's a manipulator."

Emma sighed. She paused a moment. Saying what needed to be said seemed so hard most of the time. "He was once in love with you, Patrick," she murmured. "Surely that will constrain the way in which he treats Clover."

The sound of footsteps outside on the gravel ground into the room—one of the military personnel undertaking a routine watch, no doubt.

"I neglected Clover, there is no doubt, Patrick. It's not your fault."

"Personal grief in war is a double dagger, flecked with the blood of the entire world," Patrick murmured. "For heaven's sake, Em, no one could ever blame you for grieving."

"Were we wrong to try to adhere to our principles? Do they not work in this darned world? I worry that we brought Clover up in a bubble, that we protected her too much."

Patrick's eyes were red-rimmed with lack of sleep. His hair curled on his collar, and gray shadows colored his cheeks. "I don't know," he whispered. "I just don't know."

He stood up, and she moved over to him, her head resting on his shoulder. "I don't know what to believe in anymore in this world," she whispered. "But I do know that I have every faith in you."

The sounds of gunfire ricocheted over the hills from France for the second time in their lives. The fighting, once again, knew no boundaries between day and night. Life and death, hope and despair seemed to exist on a dark and shifting spectrum, and no one could tell how their circumstances would change during these days of war.

Chapter Twenty-Six

London, 1980

A call came through the moment Laura walked into her flat. Resignation spread its own unique shadow over her when she recognized the voice on the end of the phone.

"I have good news, Laura. We can offer you full-time work." Her supervisor from the supermarket seemed enthusiastic, and Laura's heart sank at the sound of his voice. "If you need overtime, then we should be able to supply you with more hours on weekends and in the evenings."

"Thank you," she said.

"You give our regular employees a good run for their money. In fact, let me know if you are interested in our company management program. I'd be happy to recommend you for it later in the year. Can you start the additional shifts next week?"

Laura's performance exam was in seven days. "Would the following week be all right?"

As soon as they'd worked out the timing, Laura hung up and dialed the bank.

"Ivan?" she said. "I'll start paying you back the principle in a fortnight."

A vivid picture of Ivan's own resignation came into Laura's mind. "Yes, we will need you to do that, Laura, but I'm afraid my superiors are advising that we need to recover Emma's assets now in order to recoup the principle amount that is due immediately."

"Ivan. Please! She may only have such a short time left. I will pay you back as fast as I can. It was my loan. It's my responsibility."

"I was about to call Emma."

"No, please don't," she said. "Can you give me another twenty-four hours?"

"I'll try."

When Laura placed the handset back down, she ran her fingers over the shiny green phone and dialed Ewan's number.

"Laura?"

"Can I meet you after work?" The words came out as if by automaton.

"I don't know, Laura."

"Ewan. I have no choice."

Silence hung a moment. "I'll come up to Bloomsbury," he said. "How about I meet you at the Lamb in an hour?"

"Perfect," Laura said. "And thank you."

An hour later, she slipped into the interior of the Lamb, marching past the wood-paneled bar and the old snob screens that hid the bar staff from wealthy patrons who came there to drink. Laura made a beeline for the man who was already sitting on one of the leather banquettes.

When Ewan looked up at her, Laura blanched. His face was pale, and his chin was covered with three days' growth.

"Can I…" he said, his words coming out as the barest of whispers. "Can I tell you something? Personal?"

Laura nodded. "Please. I want you to talk to me."

"My father," Ewan said, "killed himself over this."

Laura held his gaze, watching the way his mouth worked. He covered it with his hand, and she reached her hand toward him on the table, leaving it sitting there, a gesture, such inadequate support.

"The whole thing was a tragic mess," Ewan said.

"Ewan," Laura whispered.

"He hanged himself in our garage." He looked at her, scouring her face, willing her, she couldn't help thinking, to turn away from him, to walk away, out of this pub, to leave him alone with his grief.

The wood under her fingers felt slippery and soft.

"Can I get you a drink?" he asked. His eyes held an ancient form of pain that Laura knew she'd never be able to reach.

"Sure." But her voice sounded as if it were some long-distance version of itself.

When he returned, placing a beer and a glass of wine down between them along with a bag of crisps, Laura reached for the packet and took one, only to find herself unable to stomach it. Slowly she pushed the crisps away.

"It's my responsibility to help you, you have to see that. I couldn't let the painting be loaned to the Tate when my father did it, and I couldn't tell you about my father because..." His words drifted off, and his hands shook as he tried to pick up his beer. He put it down again.

Laura could only stare at her drink.

"My father," he said after what seemed an age, "studied art in London when he was young. Once he'd graduated, he was fortunate enough to secure representation with a gallery owner. He was a great admirer of early twentieth-century modernism in Britain, and like Patrick Adams, he used to copy the works he admired when he was a student. It was part of his practice. Just what he did. He went to the galleries by himself and copied iconic works. When Lawrence showed *The Things We Don't Say* briefly in London at a private showing of Patrick's work, my father jumped at the opportunity to copy it."

Laura nodded.

"Unfortunately, something went wrong, I don't know what, and my father stopped painting for years. He gave up. It was the one big unspoken thing in our house. He had a career in insurance until I was a teenager. In his forties he started painting again, just for himself—he hated his job. He set up a studio in our garage. He needed to paint just as you need to play music, and I, well, I need to paint too. But all I knew was that he killed himself over something to do with art fraud…"

"Oh, dear God."

"The thing was, he'd become so happy when he finally started painting again," Ewan said. "You'd hardly have recognized him, physically even, from the person he was before."

Laura took in the washed-out man sitting opposite her.

"My father had told me he always put a secret red mark on every copy he made in order to distinguish them from the real works of art. He'd started to become completely brilliant at making copies by the time he was in his early twenties, so he marked his work. He showed me what he did. He'd left his practice pieces in storage, and one day, when he'd started painting again, he took me to see them."

Laura nodded, still mute.

"It was like going to a field of derelict old aircraft. I can't tell you what I felt when I saw his work. He'd done stellar copies of van Goghs, Cézannes… he loved the post-impressionists. He'd made several copies of Patrick's paintings.

"But after he showed me his storage unit, full of all these wonderful treasures, everything changed. He withdrew. Stopped eating, washing, painting. And started refusing to go to work."

"No."

"Are you okay?" he asked.

He caught her eyes, reaching his hand across the table for a brief moment, only to pull it back. "When I knew without a doubt that the painting was Dad's work, not the original Adams, sitting out there at Summerfield, it tormented me. I can't tell you how it tore me up inside. But now, I can't help thinking that Dad killed himself because his copy of *The Things We Don't Say* was not there with all his other paintings when we went to look at them all in storage. Somehow, I think he must have found out that his copy had replaced the original. I was never told details after his death. I was a teenager. Everyone wanted to protect me."

"Of course," Laura said, closing her eyes and thinking of her mother, and how Emma had protected her from her secret…

"But you see, the thing is this, Laura: apart from the shame and the betrayal of telling you, I simply cannot face telling my mother that Dad's painting is hanging out at Summerfield. After my father's death she went downhill, and everyone was worried about her. I thought that until I did say something to my mother about my father's work being substituted for Adams's most famous piece, I didn't think it was right to share what I knew with anyone else."

Laura took in what Ewan had told her. The ramifications of this spread endlessly, and yet, she felt as if she were locked in a long silence that seemed impenetrable.

Summerfield, 1946

Unable to communicate with her daughter, devastated at the breakdown in her relationship with Clover, Emma did what so many of her Victorian ancestors used to do: she took to her bed.

It wasn't until Clover and Jerome ended their tumultuous affair soon after the war finished that Patrick persuaded Clover to travel. She showed promise as a decorative painter and had chosen porcelain as her medium. Her pieces were exquisite, and Patrick arranged for her to meet with contacts of his in Limoges. But Clover never went to Europe. Instead, she met a butcher named Ed in a pub in the country when traveling with friends and married him within a month of their meeting.

Neither Patrick nor Emma was invited to the wedding.

Clover wrote to Emma and told her that she wanted a normal family, not a complicated bohemian utopia that was Emma's ideal.

"She wants security because she feels she's lost it," Emma told Patrick. "Why didn't we tell her the truth about us earlier? I feel we had such a responsibility to speak out."

They sat together in their studio at Summerfield on the chairs they'd set up on either side of the fireplace. Bach played on the small radio, sending a beautiful, crackling rendition out into the otherwise silent room. Emma put down her predinner drink. The sherry tasted off.

"All we can hope is that Clover is happy," Patrick said.

"I don't bear her any grudge for wanting to make her own decisions as to how she lives her life," Emma said.

Patrick placed his wineglass on the table between them. "If only Jerome could understand that I loved you and him as much as each other. Just in different ways."

Emma focused her gaze out the picture windows that overlooked the garden.

"You have been my constant, my security," Patrick said. "I'm going to feel the same way about you until the day I die. I don't want you to ever doubt it, Em."

Emma faced him.

"You know, you must not worry on your part in all this," he said, his words settling in the twilight. "I think we have to allow Clover the freedom to live her own life now."

Chapter Twenty-Seven

London, 1980

Emma placed the phone back down on its cradle after taking Laura's call. She sat on her sofa in the familiar room in Gordon Square and traced her fingers over the patterns in the fabric. How frustrating it was not to be able to leap up and stalk around the room or, better still, to take a turn around Bloomsbury, march through the squares, and have a good old think. The squares lent the whole bohemian, artistic, and intellectual suburb such a well-set-out sort of feel. Logical. Unlike the complicated lives of some of its artistic inhabitants, that was a certain thing.

And yet, a little thought was forming into a full-blown idea in her head. Yes, Jerome had been upset by the Circle, by the idea that he'd never really fit in. Emma understood that. She knew that she had been somewhat exclusive in the way she gathered those who were close to her around her and held them as if she were clasping on to a string bag that always seemed to threaten to burst.

She was haunted now by one terrible thought. And the more Emma gave it any foothold in her imagination, the more it might make perfect, yet awful, sense.

Laura's sleep was fitful. Explanations made no sense to her as she lay awake in the all-too-familiar early hours turning on her bright bedside light, only to turn it off again in despair at the slow ticking of her clock.

When Laura looked at her face in the mirror the next morning, all she could see was the same grayness that haunted Ewan. The malaise now hung over them both. She splashed cold water on her face.

Her exam loomed over her like another shadow. She'd practiced until midnight, and her fingers ached. She should put in at least six hours of playing time. Laura sighed at the sight of the score that rested on her stand. The music was so marked with her own performance notes that it was surprising Laura could see the notes when she needed to practice. When it came to performing from memory, she didn't think about any of it. It was as if she forgot all the rules in the end.

Laura fixed herself some breakfast. Drank coffee. Grumbled at the bowl of cereal she'd made and rested her aching head in her hands. She went to the phone and dialed Ewan's number, which, like the Bartók and the Bach Double that she was performing straight afterward, she had committed to memory now.

He answered on the first ring.

"Hello?" She winced at the high-pitched sound of her voice, hating the fact that she was compelled to hassle him…

"Laura."

"Your mother lives in Edinburgh?" she said.

"Yes, but—"

"Scotland, then," she said. "Today. I don't think we have any choice." Her words seemed to hang in the cold morning air of her flat. "If your mother were to find out about your father's copy of the portrait from another source, could you live with that?"

He was silent a moment. "No," he said.

"Ewan…" She closed her eyes. "Emma is more than ninety. She might have a day, a week, a month left. I understand how hard this is, but your mother is our only hope now. Wouldn't she want to know? Do you think hiding the truth from her will in any way help anyone out of this mess?"

"Look—"

"Please, Ewan."

"I can't put my mother through anything more. Losing her husband to suicide—"

"Hiding the truth from her, no matter how protective you might think it is, could have implications that go on for far longer than you ever, ever could imagine. It can span generations. Believe me."

"Laura…" Ewan almost pleaded.

She pictured her own mother and rested her hand on the table by the phone.

"I can't promise you anything by opening up to her," he said.

"I know, but what if she knows something? What if it was she who was protecting you, just as you are now?" Laura had to go on. "What if that protection, ultimately, has cost you the confidence to break out from this and to be true to your own dreams? Your father's story, tragic as it was, haunts you, but can't you see how his death and his sadness at losing his own dreams are stopping you from leading the life you were born to live?"

For a few moments, there was silence. "Laura… I'll pick you up in an hour."

"Thank you, Ewan." Laura believed fully that hiding something from a person you loved to protect them was only ever a short-term fix—it would fester like some smoldering volcano until, eventually, it belched forth over everyone concerned.

Emma woke with the same troubling conviction that had haunted her after she'd spoken to Laura yesterday. In looking for the answer, she'd come to find a pattern—the full circle that she'd seen all those years ago. Jerome had triggered it.

She'd thought, back then, that she could live under her own terms, creating a life, like some artistic vision that was separate from the reality of this world. But what she'd failed to realize was that this world was, in the end, the only one we have, and even though we all have different experiences, some things are universal.

She'd hated how Patrick's relationships had affected him, but at the time they'd happened, all she'd wanted to do was to support and protect him. In the same way she'd tried to protect Calum and Clover from anything that might hurt. And, of course, the reason she'd wanted to protect them all, the reason she had fought so hard to build up an exclusive, safe world was because she was terrified of losing them after she'd lost Frederick in such a devastating way when she was young. It was that loss that had done it. She knew that.

But she hadn't seen at the time that a circle was a closed shape.

In building up this safe world for herself, she'd not seen the darkness outside her bright circle. She'd ignored the slight twangs of guilt that she'd felt when they cast aside people who didn't fit in—resorting to organization instead: catching trains, planning meals, renting properties, being her silent, practical self. The irony was, in spite of her tolerance and perhaps because of her strident views about it, she'd blinded herself to the truth of other people's feelings. By living according to principles, sometimes, she'd not been receptive to others' hurt. To her, people she did not want to tolerate were simply the books she didn't want to open up. But by living with such firm beliefs, had she, in fact, ended up judging and treating some people more harshly than she should?

In the end, she and Patrick had been fine—she'd been worrying about the wrong thing all these weeks. Because they always had each other. A tight circle within the larger one she'd created herself. She had been the center of it; there was no doubt about that. She was the person around whom they all orbited. And yet, had she and Patrick seemed like such an impenetrable force to those who were shut out of their world?

It struck her how extraordinary it was that the way one saw one's own life was so completely different from the way others interpreted it. Like a painting and a viewer, the artist could present only *her* version of reality, and a viewer could never really know what an artist's true intention was. If the artist painted only the unblemished side of an apple, the viewer would never know that it was bruised. It was the same with life and other people. We humans could never achieve complete understanding of another person if we couldn't truly see inside them.

For now, all she could do was to try and realize that people—potential lovers, artists, friends—may have wanted to break into the close world she'd created. But something was as clear as the sound of a bell. She'd failed to see beyond the covers of those who needed her to do so the most. She'd failed to see the other side of people's anger and destructiveness for what it was—desperation, panic, and fear.

Emma reached for the pair of reading glasses that sat on the same table she'd had by her side every night for the past forty years. All her thoughts were falling into place, like some jigsaw puzzle that she'd never seen fit to fix until now. If she were not mistaken, there was one final thing she needed to do before she left this earth.

Chapter Twenty-Eight

England, 1980

Ewan was quiet as he wound his way through England's northern counties toward the Scottish border. Laura started up conversations, but every time she did, she ended up talking to herself. As the fields of England gave way to wilder landscapes and they crossed the ancient border into Scotland, Laura forced herself to stare at the moody hills and the tumbling streams on the sides of the road. The farther into Scotland they traveled, the broodier she felt.

She glanced across at Ewan as they approached the city where he'd grown up. He remained a pale, sunken version of himself, and all she wanted to do was to reach out to him, to hold him, to hug him. But that would be the last thing that was appropriate right now. He was lost in his own past with his own demons—how one event had spiraled out to such great effect. As he drove through the streets of Edinburgh, rows of gray houses seemed to match the heavy, leaden sky. Ewan wound his way through the suburb of Stockbridge until he pulled up outside a tall, old, narrow house.

He stretched his arms. Laura unbuckled her seat belt. She rested her hand on the armrest. She'd been surprised by his car. It was a Mercedes, but it was a few years old, not some new sports car. She opened the car door and stepped out into the street.

The fresh Scottish air hit Laura's senses, as if waking her suddenly after the long car ride north. Nerves danced inside her in a strange out-of-time jig throughout her system. She ran her eyes over the Georgian house that stood proud on the wide, tree-lined street.

Ewan moved around the car to stand next to her.

"She won't talk about my father's death," he said. "I've not had a conversation about it, not a proper one, since he died."

"I understand," Laura responded.

His eyes seemed to search hers for a moment.

"Let's go inside." Her words sounded soft in the still, heathery Scottish air.

Ewan's mother opened the front door and hugged her son. She seemed tiny, a small blonde woman enveloped in his embrace.

"Laura," she said, holding out her soft white hand and smiling, tucking a loose strand of blonde hair behind one ear. "I'm delighted to meet you. I'm Rosie."

"Hello, Rosie." Laura held the older woman's hand a moment.

Ewan stood aside for Laura and Rosie to go into the house first. Rosie's little feet clipped down the hallway along the polished floorboards, while Laura took in the black-and-white photos that lined the cream-colored walls. In the back section of the house, the kitchen was warmed by an AGA, and it was filled with the smell of freshly baked scones. A tray of them sat cooling on the bench.

Rosie busied herself with the kettle. "I thought you'd be starving," she said like any other normal mother greeting her son.

Laura caught Ewan watching Rosie with a warm expression on his face that was hard to resist.

When they were all seated at the long table in the middle of the kitchen, Rosie poured tea, her faded blonde hair falling now in loose strands onto her cheeks. Her brown eyes were mirror images of Ewan's.

"There," she said, her soft Scottish accent lending the word a particular charm, as if tea settled everything.

Ewan stood up. He moved over to the window, staring out at the heavy sky outside. Laura shot a glance from him to his mother, her heart aching for them both.

"Mum," he said, "there's something I have to say."

London, 1921

Emma hovered by the window in Gordon Square. Waves of loneliness flowed through her at the sight of Patrick leaving London. He raised a hand to her, tipping the brim of his hat as he ushered the man who was accompanying him to Italy into the taxi out on the street.

Italy. A place for passion, for romantic adventure, for love. Not for Emma and Patrick but for Patrick and some random man he'd met in the National Gallery while looking at Italian art.

Emma moved back into the living room. The rooms that she'd filled with such hope for a new life before the war seemed lifeless now.

Patrick assured her that they'd build up a life together here after the war—they'd go to the theater at Covent Garden like she used to with Frederick. They'd work together as partners and artists during the day. They'd fill this house with the joy that had dissipated, cut off abruptly after Frederick's tragic death and then the war. How naïve she had been, thinking things might work out for them. A few afternoons snatched together at the end of the war were not the enduring love she needed. And yet, as with so many things in life, even if it was not perfect, she would do it all again.

Emma made her way to the staircase. She would paint. But as she clipped a fresh piece of paper on her easel, she heard the sound of a car door slam. Leaning toward the window, she glanced down at the square. All she could see was a hat and a certain way of standing.

She'd know him anywhere.

Again, his timing was completely, utterly off.

Emma steeled herself. *Not now,* she thought. *Please.* But she wiped her hands down the sides of her smock and slipped it over her head. When she opened the front door and he stood there, seeming uncertain of the welcome he'd receive, Emma forced herself to smile.

"Rupert."

He angled forward and waited for her to kiss him on his unaccustomed, shaven cheek.

She took a step back. Once his anger had subsided after the trauma of the war, he and Patrick had reconnected as friends. Emma was certain that it was impossible for Rupert to keep away entirely from Patrick. The three of them had been out for a drink a couple of times. Things remained awkward on Emma's part; she had never mentioned to a soul Rupert's approaches to her, and she was still aware that Patrick, in turn, had been genuinely in love with Rupert during the war. Were he to find out that Rupert had propositioned Emma, there was no doubt Patrick would still be hurt.

"Are you here alone, Em?" Rupert asked. He clenched and unclenched his hands by his sides.

Emma took in how clean they were. She was half-surprised to see that his fingernails were not encased with farmyard dirt.

"Patrick's just gone to Italy with his new boyfriend. Someone he met at the National Gallery apparently. I'm sorry. This is not a good time."

But Rupert stepped inside and picked up a little black-and-white photograph of Patrick. "How is our absent friend?"

Emma watched the way his hand caressed Patrick's face.

"Rupert," she warned.

He placed the photograph back down on the table. Facedown, so Patrick was obliterated from sight.

Rupert moved toward her. He took her face in the palms of his hands.

"No, Rupert," she said. And took a step back, disgust and an odd sense of confusion lurching around inside her at the old pain that still haunted his face.

Hampshire, 1980

Emma eased her way out of the taxi and stood on the smart doorstep of the elegant Georgian house. She'd not been here for a decade. Her last visit, with Patrick, had been odd in the extreme. She leaned heavily on her cane and gazed out at the valley below the house. Old villages sat nestled in perfect view from the terrace as if they hadn't been touched for centuries.

Civilized gentility.

"What now, Emma?" she muttered aloud to herself. She watched the taxi disappear into the countryside.

Emma made her slow way up the wide front steps to the house and reached up to hold the door knocker firmly despite her shaking old hand. She tapped with three loud knocks. A flurry of canine feet sounded inside the house, and a series of yaps resonated out into the warm afternoon air.

When the door opened, she raised what was left of her once fine eyebrows.

"Afternoon, Rupert," she said. "Do you mind if we have a chat?"

If Emma could have put a name to the color that flushed over Rupert's cheeks, she would call it shocking pink.

Edinburgh, 1980

Laura fought with the compulsion to reach out a hand toward Ewan's mother. Rosie sat, ramrod straight at her own kitchen table, like some valiant soldier returned from a foul war, her own personal battle stains running deeper than anyone could understand. Ewan's mother's face was mottled and blotched. Pale pink stains spread across her cheeks, and she pushed her tea away, letting it slide, too hard, across the table.

Ewan caught it midpush. He placed his head in his hands. "I couldn't tell you, Mum. I just couldn't do it. And yet, in keeping it from both you and Laura, I let both of you down. I am so very sorry."

Outside in the garden, a lone bird started up a song.

"I am certain Dad would never have done anything dishonest, that he only found out the painting was missing after he showed me through his studio. I'm sorry. It all makes ghastly sense to me now."

Rosie stood and moved toward the back door, opening it wide. She faced outward at the garden. Laura caught glimpses of a long, well-tended lawn bordered by flower beds, the colors bright. Rosie's small, slim frame. If Emma painted it, she would capture the scene and the emotion behind it all so well.

"I'm sorry, Mum," Ewan said again.

"Don't be." Rosie's voice was hard, cracking on the upward swing. "Because I already knew." She remained facing out at the garden.

Laura reached a hand out to him instinctively across the table.

Ewan didn't seem to see her; his eyes were locked on his mother's back. But he allowed Laura to place her hand on his own.

"It was after your grandfather's death that your father started painting again. But, Ewan, your father found the original Patrick Adams portrait of Emma Temple stored away in your grandfather's house when we were cleaning things out together. That was what killed your father. Going through his collection of meticulous copies with you, that was something he was so proud to do. When he saw the Adams copy was missing, he assumed it was just sitting in his father's storage facility. Until your father finally unwrapped the canvas when we were tidying your grandfather's things to show it to you, as it was his favorite piece. I will never until the day I die forget the way Hamish cried when he saw that it was the original in your grandfather's collection, not the copy he assumed it was."

Laura felt as if she'd been stabbed with a knife.

"I'm certain... I'm certain that your father killed himself because he could not stand to have his name linked to any deception, especially on such a monumental scale. It was unthinkable for him."

Laura's hands were wet with sweat, and her heart was thumping in her chest. She pushed back her chair, then pulled it back in.

"Laura," Ewan said.

Rosie went on in a strange, disconnected tone. It was as if she was speaking with a new voice. "It wasn't in any way your father's fault. The painting was swapped by the owner of the gallery where he worked—"

"Mother!"

"Your grandfather, Ewan. He owned the gallery where Ewan now works, Laura. Duncan Buchanan was the one who did the entire deed when Ewan's father, Hamish, was just a young art student toward the end of the war... Your father had no idea it had happened, Ewan, no inkling that the paintings had been swapped until twenty years afterward. Until you were a teenager, and when your father had just reconnected with the passion he'd tidied away for his art."

Laura tried to focus. But everything swam.

Rosie sat down at the table, her eyes and her face a little clearer now. "You were at art school when your father died so soon after the grandfather you also adored. Eighteen—with such hopes of being an artist. I could not put you through anything more after you had to go through both of those deaths in such quick succession. I simply couldn't tell you what your grandfather had done, not that he had unwittingly, yet entirely dishonestly, caused your father's decline and death. You were being groomed to take over your grandfather's gallery someday. And you adored your grandfather. I couldn't bear for you to lose your fond memories of him, not after you'd already lost your father. You were struggling with more than enough disillusionment as it was."

Something worked in Ewan's cheek, and a sharp, straight line divided his brow. His chest heaved. "No," he said.

Laura reached out again, but Ewan pulled his hand away from her.

"Any scandal, any hint that came out, would mean that you were the son of the man who had copied Patrick Adams's portrait and the grandson of the man who had elicited an illegal swap out at Summerfield. Any such thing would wreck any chance you had of building a career in the art world. I knew how much you cared about art. I also knew that after your grandfather's death, you'd do the right thing. Step up to the plate and take on the family business. I knew you'd forsake your own passion for painting to protect his memory. And I admired the fact that your father never put his own father down in your presence. He allowed the two of you to bond in your own way. It was… complex.

"And yet, I saw the fire in you, the need to be an artist, just like I recognized it in your father. He stifled it. He never allowed it to rise to fruition. Not until it was too late."

"Why?" Ewan whispered the words. "I had to take on the gallery, and yes, I wanted to for… Granddad's sake. But why did Dad not just paint?"

The irony of his question seemed breathtaking right now.

"Because the person who drummed his passion for art out of him was his own father. Duncan pressured him. And I saw him do it to you. But you are made of different stuff. I knew you wanted the gallery. Your father never did. And I knew that equally well, you could paint. I just had to have faith that you would blend both your passion for painting and your talent for running a successful business. Your father was… not so strong. Not being able to paint killed him. It would have been impossible for him to work alongside his father. Their relationship was always complicated. Your grandfather treated you quite differently, Ewan."

"I sensed that," Ewan whispered.

"Your grandfather Duncan never wanted your father to be an artist. He saw it as the stupidest of career options. Oh, he encouraged him to study it, to understand it… in order to gain expertise to work in commercial art—a real job. Your grandfather saw me as a bad influence because I encouraged your father to follow his desire to paint."

Ewan rolled up his shirtsleeves and rested his head in his hands. "I know," he said. "I tried to see both sides of the argument. Yours and Grandfather's. I guess I just ended up thinking that both worlds needed to coexist. Art needs both."

Laura looked at him. She recalled her own mother's words: "The stupidest of careers…" How many times had she heard Clover utter those very words? How familiar this all was, no matter how strange.

"If there were any hint at your father being an artist, at using that incredible talent of his to get anywhere, your grandfather didn't want to know about it. Not that it stopped him exploiting your father," Rosie went on. "I think, to be honest, your grandfather was jealous—your father's talent was something your grandfather never had."

Laura turned her teacup on the table, hands and mind busy.

"You see, your grandfather swapped the two paintings. He organized to have your father's copy hanging out at Summerfield. It was his final cock of the finger at the Circle. Because Patrick had turned his gallery down when he'd offered him and Emma representation years ago, when they were working in London. Your grandfather genuinely thought Patrick was mad not to want a part of a smart art gallery in Piccadilly, when instead, he insisted on working exclusively for the collective workshop in Fitzroy Square. Your grandfather was furious, and yet Patrick remained oblivious.

"Your grandfather's business partner in the gallery had a deeper grudge against the Circle and Patrick, it seemed. A personal connection."

Laura's head shot up.

"Your father's partner had never quite fit into the Circle himself, you see. So when the time was ripe, they acted. It suited your grandfather's dishonest, commercial nature and his partner's need for revenge against Emma and Patrick."

Ewan caught Laura's glance, swift as a hawk. She sat up, her breathing quickening. Understanding hit her like a brick.

But Rosie's Scottish voice was firm.

"Ewan and Laura, dear," Rosie said, "there's still more to it, I'm afraid."

Hampshire, 1980

"I think you'd better let me in, Rupert. Long time, no see, but sometimes that's the way things move, don't they? In circles." Despite the dark images that haunted her—this circle was not a clear, honest one at all—Emma managed to keep her tone even. There were boundaries, and Rupert had crossed every one. Why hadn't she seen it before?

His brown corduroy trousers were neatly pressed, and around his soft cashmere cardigan, which was the color of a gaudy marigold, the delicate scent of aftershave lingered. His fair features were no longer strong in his older face, but his blue eyes still peered at Em. Emma stopped herself from turning up her nose. There'd been enough of that for one lifetime… she had to think about her own role in this. Put herself in Rupert's shoes.

"Well?" she asked.

"Em?" He peered at her. "Good God, it's been more than ten years."

"Who on earth else would it be?" Emma tapped her cane on the ground. "The journey has been quite long enough and tedious,

Rupert. Lengthy car rides are not something I do these days. Unless I have good reason."

After what seemed an age, he led her into the hallway, turning right into an elegant sitting room filled with the sorts of antiques that Emma's father would have approved of without a doubt. The complete antithesis of everything to do with modernism.

Emma decided for once to speak out. She gave him a blow-by-blow version, sparing him no details of Laura's predicament nor her own. At the end, she simply eyed him.

He stood up and went to the drinks cabinet. "Gin?"

"Yes."

Rupert took a sip of his own drink and finally he spoke. "I admit, things got a little out of hand."

"Out of hand?" Emma placed her glass of gin back down herself. The astringent drink, which she hated, had given her strength. "What a ridiculous euphemism. I am sick, Rupert, of not telling the truth."

Rupert shot his head up. "Your utopia, if such a thing exists, and it doesn't, was my bloody apocalypse. I made the heinous mistake of falling in love with you both. And forgive me, but I couldn't help my feelings, nor the fact that they were never returned. By God, it was hard to stay away, and God knew that I tried. But in the end, staying away from someone or, in my case, two people whom I loved, well, it was impossible. Because, you see, my love did not fit in with your theories."

Emma stared and stared at his smart mantelpiece. "Patrick was in love with you during the war. You know he was. And yet, you wanted me as well."

But Rupert seemed to be miles away. "I didn't swap the painting for myself. I did it for Clover," he said.

As the words circled around the room, flying like some long-trapped nightingale that had been let out of its cage, Emma reeled backward against Rupert's silken cushion. "Clover?" she said.

Edinburgh, 1980

"Mum." Ewan's gaze ricocheted from Laura to Rosie. "Where is the original? If it was swapped for Dad's painting, then where is Patrick's original work?"

Rosie's lips were white. "I have it," she said. She spoke with complete dignity.

He pushed back his chair with a clatter.

"Safe," she said, holding up a hand. "When your grandfather died, I insisted on taking back all your father's works. Your grandmother, when she was alive, had no idea it was the original. Your grandfather must have been hoping it would go up in value. He'd sell it when the time was right, I'm sure of it. So I'm afraid, favorite person that I am of his, I took it and kept it safe. Until the ghastly mess resolved itself. It's under the house. I was just waiting for…" Her eyes widened, and she looked scared. "I don't know what. You, Laura? *The right time?*"

Ewan swore silently under his breath.

Hampshire, 1980

Emma took in the replica of that once handsome blond man who sat opposite her. She had to get him to talk. The reasoning that she had tried to use before she came here in order to elicit some sort of empathy for Rupert was dissipating faster than she could think. She felt Rupert's eyes on her.

"Rupe." She sighed. "Everyone was in love with Patrick."

"I was in love with you too, though," he insisted. "You always did underestimate your own allure. We certainly operated in complex patterns. It was far more than a simple circle."

"An unfathomable kaleidoscope, I think. And was I the one turning it, or was it Patrick? You, during the war? It was hard to know at times."

"All of us in turn, I imagine," Rupert said.

In spite of all the complications, a sense of almost unbearable loss for it all washed over her.

"Talk to me," she said.

"It's not so easy to talk, despite what you just said about the truth, Emma."

Emma clasped her old hands together. "You are not telling me a thing."

The expression on Rupert's face softened a little. "I met Clover in London toward the end of the war. She was gorgeous and charming and delightful."

Emma shot him an alarmed glance. First Jerome, and then *Rupert*? Had she underestimated her and Patrick's daughter entirely?

"No," he clarified. "Nothing happened, my dear."

Emma sank back in her seat.

"We talked about things, though. About it all."

"Clover talked to *you*? Well, that is just grand."

"Clover was confused. Upset, hurt by what she saw as Patrick's and your betrayal toward her. She had just ended things with... Jerome."

Emma wiped her hand across her brow. She had thought she was of the interesting generation. What a mistake that was!

"And by God, I was open to listening to her talk about that and about your not telling her she was Patrick's daughter. She was so young, twenty, charming, innocent... so I cooked up a plan. The most precious darned thing in Summerfield was that bloody artwork. As a dealer, I managed to convince her to place *The Things We Don't Say* into safekeeping for the duration of the war. To protect the only thing she was going to inherit from you both that was of value back then. I wanted to help her gain some semblance of... I don't know what, exactly..." His voice trailed off, and Emma found herself seeing him as vulnerable. Not the other way around.

"Summerfield was too close to the coast, Em. You'd already had your studio in London bombed. You'd lost all your work there. I asked her if the portrait was insured. We did a lot of that sort of work, you see. It wasn't unusual for our clients to move their paintings into safe storage. My partner, Duncan Buchanan, and I, well, we were familiar with this."

Emma looked at him, incredulous. "What did you just say?"

"Duncan Buchanan. I had an interest, a financial one mainly, in his gallery in Piccadilly. We were old friends. He owned it, of course; I just had a financial stake in it. As you know, I was able to afford not to work after I inherited my father's estate. But, quietly, I always kept an interest in art."

Emma narrowed her eyes. And her thoughts rolled back, to that dealer who had approached her when they'd been working in Fitzroy Square. She had dismissed him out of hand as nothing, and so had Patrick. He'd turned the dealer down with no discussion. But they'd never heard anything of him again—until now…

"I thought at the time that there was no point trying to convince you to place the portrait somewhere safe. I knew how bloody-minded you could be about Summerfield, that you'd never see it as anything but the darned haven that it never was to me.

"So we decided the only way to protect the original portrait was to switch it over with Duncan's son's copy. It was easy enough for Duncan to suggest his talented son, Hamish, make a copy of the Adams portrait when Lawrence took it up to London to show. Duncan's son was studying at art school. Sensitive. Talented. An earnest, deep-thinking young fellow. Trusting. Wouldn't hurt a flea.

"Clover, your daughter, did the switchover. She was young; I convinced her to do so, convinced her that it should never have been left out at Summerfield in the first place… It wasn't her fault—she thought it was the right thing to do, in fact, could see it needed protecting. In some strange way, it meant everything to her; it was representative of the love between her parents, although she would never, ever admit as much, feeling so left out by you as she did.

"She became convinced that someone had to be sensible in your world, Em. Someone had to start behaving in a normal, responsible manner. She's a more practical girl than you ever were, darling."

"Oh, dear God," Em said. She fanned her face with her hand.

"So she agreed it needed to be taken out for safekeeping, but then, she went off and got married to her butcher husband and didn't want anything to do with it or the Circle—let alone me! Duncan hung on to the portrait, and well, if I were honest, I think he would have sold it a few years ago had he still been alive when Patrick died and the value of it skyrocketed, the rest of his work being held in museums, of course."

"Rupert!"

But Rupert bent forward and rested his old hands on his knees. "I'd created my own little circle, you see. One based on good financial sense. Protecting the painting from people who were so airy-fairy they had no idea about its value at all. It was, in the end, quite different from your approach, I know that, but there was nothing wrong with Clover looking after her own future. After all, you'd kept a pretty darned serious secret from her yourself, Em... She told me all about it, you see. It didn't seem wrong to have a few secrets of our own... Bring things full swing and all that."

Emma felt the sudden need to rest right back in her seat. The swell of pain that spread through her chest was like a heavy butcher's knife cutting into one side, soaring up her arm, down her back... She gripped the sides of the sofa and felt her head throw itself backward. Then everything went black.

Chapter Twenty-Nine

Hampshire, 1980

Faces and images blurred. Emma focused on colors, trying as if with some last desperation to keep her eyes open, but she was unable to control the way her eyelids fluttered. People surrounded her, their uniforms, she tried to think valiantly, were a pale green tinged with a touch of blue, like the sea at its most mysterious and beautiful in Provence. But all she could do was lie there, her breath laborious through the hideous mask they'd strapped to her face...

Her mind drifted on through the fog. Now she was lying in the grass in Kensington Gardens, staring at the vivid sky through the canopy of trees. The sun shimmered on the vines in the South of France, and a few moments later, she was flying over Summerfield, the low rise of the South Downs below her young, floating self. And back to the first time she laid eyes on Patrick, the sting of that baguette piercing her lips and salt licking the cut.

Perhaps someday people would appreciate her meager efforts to try to make sense of any of it on canvas—beauty, children, family, loss, war, hope, and, ultimately, love. As she lay there, prone, the whole lot seemed to merge into a great swirl...

As the ambulance made its way back to London, she became aware of a cold hand clasping hers. Emma wrapped her fingers tight and held on, just as a newborn baby does, as if needing some form of contact—except Emma knew this would be the final one for her.

With her other hand, free from needles and drips, she pulled at the mask on her face.

"Only a moment, then you need it back on. Oxygen," the voice that belonged to the hand said.

"I have a daughter." Emma pushed out each word, her old eyes scanning the stranger's face. "If I die before we get back to London, I need you to tell her two things."

Emma saw the way the woman's eyes caught with her own, as if in some unspoken acknowledgment. She was not going to say that Emma would make it back alive.

Emma held fast to the nurse's hand.

"Tell her that life was always a matter of wishing and dreaming for me... I'd always tried to create something better than the world I found myself in, both through my art and the way I lived and in the way I very much wanted to love someone," Emma whispered, the words seeming almost impossible to form right now. "It wasn't a matter of keeping it from her. I just didn't want this world to hurt her if I could help it. But in not telling her, I can see I did just that. Please tell her that I love her and that I always will."

Emma saw the slight incline of the young woman's head. She closed her eyes and let herself drift away as the young woman who still held her hand stroked her aching head. It seemed odd and yet comforting that the touch of a stranger whom she would never know was the last thing she would ever feel in this life.

Chapter Thirty

London, 1980

Laura sat next to Emma's bed. The sound of the hospital monitor's beeping was alien, taking up the space where Emma's voice should have been. They'd told her it was unlikely Emma would ever wake up. Laura rested against Ewan's shoulder. He'd driven her straight back to London after a resourceful Lydia called Ewan's office and tracked them down. He'd sat up with her all night.

Dawn light was sneaking through the hospital curtains now, sending strange patterns onto the linoleum floor. Waiting for Emma to leave this world, in turn, was one of the strangest things that Laura had ever done. She'd never imagined that what she'd dreaded for so long would become the thing that she wanted for her beloved gran. But now, she wanted Em to be able to rest in peace. The inevitable wait for death to lend a final stroke to a person one loved seemed like one of the most impossible things to endure.

When the door to the room cracked open and a tentative footstep edged inside, Laura laid Emma's cool hand down on the still, white sheets. She moved across to hug her mother. Clover's face blanched as she caught sight of Emma, and she brought her long-fingered hand up to her throat. Clover took a step backward when she saw the old man sitting in the shadows in the room.

"Rupert?" she whispered. "What on earth are you doing here?"

"Hello, my dear," he said.

Laura pulled open the curtains, suddenly desperate for light.

Ewan stepped out of his chair and offered it to Clover. Laura sat next to her mother now, while, tentatively, Clover reached out and stroked Emma's still hand. Laura winced at the awkwardness between them, her mother and Em. And yet, there was a slight murmur of movement in Em's fingers at the feel of her daughter's last touch on the hands that had painted such treasures to leave behind in the world.

When the nurse came in, she asked that same question that she'd asked Laura only a few hours ago, and they all looked at each other, this odd little family of sorts—the extension of the Circle that was Laura, Clover, and Rupert. What was left. And they all agreed it was time. Time to turn off Emma's life support. Everything that had needed to be expressed in one beautiful life was done.

In one roundabout way or another, Emma had finally sent her message of tolerance, peace, and love to everyone she'd known and to people she'd never met, whether through art, words, or love, no matter how human she was, no matter that she'd loved, sometimes painfully, and had been loved, sometimes imperfectly, in return.

It was time now; the Circle had made its full round.

Laura stroked Emma's head.

"Goodbye, Gran," she whispered. "Goodbye, our darling Em."

Laura held the door open for Ewan and Jasper to make their way into the bank. Ewan held the real portrait of Emma, while Jasper carried the copy. They both stood in the entrance hall, hovering while Laura closed the glass door with a soft, final thud. She managed to smile at both of them.

"Okay?" Ewan asked.

"Yes." She nodded. Em would never want her to collapse. "I am."

As Ivan invited them into his office, Laura felt the hint of a smile pass across her face at the sight of the odd yet strong group that was gathered today.

Clover, Rupert, and Rosie Buchanan were already seated in a half circle around a small table in the middle of the room. It was Clover whom they'd agreed would talk to Ivan, telling the story of a painting that was inextricably linked with all these lives.

Once Clover was done, her story clear and dignified, Ivan regarded the circle of friends—almost a family of sorts, was that what they were? Through a century of turbulence, through two world wars and a gentle social revolution carried out by the extraordinary Emma Temple, this group of people had delved into past passion—of both the destructive and beautiful sort—into secrets that had been held close to private hearts, and into worlds that had circled around, linked because they were polar opposites and yet also because nothing existed as an entirely separate entity from anything else.

Ivan was quiet for a moment before he laid his glasses down on the table. "Well, I am relieved to tell you all that Laura can have her music back."

Relief washed over Laura at the sound of the words she'd so longed to hear. She caught her mother's eye. Clover's face was clearer than Laura had ever seen it in her life.

Summerfield, 1980

Two days later, on a hot day in Sussex, the same little group hung the portrait back over Emma's bed at Summerfield, only this time, they were open about the fact that it was Hamish Buchanan's soaring copy of Patrick's work that would delight anyone who cared to come into Emma's room. The fact that the Tate was holding Patrick's original for possible acquisition after the exhibition of gay artists in the early twentieth century was something that sat well with Laura. It turned out that Laura's loan could have been worth ten times what she'd borrowed, and once the Tate had acquired the painting, there would be more than enough to put toward the proposed Emma Temple and Patrick Adams Trust to turn Summerfield into a museum in memory of the Circle and all their lives' work.

They made their way out into the garden. Laura sat between Jasper and Ewan, those two men whom she knew would always be so very dear to her. Somehow, they'd helped her form a complete little triangle, which, perhaps, was the most stable shape after all.

As the guests settled quietly in the rows behind them, an old man stood at the podium. He peered out at the crowd gathered on the lawn to say goodbye to Em. Laura turned a moment. White funeral programs fluttered in front of hot faces, and people's legs stuck to the white plastic seats that had been set up in the heat. If Emma were here today, Laura knew those utilitarian, unornamented chairs would never have been allowed through the front gate.

"Very few of us can leave this life without suffering any regrets, but I believe that Emma Temple can rest without any misgivings." The old man smiled as if he'd reached a conclusion of sorts. Perhaps it was because he was the last person anyone would have expected to see here, let alone speak.

Butterflies fluttered in the shady nooks at Summerfield, where the grass had been allowed to grow wild and long, its graceful stems wafting as if in accompaniment to Em's funeral by the lake.

Two empty wooden chairs sat on the stage next to the man who spoke.

Jerome leaned as if for support on the chair closest to him while he spoke, his hand resting on the decorations that Emma had wrought along its back. Her particular painted circles were rendered in pale greens and terracotta, from paint that had been mixed with alabaster chalk from the soil here in Sussex. Glorious athletic male figures languished across the back of the second empty chair—Patrick's work.

Emma's and Patrick's art would outlive them both; perhaps the beauty of their work would speak to future generations, to those souls who would take the time to discover Emma's story, a story that was not only unique but one that would always be intertwined with Patrick's, no matter that some line of convention should have kept them apart.

A breeze riffled across the surface of the pond. Laura looked at the water, wondering whether Emma and Patrick were, in some way, aware of what was going on at Summerfield today.

The entire house and garden might be a testimony to a world that was long gone now, even though the inhabitants were both a product of and a rebellion against their time. Their spirits still seemed to whisper around every room and linger out here in the garden.

But just because people had gone, it didn't mean they didn't have anything left to say.

Jerome cleared his throat. Laura glanced up at him, her nerves pirouetting below her ribs.

"Progressive in her approach to both art and life, Emma Temple forged new ideas about personal freedom, love, and what makes a family—issues that we still grapple with today."

Laura's gaze was fixed on her grandmother's coffin. Roses in an array of sunny morning yellows and sunset-infused pinks were arranged on the closed lid. Color was both her fascination and her gift.

"Much has been written about Emma Temple as a woman and as a mother but not as an artist."

Laura looked up at the sound of the second voice. The smaller, lighter man appeared like some second player on a stage. Rupert and Jerome might have hovered around the edges of the Circle, but they had outlived everyone else.

"We must remember that Emma was a bold, modern innovator in her own right, a woman who practiced her craft every day, a dedicated practitioner with a strong vision who was not afraid to strike out and take a risk. Her sixty-year relationship with the equally gifted artist Patrick Adams had this same distinct trait, and that thread is what made their relationship one of the most remarkable in the art world in the twentieth century."

Ewan reached out. Laura placed her hand in his, and he held it fast between them.

"Yes, she was unconventional; yes, she suffered because she and her extraordinary family lived well outside society's rules, but Summerfield and all the work both Patrick and Emma have left for us are a testimony to a bold, innovative modern couple, who viewed their family and their home not as a place of restriction but as a vehicle for personal freedom for all," Rupert exclaimed.

"Well said," someone murmured a little farther down Laura's row.

"The only way the artists in the Circle could cope with the wars that blighted this century was to refuse their involvement and simply to paint. They were pacifists," Jerome finished.

He removed his reading glasses and looked over the guests. Laura reached up and wiped a stray tear from her cheek. The more the Circle were ostracized by society during both world wars, the more Emma retreated, and the closer she drew her loved ones around her, the more she supported them and loved them no matter what.

Rupert made his slow way to the record player that Patrick and Emma used to keep in their studio, the glorious light-filled space at the back of the farmhouse with its vaulted glass ceilings and all-day steady southern light. He lowered the needle onto the black LP before making his solitary way to one of the two empty chairs. The chair he chose was the one Emma had painted, which was telling in itself.

Bach's Double Violin Concerto soared around the garden, the two violins calling to each other like a pair of birds in simultaneous flight, one winging ahead for a moment while the other supported it until, in a glorious switchback, they would swap so that the other one led for a while, until the pair of them would come together in unison as if in a perfect partnership.

The old record player brought to mind Patrick and the jokes he used to play when Laura was young. He loved tricks… but Emma's deep love for Patrick, alongside his enduring love for her, like Bach's music, would always live on.

The Royal College of Music, 1980

Laura glanced down at the small audience that sat in the concert hall—three examiners, her teacher, and, up at the back of the room, there was Ewan. She caught his eye, and he blew her a silent kiss. She'd made it through the Bartók, weaving her way among the challenging jumps, her hands playing multiple tricks between bows and pizzicato alike. And now, she paused a moment.

As Laura raised her bow to the Guadagnini to play the glorious Bach Double, a sudden strong yellow light beamed in through the tall windows, shining and spreading all through the concert hall. The light dazzled on Laura's face just for one moment before glinting on the cherry-colored wood of her adored violin. As she turned to Jasper, they smiled at each other, and she was grateful he could play the violin as well as the viola because right now—after everything that had happened—he was the only person she wanted next to her on this stage while she played this exquisite piece. If Emma's portrait captured Patrick's feelings toward her, then Bach's Double Violin Concerto was a pure expression of the way Laura felt toward them both—her inspiration whom she would never, ever forget. She and Jasper began, in unison, to play the timeless music together that was, in the end, divine.

A Letter from Ella

Dear reader,

I want to say a huge thank you for choosing to read *The Things We Don't Say*. If you did enjoy it, and want to keep up to date with all my latest releases, just sign up at the following link. Your email address will never be shared and you can unsubscribe at any time.

www.bookouture.com/ella-carey

I hope you loved *The Things We Don't Say* and if you did I would be very grateful if you could write a review. I'd love to hear what you think, and it makes such a difference helping new readers to discover one of my books for the first time.

I adore writing, and each of my characters are so special to me. I travel all over the world to research the settings for my books. It means so much to have walked in the places you've read about here—it's a privilege to be able to learn about other people, places and times. Once I've traveled to research a book, I read and read about the time, place and stories surrounding the real people who lived through the historical time period concerned. When I've interviewed those who know about the topics in the book, it is wonderful to find my characters and story evolving, almost as a simple tribute to those who have gone before us and who have lived through times that seem so different to our own—but, in many ways, there are always links, always ways to find empathy, always pathways to understand. I am a huge believer in the power of stories to connect us in the present and to help us understand the past.

I would love to share my future books with you, and would love it if you would like to join me and my readers on my Facebook page, through Twitter, Goodreads or on my website, where we chat regularly, and where many of my loyal readers have become friends. It's always me at the other end!

With love,
Ella Carey

ellacareyauthor

@Ella_Carey

www.ellacarey.com

Author's Note

While this novel is inspired by the twentieth-century Bloomsbury group of artists and writers, the characters and story in this book are products of my own imagination. I have long been intrigued by the artist Vanessa Bell and her relationship with her fellow artist Duncan Grant. One of the most profoundly moving experiences I had while researching this book was standing at Vanessa Bell's and Duncan Grant's simple gravestones, which lie together in a small village cemetery in Sussex, not far from Charleston—the old farmhouse where they lived and created art and a beautiful life inspired by tolerance and acceptance during all the upheavals of the twentieth century. No less moving was walking in Vanessa Bell's and Virginia Woolf's footsteps in Gordon Square, seeing university students studying in the living room of Vanessa's house in Bloomsbury, and standing at the site of the real Omega Workshops where Roger Fry set up a collaborative workshop for London artists in the early part of the twentieth century.

Acknowledgments

My thanks to my editor, Maisie Lawrence, and to my agent, Giles Milburn and everyone at The Madeleine Milburn Literary Agency.

My sincere thanks to everyone at Bookouture. Especial thanks to Kim Nash, Sarah Hardy, Alexandra Holmes, Peta Nightingale, and Alex Crow. Thanks to everyone else at Bookouture who has worked on this book.

Thank you to the talented cover designer, Debbie Clement. My thanks to proofreader Anne O'Brien for your careful work.

My thanks to my readers for your enthusiasm and excitement about this story. Many of you have been with me since the publication of my very first novel, and I appreciate every one of you no end.

I am grateful to my sister, Jane, for taking care of things at home so that I could travel to London and Sussex to research this book, and as always, love and thanks to my children, Ben and Sophie.

Lightning Source UK Ltd.
Milton Keynes UK
UKHW012008190522
403254UK00004B/852

9 781800 191518